Cookies Kale & Coffee

RON KRIT

This book is dedicated to my family and friends.

Especially my boys.

A LITTLE HISTORY

The hardest part of chess is anticipating the competition's strategy. You see, one move could be a ruse. Aggressive players telegraph their intentions a little more than others. All that thinking is what I loved about chess. And I was good. From tournaments at the library when I was five to travel competitions when I was ten, it consumed me. Chess books, movies, and YouTube videos were my obsessions.

My parents never really pushed me. My mom guided me, taught me how to play, took me to the chess section of the library, and never forced me to go to bed when I was still reading at midnight. Life revolved around chess, judo (my parents didn't want me to get beat up for being a geek), and basketball. Those were my interests. This might sound selfish, but I have no idea what their interests were. They both worked a lot.

My mom, Sue, was an angel. On Sundays before work, she would make restaurant-quality pancakes. They were fluffy, buttery, and just a little crisp on each side. Working two jobs kept her busy, and although the money wasn't great, she just loved being a nurse and baking. Her only real flaw was timing. She would show up late to school events, family plans, and dentist appointments. The only thing she did early was die. Fuck cancer.

My dad, Jerry, works in logistics. Because my mom was a super-woman, he didn't have to do much, but he tried harder than my friends' dads. You know, those dads that skate by. They show up late to a few games, crack a beer at dinner, and then retire to the couch. He was a step above those guys. However, my quitting baseball at five personally insulted him. That was the sport he could coach. Judo he tolerated, basketball he accepted, but chess confused him. A few months into my chess career, he stopped playing against me. He did not like losing to a kid. With my mom working all the time, the old man resentfully took me to my weekend tournaments. Occasionally peering up from his phone or a paper, he would yell, "COME ON, ALEX!" It was slightly embarrassing, but deep down, I loved it. The best was when he did it at a chess match, and it broke complete and utter silence. The judge would whisper yell, "SILENCE!"

After mom's diagnosis and subsequent sickness, my dad surprisingly picked up his game. He tried to be more caring and loving to mom and me. Not known for affection, he became a hugger. These hugs were slightly awkward at first, as I wasn't used to him showing me love. Once my mom died, he fell apart. My mom was the rock. She made dinner for the week on Sundays, did one load of laundry per night, and baked every Friday night. Most people ordered birthday cakes, but brownies and cookies were her specialty. I sold them during lunch to both kids and teachers. The reaction from anyone who ate her fudge brownies was always, "OH MY GOD!" Even after multiple orders, it was like you forgot what heaven tasted like. That, and most cookie recipes, are deeply ingrained in my memory.

Laundry became my chore at 16. I also cooked dinner because dad burns everything. Cleaning the house didn't really happen for a year unless it was done by a maid. I was never into cleaning, but that's changing. I miss the smell of cookies and now I'd settle for the smell of lemon cleaner.

My dad has been dealing with depression for two years and it is really starting to affect me. He feels bad but can't pull himself out of the funk. Therapists, drugs, and hobbies haven't even done the trick. He still makes it to work, so that's a win.

The pity piled upon me at school after my mom's death helped my GPA, but that's about it. My interests and college dreams faded. Before my senior year of high school, I quit chess. My focus disappeared, and it's hard to win without it. My lack of height ended my basketball career, and judo stopped because I didn't have time for four workouts per week plus homework.

TODAY

Since my parents saved up some money for college, my dad said I had to use it. So, I'm at the College of Lake County. Not Duke or the University of Wisconsin, just junior college. I worked so hard, was a state chess champ, a member of the National Honors Society, a two-year sports letterman, and here I am.

The good news is that I'm about to become rich. My best friend, John, hooked me up with a gig selling knives. Calling from college, John was practically yelling, "DUDE, MY BROTHER MADE NINE K LAST SUMMER! You're going to make some cash, rock JUCO, and move out."

Facebook has landed me my first lead. Jane Frisk saw my post, "Whose parents need knives?" Her father, Joe, apparently needs some. All I know is that Jane has two older brothers from her dad's first wife, and she's nice. Her mom still works, but Joe is retired and plays a lot of cards. Here goes nothing.

Highland Park has some nice houses, but this house is one of my favorites. It's not on the beach, but across the street from the entrance. The mostly white house has a cool red front door and a giant U-shaped driveway surrounded by flowers and perfectly cut grass. Trying to calm my nerves, I take four deep breaths.

Before I knock on the door, an older man sticks his head out.

"Come on in, son." He smiles, this warm, sincere, I'm bored smile. I'll take that greeting.

I offer my hand. "I'm Alex, Jane's friend. Nice to meet you, Mr. Frisk."

He laughs, "It's Joe. I think we've met before. Take off your sports coat. You're selling me knives, not life insurance." Ignoring Joe, I stare into a house that should be on the cover of a magazine. I can see the entire first floor after only two steps. Noticing my awe, he says, "I'll take you for a tour after we talk business. Don't be impressed."

Trying to keep my composure, I say, "Your house is really impressive. I grew up on the West side. We have some nice houses, but this ..." My thoughts are interrupted when I notice the nicest chess set I've ever seen. It looks like it's made of ivory or crystal.

Catching my gaze, he says, "You play? I've got two older boys out in the Bay area. They used to play."

Joe guides me to the set, and I sit down opposite him. "Well, I was decent."

"Don't bluff me, boy. Listen, I'm buying knives no matter what. Don't go easy on me."

The endorphins exploding in my head are unexpected. I can't even rate this level of excitement. I haven't played chess in a year. All the moves rush into my head like I'm Bobby Fischer or something. Before I can stop myself, I've won in three moves.

Joe lets out, "What the heck? One more."

Trying not to win in a few moves, I start giving Joe hints. "Block with your rook. Wait, that's not how the knight moves. Only move the pawn one step forward."

Standing up in disgust, possibly amazement, he says, "Are you kidding?" He grabs his phone. "What's your last name, Alex?"

I've never watched anyone Google me before. "Why are you selling knives, kid? You're like a genius. I didn't know there was a state chess championship. Judo?"

Fighting back the tears, I explain, "My mom died, and it just messed me up. I haven't played in a while. And my parents didn't want a chess geek to get beat up, hence the judo."

Sensing my emotions, Joe puts a hand on my knee. "Sorry, kid. Lost my first wife. Sucks. You kicking my butt in chess is way more impressive than a big house." I notice Joe has a slight limp when he runs out of the room yelling, "I've got an idea!"

Wiping away a few tears, all I can think about is my mom. If she knew I was living at home, selling knives, and not out of state, she would be so upset. I can see her brushing her wavy brown hair behind her ears and yelling, "I didn't work two jobs for you to stay at home!" Before I can carry on this imaginary conversation, Joe hops back into the room with a deck of cards.

"What about poker? Do you know how to play?"

I am trying to play it cool. "Can you show me how to play?"

Reading through my nonsense, he says, "Sure you don't. Omaha or Texas hold 'em?"

"Let's start with Texas hold 'em."

My social circle in school was tame. I knew the chess club kids and the basketball players. Talk about a dichotomy, the only thing these kids had in common was cards. They all loved poker. The chess guys were better at strategizing, no surprise there, but the ballers could bluff.

"I'm going to teach you a few things about business, kid. You need to make small talk. I see your focus, but you need to carry on a conversation between hands."

My mom called it the Alex Zone. When I start doing something, my focus is all in. "Sorry, Joe, I'm not the best multitasker. I'm trying to figure out all the possibilities. What you have, what the next card might be, what's my best hand, and what's the probability the next card is an ace."

"You should be a trader. I did that for years. Made good money, but the grind and pressure suck. I switched to being a stockbroker. I think they call them money managers now. Something like that."

Losing most hands doesn't bother Joe. "You seem very excited about losing. Are you letting me win?"

Joe smiles. "Kid, this is great. You're coming to my Thursday night game. It's a friendly game with some of my neighbors. I usually win, so you'll do well." Suddenly, my phone buzzes, and I'm not sure what to do.

"Is it rude to check my phone during a business call?" He shakes his head no, so I go ahead and check my phone.

All of a sudden, I am snapped out of my reality when I see it's a text from my dad. In my head, I read, "Taco Vida? Or do you want to pick up dinner?" Since my dad drinks way too much when we are out, I text back that I'll get us something.

With the joy sucked out of my life, I tell Joe, "I have to leave soon. This was fun."

With a concerned look, Joe asks, "Everything okay?" Shaking my head yes, I pull up the ordering form. Joe circles the deluxe package. "I have this great girl doing some meal prep for me. She said my knives suck. Come Thursday night, play some poker, and sell more knives."

I have mixed emotions. "To be honest, I don't have a lot of money to gamble. What's the buy-in?"

"Can you hook up all of my TVs to a Roku-type thing?" I nod yes, and he replies, "Come over at eight o'clock, help me out with my tech, and I'll cover your buy-in. It's two hundred dollars."

Walking toward the door like he sold me something, we shake hands. "Thank you for your business, Joe. And I'll see you Thursday."

There's no way the other sales will be this easy, but I can handle this. He didn't ask about the quality, warranty, or what comes in the package. After all that preparation, what I really needed was to brush up on my social skills.

CRAM COURSE

Cleanliness is something I appreciate. It's not a compulsion, but ever since my mom's been gone, I secretly enjoy it. I tell my dad to at least put his plates away. He usually falls asleep with his dinner on the coffee table, the television on, and a bottle of vodka on the floor. It's disgusting, but waking him up is nearly impossible, so I clean up.

Tonight is no different than most, but after cleaning, I start researching poker instead of reading. I played a lot of poker in high school, but that was with kids. Grown men are probably more serious.

Buzzing interrupts my video bingeing. "What up, John?"

"When are you going to visit me? College is amazing. I hooked up with this chick on a Tuesday night! Girls wouldn't even look at me twice in high school."

Happy and a little jealous, I reply, "Good for you, man. I think your diversity is starting to work in your favor."

A little drunk, John responds, "They like a little Asian infusion. Who would've thought it in Madison? Got to go, bro. I don't have class until eleven tomorrow, so we're going to drink and play cards."

"Funny, I'm playing cards tomorrow night. Have fun."

He seems sincerely happy for me when he replies. "That's great to hear. I knew you would make some new friends."

In high school, John was a good friend and always made time for me. Never comfortable in his skin, he stayed quiet in class. No one cared that he was Japanese, but he cared. He must have told me a million times, "I hate that I'm good at math. I'm a living stereotype." The truth is, he excelled in every class.

Out of all my friends, he's the only one that's reached out since college started. Maybe he's all I've got. I remember my sociology teacher talking about how friend groups change. I thought I would hold onto a few more people. Truthfully, I only had a few friends, but it feels like much less now.

After watching three hours of instructional poker videos, I feel like Keanu Reeves in *The Matrix* when he says, "I know kung fu." Except in my case, I know poker. I feel my eyes closing as I shut down my computer.

Per usual, the smell of coffee wakes me up. I love that smell, as it reminds me of my mom. She drank it in the morning and when she started a baking project. Sue was old school. She roasted her own beans and ground them. Her thorough process spoiled me. I can only drink at certain coffee houses; otherwise, the coffee tastes burnt. At least I learned the process. The first Sunday of the month, I prepare a few pounds of coffee. The house smells like a Starbucks. If selling knives doesn't pan out, maybe I'll be a barista.

School feels like a bad dream. In life, I'm not a snob, except for academics. The only thing kind to me in high school was grades. I received two Bs, in English and Advanced Economics. Econ was no joke. The teacher was known as Mr. C because that was the grade he doled out most often. The first exam everyone failed; he told us, "If you want college credit, work harder." He was a total dick, but he forced me to think. Currently, I have a perfect GPA and it has been a little too easy. High school was very competitive. I hated it, but it prepared me well.

Interrupting my thoughts, my dad pops into my room. "Have a great day, buddy. Coffee is on. Maddie texted me, and she's dropping off a casserole soon. Offer her some coffee, and maybe one of those cinnamon rolls you made. I can't eat another one."

Trying not to answer annoyed, I say, "Sure, dad. She always stays a little too long."

With a smile, he says, "I know. Love you."

Before finishing my first cup of coffee, I hear the soft knock of Maddie. I think she has a crush on my dad. Why else would she stop by once a month to drop off a casserole? That option as a meal should really end a few weeks after a funeral or childbirth.

"Come on in, Maddie. I made cinnamon rolls. Coffee?"

With a hug, she says, "How are you?"

Without meaning to, we always have deep conversations. "First off, stop by whenever, and you don't need to bring food. She's been gone almost two years. We don't need sympathy meals. But thanks, it's one less meal I have to make."

Shaking her head like she gets it, she says, "That's why I do it. I double a recipe here and there and then bring it by. Maybe I'm just a nice person. And, you do have the best coffee in the neighborhood."

Feeling a little too comfortable with Maddie, I say, "Or maybe you just like the company."

With a huge smile, I can see all her white teeth. My guess is that she's in her thirties, maybe forties. "I love the company, but seriously, this coffee is so good. How's school?"

"Fine. These classes are a joke. I had more homework in high school—not that I'm complaining. The group aspect is annoying. I need to figure out how to work better with others. I usually end up doing all the work."

Combing her long red hair with her hand, she pretends to be a school counselor. "Is that because you have trust issues? Or control issues?"

"Well, doc, since you asked—a little of both. My last partner on a stock market project showed up to the library baked. His eyes were so red, there wasn't enough Clear Eyes at Target to help him out."

Laughing, she continues to probe. "What did you do?"

"I got us an A. He gave me this." Holding up a bottle of CBD/THC balm, "It works like a charm on muscle pain."

Not done poking around in my head, Maddie asks this doozy: "Have you been talking to your friends?"

"Do nosy neighbors count? I'm kidding. Yes, one. The others suck. I am playing cards tonight with some guys."

With excitement in her eyes, Maddie remarks, "That's great Alex. You know, you could always reach out to friends."

Very appreciative that I don't have to cook tonight, but ready for this conversation to end, I thank Maddie and head to school.

GAME NIGHT

When your mom is a baker, you learn some tricks. I learned to take the cookies out a little early to keep them chewy, to add toffee bits for a little sweetness, that big chips are better, and then to drop some sea salt on top. You also learn never go anywhere without bringing something delicious. If you bake it, they'll appreciate it even more.

The cars lining up in Joe's driveway are fancy. A sporty BMW, a convertible Mercedes Benz, and a Porsche sedan. The Tesla SUV in gun metal might be my favorite. My car looks like the delivery guy's car. Although cool to look at, cars mean nothing to me.

The door is ajar. Poking my head inside, "Hello, Joe?"

I hear his deep voice yell, "Come on in, kid. We are in the kitchen." The spread in the kitchen looks like Joe's entertaining a small army. The kitchen island is covered with wings, grilled veggies, hummus, and lots of deli meat.

I hand Joe my cookies. He says, "Thanks, kid."

The first person I meet, Rob, takes a cookie and devours it. "These are the best cookies. Really. Where did you buy them?"

"I made them. Thanks! I'm glad you like them. My mom was a baker."

Rob's raving review leads all the other guys to skip dinner and try a cookie.

Joe gives me a handshake and a one-handed hug, "Kid, follow me for a second." Taking me upstairs, he continues talking, "I have two TVs that I need help hooking up to a Roku. I wanted to do this before everyone got here. For some reason, people came early. Sorry."

With a smile, I say, "I don't care, Joe. This will take no time." Walking into his bedroom feels a little weird. It's huge, a massage chair like the ones at the mall sits next to a massage table, a bed made for a giant lays wrinkle free, and against a wall rests a pretty average size TV.

Sarcastically I say, "You really went all out with this television."

Handing me a sheet with passwords, he replies, "Listen, asshole, I didn't need anything fancy for the occasional movie. Are you already done?"

"Hand me your remotes." With a quick search on my phone, I set up his universal remote. "This is how you get to Netflix, other movie channels, and YouTube. You got anything else?"

"That was fast. I feel like I overpaid you. It's cool how you programmed this remote."

With a grin I say, "You did. Where's the other set?"

"Basement. I think you'll find it a little more acceptable."

The basement is better than I imagined. The main room is massive. One corner has free weights, a stationary bike, some weight machines, a heavy bag, and a treadmill. All the exercise equipment faces a wall where a projection television is displayed. In front of the screen is a brown leather couch that sits a small army, and the poker table sits behind the couch. The gamer corner is home to a dartboard and a few pinball machines. My favorite items are the ping-pong and pool table, which are parallel to one in other. That area gives off a cool bar atmosphere.

Sensing my awe, he says, "I splurged in this room. It was a great hangout for the kids, and now I'll get to use it. My boys only got a few years of use down here before college. Jane and I played a lot of ping-pong down here. She's a player."

While hooking up his television, curiosity takes over my thoughts, "Can you tell me a little about the guys?"

Wasting no time, he responds, "Rob is good guy. He works in sales and loves poker. He goes to the Poker World Series. Plays bigger games around town. He's very consistent and doesn't really waver. Mike is a mess right now. He's a lawyer and in the middle of an ugly divorce. He spends more time reading others than playing his cards. Rick is super smart. He works with hedge funds. Prints money, that guy. Love the guy, but he thinks he's great. Dave is closest in age to you. He's probably around forty and started some tech company. Then he sold it and made serious money. Now he's on to the next thing. Nice guy, and he takes risks with hands."

Making eye contact, I say, "That was thorough."

With a hand on my shoulder, he replies, "You work quick. My girl made some good stuff. Let's eat."

When we step back into the kitchen, Rob asks, "Beer? Cocktail? Coke?"

Since I don't drink alcohol, I say, "Coke sounds good, thanks." The Coke is in a glass bottle like in an '80s movie and tastes amazing.

Extending his hand, another guy says, "I'm Dave. And nothing beats a Mexican Coke. Real sugar in that bad boy."

"Nice to meet you Dave, I'm Alex."

With a big toothy smile, he says, "Joe warned us about you. Chess champ, baller, card shark, knife salesman. What else? Are you a ladies' man, too?"

"That's next on the checklist. Usually, chess skills and women don't go hand in hand."

Dave continues, "I still don't get women. The only advice I can offer is to listen when they talk, smile, pay most of the time, and plan fun dates."

As Mike approaches, Dave adds, "And whatever you do, don't listen to Mike."

With another handshake, Mike disagrees. "Dave has a hot wife. I'll give him that. Jessica is sweet and caring, but she's pretty much the only girl he's ever dated. I worked at a bar in college. If you want to get some tail, be nice-ish."

Shaking his head, no, Joe cuts in, "Dave had it right. Don't listen to Mike. And who uses the word tail? What are you, running for president now?"

Confused, he says, "Sorry, old man. Is 'vagina' better?"

The group laughs and heads down to the card table. "If my wife was home, she would kick you out. Just wait until your daughters are a little older."

Rick adds, "Stay away from women. Divorce sucks. Focus on making money and you won't have to worry about the women. Right, Mike?"

Mike says nothing, but feeling left out Rob weighs in, "He's so bitter. Ignore them. Whatever made you successful at chess, apply it to everything else."

Joe deals the cards and all the chatter fades. My first task is to look for tendencies. I fold many hands as the others keep going. Rick pushes his luck and usually does not have the cards to back it up. Dave only stays in it when he has a full house or better. Rob wins most of the hands. Joe wins a few, but only with a full house or better. Mike and Joe remain quiet.

I have aces and three queens. Everyone else is out but Rick. "Alright kid. What have you got?"

Flipping his pair up, I show him my hand. I can't help but smile. "Thank you, Rick."

Laughing, he says, "Fuck you, Junior. I'm out."

Mike, clearly avoiding going home, says, "I'll keep playing, anyone else?"

The others thank Joe and yell out, "Nice to meet you kid."

As Mike packs up he says, "Kid, I'm going to need some knives. Here's my card. Call me tomorrow. You're a hell of a player."

Rick, being a good loser says, "Call me, too. We have the same crap we've had for twenty years."

Trying not to be bad a winner, I say, "Thanks, just beginner's luck." As Mike follows the others upstairs, I count my winnings. $900! I hand Joe $200 back.

His visceral reaction was as if I held up a gun to his head. "Are you fucking kidding me? Put that in your pocket. I've been waiting on this TV project for three months. My wife already texted me THANKS. And she never texts. She's probably passed out in our room watching some sappy movie."

Placing the money back in my pocket, Joe asks, "What did you think? Was it too easy? You left what, three hundred dollars on the table?"

Responding to Joe, "Dave doesn't like to bluff and Rob only had one bad play all night. You smile too much when you have a good hand."

With a proud dad smile, he says, "Good job, Alex. Hopefully you can make it next week. I'll send you everyone's email. You should follow up with a nice to meet you email and ask if you can demo your knives."

Carrying up a few leftover drinks, I reply, "Anything else I can help with?" All the food has been magically cleared away. "My wife loves poker night. She eats the leftovers, packages up the rest, and watches her shows. Now go home. Don't spend it all in one place. Next week come earlier and we'll open a high yield savings account for you.

As I unlock the tremendous bolt, I reply, "I might have one. I'll ask my dad. Thanks for everything." When I was not tuning everyone out, there was a lot of financial bragging and suggestions thrown around. One guy spoke about no-load mutual funds.

Before walking inside my house, I Facetime John. "So glad you are up, J. I needed to tell someone that I just won nine hundred bucks!"

Looking a little drunk, he exclaims, "Nice, BOY! What are you going to do with the cash?"

"I have no idea. My dad started buying some workout stuff, so maybe I'll get more weights. I need to put some muscle on this frame."

Shaking his head in agreement, he says, "You are pretty skinny, dude. I need to chill on this beer. We drink Thursday through Sunday."

Unsure of what he just said, I yawn, "Don't flunk out J. I'm heading to bed."

Catching my yawn, he replies, "Don't worry mom. I've got mostly As. I do all my work right after class. In two hours, I can bang out all my work. I'm beat. We played cards, but it was just a drinking game."

RICK SLOAN

Each poker player agreed to meet me for a knife demo. I was a little surprised, considering they couldn't have cared less during the game. I think I was asked three questions the entire night.

Rick told me I could stop by at noon, which gives me lots of time before my night class. Signing up for three hours of economics was not my smartest move, but the teacher is decent and works at Abbott. He suggested we find him on LinkedIn. I thought that was a nice offer.

Holy shit! My GPS has led me to a monstrous house. Lake Michigan is in plain sight through the large windows that sit above and next to the front door. It looks like from his backyard you can walk to the lake. Because the windows are so huge, I can see Rick walking to let me in.

"Come on in, kid. I'll take you to the kitchen. I'm on this new health kick. I have extra food for you, but if you prefer a burger, you're on your own."

"Thanks, Rick. This house is unbelievable."

The all-white kitchen is made up of two huge islands and a large rectangular table. A generous bowl of salad, chicken breasts, and seasoned avocado slices are waiting for us.

I remark, "This food looks like it's out of a magazine."

Rubbing his dark brown and gray stubble, he says, "When you get old, the weight sticks more. I hired the woman that works for Joe—Roberta. She's a good cook. I don't even have to track or log my food. I just order the seventeen hundred-calorie plan. My wife is into it, too."

Staring at my bag of knives, he says, "Just tell me what to buy. My wife said we need everything. We've been married twenty years and still have the same set we got for our wedding."

"This is easier than beating you at poker. Are you sure? Tell me what you want to spend, and I'll put a package together." I handed Rick my product sheet.

"Kid. We need knives. Five hundred bucks enough for a set?"

Trying to control the sudden burst of excitement building up inside of me, I blurt, "Perfect. I'll get you a great set."

Aside from a few decorations, pictures of two kids surround the walls. The older one is a girl who looks sporty. She's either holding a lacrosse stick or a tennis racket. Of course, his son is a golfer and tennis player. I think he graduated when I was a freshman.

Picking up on my glances, he says, "Kim and David. They are the best. Kim is finishing veterinary school and David is at Stanford. I have no idea how he got in, but he loves it out there. He's on the golf team. He's trying to be like Tiger."

A little nervous, I reply, "I don't want this to sound rude or nosey, but what do you do? This house is out of a movie."

A huge grin forms on Rick's face, and I can see the crow's feet next to his eyes, probably from too much golf with his son. "It's not rude it all. Do you want the long story or short one?"

"I have three hours before night school. Take your time."

Shaking his head, as if he can't believe it, he says, "This is fucked up. My dad is an asshole. He made decent money with a car service. That led to car wash businesses, and then he started buying buildings. He was never satisfied."

After taking a break to chew, I ask, "Satisfied with you, or with work?"

After swigging some coffee, he replies, "Nothing really satisfied him except my mom, who doted on him. My brother and I were always pushed to do better at anything we did. I would come home with one B, and he would ask what happened. I couldn't wait for college. I was never coming back to Chicago. My brother, older, came home and was given the driver business and car wash."

I feel like I'm listening to an amazing audio book. "What happened to him?"

"Jim, my brother, sold all the cars and eventually the car washes. He then moved into logistics, buying freight trucks. Smart move. My dad was involved, partially. At this point, he and mom spent a lot of time in California, and he begged me to move to Chicago. He promised me I could run his other buildings. That sounded awful to me. I graduated from Madison with all of these kids from New York. They helped me get a job on Wall Street as an analyst. I researched technology firms. I spent ten years busting my ass, learning what makes firms successful."

Picking up his phone, he says, "Sorry. Making sure it's not a kid. Anyway, after ten years away from home, my dad visits with Jim. He has this look in his crazy old eyes and tells us this crazy challenge. He said he would give us five years, and whoever delivered the highest return on his investment would get the house in Utah. The loser got the ranch in California."

I'm done eating and sitting on the edge of my seat. Rich people are crazy. "Wait, he's challenging you two, almost trying to tear you guys apart to get a house?"

"He loves a good battle. Jim and I are tight, but also very competitive. I mean, my dad made us that way. And truthfully, I was sick of New York. My girlfriend at the time, who became my wife, is from Michigan. She was okay with this because she wanted to be closer to home. He handed me the deeds for all his condo buildings."

"How many?"

"He had about eight buildings. We are talking about small to midsize, eight million dollars or so. I sold every one of them. He's pissed and calls me all these names. Two years go by, and he stops talking to me."

Curious, I ask, "What changed?"

Shaking his head in disbelief, he says, "My mom told him my wife was pregnant and he would never see his grandkids. So, he came around. Of course, he yelled at me, and said he worked his ass off to buy those buildings and I just sold them in a few months. It ripped his heart out. I also paid off all the debt and walked away with four million dollars. I know I can't complain. Since I knew technology, I invested the money. I met all these founders when I worked in New York. I knew what to look for in a company, from culture to cashflow. In five years, I took his money and made millions. I paid him back with interest. And yes, he took the money. He donated it the next day to a charity. So that's good."

Grabbing his arm as if he's telling me a bedtime story, I ask, "Who won the bet?"

"I did, silly. My brother did great, but the tech boom was just starting. My dad said not to spend it all because you could lose it when the recession hits. I saved a chunk of money because what if he was right? However, I kept investing. I got extremely lucky with Apple and Google. HP and a few others hurt me, but I was out of most of them before the bubble burst. I never thought I would make this much money. It's fucking crazy. My wife is an architect. She designed this house." Taking a long breath, "And we sit, drinking wine, staring at the lake in disbelief."

"What happened to your dad?"

With little emotion, he says, "He died a few years ago. I thought that asshole would outlive me. He somehow, even in his nineties, died with millions in the bank. He donated almost every penny to charities. He left each grandchild a hundred thousand dollars that they can't touch until they're forty years old and marry another Jewish person."

Throwing my hands up in the air, I ask, "Really? You can do that?"

"I have no idea. Now my kids aren't lazy, but that money is in a trust and it's going to be worth a lot more than a hundred K. So, I'll probably have Jewish grandchildren. I can't make this shit up."

"Rick, that's a crazy story. Thanks for sharing. I can't believe it. Also, thanks for lunch and buying all the knives. Do you know anyone else who might need some?"

Putting a hand on my shoulder, he says, "Excellent selling skills. I'll send you a few people. Let's figure out your next move."

"Thanks again. Tomorrow I'm meeting Dave. Any tips?"

"That guy sold a start-up to Google. He can buy some knives."

NORMALCY

A surprise call from my dad catches me off guard as I drive around in search of an early dinner. "Hey, dad."

Sober, he says, "Hello, buddy. I'm heating up the mystery casserole Maddie left. Can you get home for dinner before class?"

"I'll see you in a few." We try and break bread a few times per week. With classes and his work schedule, it's hard to fit in more than that. With encouragement, he bowls one night per week with coworkers and plays in their softball league. Between broad shoulders and stocky legs, he can hit the ball pretty good for an old guy. I've filled in a few times and it's a little embarrassing when your dad hits the ball farther than you.

My mom demanded three dinners per week together. With basketball practice and other extra-curriculars, it was hard, but she always made it happen. Sometimes we drank our dinner. She would make us these shakes with peanut butter, frozen bananas, and Greek yogurt. They were so good, but I still can't figure out the secret ingredient.

Pulling into the driveway, the struggle hits me. Do I tell my dad about poker? Would he care? Would he want some of the money?

A hug greets me. I haven't gotten one of those in a while. Mostly because I avoid it. He has this way of gripping you with his hands, that makes you feel loved. He stole the move from my mom.

Not trying to ruin the moment, I ask, "Dad, did you ever notice you're extra caring when Maddie comes over? Why is that?"

Never one to sugarcoat things, he explains, "She told me to be a dad. Soon you'll be at college, and I have this rare opportunity to start being present before it's too late. I'm also going to start going back to meetings."

Sitting down, I'm trying to hold the tears back. His blue eyes are fixated on me, "Two years of being a drunk is enough. I'm sorry. I know that I'm going to screw up, but I'm done being a loser. This has nothing to do with finding a wad of cash in your underwear drawer. You do know you have a bank account, right?"

I point at him and explain, "I'm still good at games, old man. Long story short, I sold knives to this guy, and he begged me to come to his poker game. He paid the entrance fee because I hooked up his TVs. These guys were not very good."

I was unsure what his reaction would be, but he exclaims, "That's my BOY! Considering we don't have a lot of money, don't lose more than a few hundred. Trust me, at some point even wonder boy will lose."

"Don't worry. These are not big buy-ins or anything. It's great networking. Today I sold five-hundred dollars' worth of knives to one of the guys. His brother is in logistics. Does the name Jim Sloan ring a bell?"

His eyes widen, "You were in Rick's house? I heard it's amazing. I worked for Jim years ago. He's a nice guy. His old man was crazy and mean. If Jim ever comes to a game, tell him 'hello' for me."

Enjoying a meal with my dad for the first time in months starts to feel fake. What the hell is the matter with me? Why can't I take this moment and enjoy it? I ask, "Dad, is everything okay?"

With a warm hand on my shoulder, he explains, "When Maddie called me, she said something so simple. She said that I can be happy and a good dad, and I have to make the choice. And I did. I'm going to be better."

At this point, the tears are running down my cheeks. I want to believe him, and I want to enjoy this moment. Wiping the tears, "Something in you and me broke. It's going take more than one meal to fix it."

With a smile my dad says, "This is me. I'm going to get a new shrink, and I went for a jog after work. I'm putting my life back together."

Kissing my forehead like he did when I was kid feels forced but I'll take it. Taking a deep breath, I say, "I hope this continues. Got to head to class."

The moment I get in my car, I dial Maddie's number. When she answers, I blurt out, "What the fuck did you say to my dad?"

Confused, she explains, "Um, I told him you seemed sad. And he needs to man up and stop sulking. He needs to be a dad. Everything okay?"

"I came home, and it was like *The Brady Bunch*. He was a dad. I hope it continues. If it was just a tease. If I come home and he has a glass of booze next him and the TV blaring, I'm going to lose it."

I sense her smile through the phone. With a caring tone, "You are one hundred-percent normal. Those feelings are exactly spot on. If you come home and he's drunk, get all your stuff and come to my house. Anytime, seriously."

With controlled breathing, I reply, "Thank you. I appreciate the offer. I didn't really like my therapist, but maybe we could talk once in a while?" The words just slipped out of me.

With a parental tone, "You got it! Now stop driving and talking."

All of these emotions flood through me, and it only gets worse as "Poker Face" comes on the radio. My mom played that song for me all the time. She would take her hands that always smelled like sugar, and place them on my face, "You have the sweetest poker face." Good old mom was preparing me for these card games.

Concentrating in class is easier than normal. Since I took most of these classes in high school, I tune out most of the hour, or in this case almost three hours. Homework in high school was ridiculous. I had hours of work. It was like I was working on a thesis. I'm taking three classes right now, and I maybe study for an hour every night. I'm not complaining, either my expectations were too high, or my school prepared me well.

Driving home, a million thoughts zip through my head. Will my dad be passed out? Will booze be involved? Will I be able to hear the television from the garage, or will it be set to a normal volume? What will the wardrobe situation be—tighty-whities or boxer briefs?

Reruns of some cop show greet me as I open the door. The old man is out cold, no booze, and he is wearing sweatpants, no shirt. I can get used to this.

DAVE KAZAN

For the first time in months, I wake up to a silent house. Sleeping until seven o'clock feels refreshing. Only one cup of coffee is needed as I work on homework and prepare to sell more knives to my new poker buddies.

Pulling up to Dave's house was not like Rick's house. Then again, not many people can have a monstrosity on the lake, and Dave is probably 20 years younger than Rick. Don't get me wrong—this is a big house. It's just not ridiculous.

Barefoot, with shorts on and a Dave Mathews Band shirt, Dave greets me with a handshake. "Come on in, bro."

The smell of coffee permeates the house. We walk past a dining room table that has a bench on one side and chairs on the other. The kitchen looks like something out of a restaurant. The oven is huge and there's a walk-in pantry organized by a pro; there are even tins labeled in thick ink. I really want to check out what's in the granola box but have no idea why. Catching my glance, he says "You can have some granola, Alex. Or anything else."

"Maybe just some granola." More than anything, I want to see what's inside a bin marked, in bold, "GRANOLA!"

With a warm smile, Dave offers, "Coffee? It's kind of like my obsession."

"Me, too! I roast my own beans every Sunday for the week."

Looking at me like I'm crazy, he says, "That's intense. I just splurged on this organic bean and my in-laws got me this fancy coffee maker. It's good, real smooth."

While Dave pours me a cup in a pink mug, I pillage through the cereal offerings. From grain free, to chocolate almond, there are lots of choices. Is it rude to try multiple options?

Taking a seat on a stool, I select two granolas. Dave asks, "Milk, fake milk, yogurt, what do you want with it? And how do you like your coffee?"

"All of these decisions to make! In my house, it's only milk. Let me try almond milk. I usually put that in my coffee, too."

Dave turns on a burner and takes a pan off the rack above the kitchen island. "Do you want an egg? I've been on this egg sandwich kick this month."

Feeling extremely comfortable with Dave, I say, "Full service at the Kazan house. I'm fine. The granola is perfect. I'm not a big breakfast guy."

Cracking the eggs right in the pan, he explains, "My wife says we need new steak knives and a bread knife. Oh, and a few pans. I didn't know they made one just for bread. I want a block too. We have them hanging on this magnetic strip, but now that we have kids, that scares the crap out of me."

"I can do that. How old are your kids?"

Still making eggs, he says, "Five and seven. We knocked them out a little too close, but we are done now. Two boys."

"I always wanted a brother. Do they get along?"

Walking in the kitchen and answering the question, a woman says, "They fight all the time, but love each other. Hi, Alex. I'm Jessica."

Trying not to drool, I say, "Nice to meet you, Jessica. How did you two meet?"

Sitting down next to me, curling her blond locks with a manicured finger, she says, "We both went to Drake University. Of course, I'm younger. We met at a house party. It's a small school, but we were three years apart and had never met before."

Joining us at the table with his breakfast sandwich, Dave adds, "We were also taking classes in different buildings. She was an education major, and I was business."

With a smile, she says, "And now we work together. Speaking of which, I'm heading to the office. Nice to meet you, Alex."

Kissing her husband on the cheek, Jessica walks out. As if I wasn't there, Dave says, "Babe, your butt looks amazing in those pants."

Grinning ear to ear, Jessica explains, "I knew I had to impress Alex. Thanks."

Trying not to stare at her butt, I reply, "She's funny. What do you guys do? Is this your first start-up?"

Pulling his chair in closer, Dave explains, "This is a long story. I'll try to get it done fast. I grew up in Iowa and needed to get away. My junior year, I interned in Chicago as a consultant. I lived with a guy who graduated the year before I did. He started this paid search firm. It was just him and two other guys. He told me I could work remotely while I went back to school. He needed someone to research competition, software, and trends. With Google ads just starting to get big, we were ahead of the curve. I loved it. I worked about ten hours per week because that's all he could really afford, but when I graduated, he gave me a nice salary and shares. We were bought out two years ago."

"Sounds like a wild ride."

Shaking his head, he agrees. "You have no idea. We worked a lot. Once we got down our system and hired salesmen, things just started happening. We grew quickly. I'm shocked how it went down. Jessica was a teacher, but she quit when we had number two. Sitting at this table with a friend that works on the tech side, we started talking about educational tools. There's so much out there on the STEM side, but not really the history and arts side. So, we developed a tool to help kids learn to use technology by creating videos."

"That's really cool."

A serious look takes over Dave's face. He asks, "Why are you selling knives?"

I don't think he's trying to offend me, but it hurts. "I wanted to go away to college. When my mom got sick, I just needed a break from everything."

"Where did you want to go?"

With no hesitation, I reply, "Duke."

Taking a bite, following it down with some coffee, he asks, "Basketball guy?"

"I love basketball, but their graduates have the highest starting salary. Well, they did when I was applying."

With a toothless smile, he says, "That's cool. I like money, but really, I love to build things. Don't worry about the money. You are smart, hard-working, and you're making great contacts. Joe, Rich, and those guys are connected."

I love how rich guys tell you not to worry about the money. It's so easy for him to say this from his million-dollar home, garage full of fancy cars, and gourmet coffee maker.

After signing the knife contract, Dave thanks me. I don't want to overstay my welcome, so I stand up and extend my hand, "Don't thank me. Thank you! If you have a friend, neighbor or anyone who might be interested, let me know."

Walking to the door, I forget I have his Secret Search coffee mug in my hand. "I don't want to steal your mug."

With no hesitation, he says, "Take it. I have so many. I'm trying to get rid of them. They keep the coffee too hot. I know that sounds odd, but I don't like super-hot coffee."

"Thanks, man." The caffeine buzz hits me as I drive to class. I won't fall asleep today.

FRIENDS

When class ends, I review my notes and do my homework right away. My friends in high school made fun of me because as soon as class ended, I read my notes. My dad once said it's the best way to get things to stick. I'm not sure if that's true, but now it's a habit.

Ripping through my homework and studying after class frees up my time. The sad thing is, I really have nothing to do. No friends to see, just emails and calls to sell knives. That's my life. I need a hobby and some friends.

Sitting at my kitchen table, pondering my friendship game, my phone rings. It's Joe. He might be 50 years older than me, but that's okay—right?

"Hey, Joe. You just interrupted my internal monologue. How are you? TV's working?"

"Hello kid. Are you good with computers, too? I need to load software onto a new computer and load a few old files. They are mostly pictures of my kids and grandkids."

Looking at the clock on the microwave, I see that it's 3 p.m. and I have nothing to do. "Sure. I can be over in ten minutes."

"You're a lifesaver. I pay my computer kid forty dollars an hour. Does that work?"

This guy is just throwing money at me. In need of company more than cash, I respond, "This is on the house. Maybe just a snack."

I can hear the joy in his voice, "Kid, I have the best snack. My girl made these peanut butter balls. They are awesome. She put M&Ms in them too. She's bringing more goodies tonight."

"You love Roberta."

I can sense Joe smiling through the phone. "You would, too, kid. See you soon."

Is it bad that my new best friend has grandkids?

When I arrive, the front door is open. Through the screen door I holler, "Joe?"

"Come on in, Alex. Thanks again. I owe you."

Heading straight to the kitchen, I hand Joe a bottle of wine and a card.

He looks at me surprised. I explain, "My dad says if anyone gives you a referral, bring them a bottle of wine and a thank you card. He's a vodka guy, my mom didn't drink, so we accumulated a stash from people bringing it over."

Patting me on the back, he says, "That's good business. Thanks, man. You have to try one of these." Holding out this peanut butter concoction with oats and chocolate, I grab one.

With my mouth half full, I say, "I love Roberta, too."

Pointing to the table, I see a computer, CD drive, and a few disks. These are old files. While reading over everything, I get to work. My phone, sitting on the island, buzzes. "Can you read me the text?"

Pulling his glasses down from his thinning hair, he reads, "I have a meeting in Morton Grove today. Peqoud's for dinner?"

My dad is really on a roll. He knows I love that place. I tell Joe, "Respond 'yes please.' Toss in a bunch of exclamation marks. That's my favorite pizza spot."

Whatever computer Joe bought, it's super fast. As I load the jump drive, I still can't believe my dad. Turning to Joe, I ask, "Couldn't this have waited until tonight? Can I also ask you a random question?"

He nods, and I ask, "Can someone change overnight?"

With a serious look, Joe pulls up a chair and joins me at the table. "First off, I didn't want you working again before playing. Back to your real question. It happened to me the day I met Jane's mom. I was at this charity event in the city. I had just called the boys to see if they were okay, and this woman, a stunning brunette with perfect teeth, introduces herself to me. She put together the event."

With a sudden pep in his step, Joe hops to the fridge and shows me a picture of himself and his second wife. "That's the night we met. Yes, I was enamored with her looks. But she said to me while we were talking, you can be happy. And it was like this light switched in my brain. I got her business card and thought nothing of it. She's twelve years younger than me, so I thought she was just being friendly. I came home and my oldest looked at me at breakfast. I made them pancakes out of the blue, and he said, 'What the fuck happened to you?'"

Shaking his head in disbelief, Joe continues, "It was like I needed someone to tell me, it's okay to be happy. It's okay to move on with your life. Crazy. I told the boys about Val, and they told me I had to do coffee with her. My youngest joked, 'Bring some protection.' We all laughed and cried."

After a quick reboot of his computer, everything looks to be in order. "Thanks for sharing that. I haven't had that moment yet, but I'm working on it. My dad did. I wonder if he met someone."

Walking me out, Joe says, "First off, I do owe you. Thanks. See you at the game. Come a little early and you can say hello to Jane. She's got some cute friends. You should try and stop by her campus. Second, if your dad does have a lady friend, don't hate her. My boys, despite the encouragement, resisted Val for the first six months, but now they love her."

Heading out of Joe's house, I wonder, is Maddie my dad's girlfriend? I wouldn't blame him. She's got a nice body, the bluest eyes, and is the nicest person. Is that why she stops by? I ponder this all the way to Mike's house.

When I called to set up the appointment, I could hear the depression in his voice. The sarcastic wit from the poker game was gone, and he was matter-of-fact, telling me he needed a full set of knives because of the divorce.

Living walking distance from Joe, I have no trouble finding the house. It looks like an office building, all geometric with a lot of wood. A 'For Sale' sign practically waves hello to me as I pull in. Picking up his newspaper, I head to the door. He sees me from the glass next to the door and slowly gets up from his chair. As if he's given up on life, he's wearing a robe at four in the afternoon.

With a melancholy tone, he greets me. "Hey, buddy. Come on in. You want to buy a house that doubles as an orthodontist's office?"

Hoping to cheer him up, I laugh. "This does look awfully like an office building. Not sure it's a medical building. Maybe."

Mike looks up from his desk, "I printed up the form you sent me." Handing me his order, he says, "Sorry I'm such a sourpuss this morning. Divorce sucks. I'm bitter today. My wife moved out and into her boyfriend's place."

Having sat through countless therapy sessions, I try to help. Each session started with some statement like, "I'm sorry you're going through a rough time. How are you going to get through this?"

Stroking his gray and brown beard, he explains, "I wish I fucking new. I was seemingly the last person to know Jen was fucking her personal trainer and I was paying him to work with her three days per week. I was this guy's pimp and customer. But he did not have enough money for Jen, so she moved on to the real estate agent. That piece of shit was so stupid."

Pausing for a minute, Mike looks at me and shakes his head. "He came to the house wearing a robe and rings the doorbell. I'm in a meeting at work, but I look at my phone because anytime someone rings the doorbell, I get an image texted to me. I'm sitting with my boss and he looks at the picture and says, that man's fucking your wife."

Making two fists, he continues, "My boss is seventy-five years old. I've never heard him swear and for a lawyer, that's saying something. I lost my shit. As I head out the door he's yelling, "If you kill him, I'll get you off."

Watching a thriller in the movie theater doesn't have this much tension. "I open the door quietly. The rage bubbling over me. This asshole had no chance. They must've heard a footstep. I could hear Jen yell out, 'HELLO?' It was coming from the basement. I race down the steps. Being a tall guy, I can intimidate people easily. I stand over him while he is on the couch, staring up at me. My wife is yelling, 'Don't hurt him Mike! It's me, it's all me.' It was some bullshit like that, but I was tuning her out. I smacked him in the jaw and he passed right out."

Standing up to replicate the action, Mike gets up and smacks the air. "After he passed out, I felt much better. I know, it's not right. Violence is not okay. But I'm a lawyer, so I knew to hit him with an open hand. It looks better in court because there's less bruising. I take a deep breath and turn to my wife. 'Pack your shit you dirty bitch. I'm hiring a new real estate agent. And get a lawyer.'"

Absorbing the story I say, "Mike, that's crazy. I'm sorry. What happened next?"

Taking a sip of coffee, he explains, "She moved out. He called and apologized. I mean, I knew this guy for years. The kids are in college, and are slight fuckups, so the only thing we are figuring out is the money. Don't get me wrong, I was a shitty husband. I worked all the time, drank a lot, and missed most things. But I never cheated on my wife, and from day one I told her I'm a work-acholic. Now I just need to get my life together. Maybe I will head to Vegas, pay for some sex, and feel better."

Staring into his dark eyes, I say, "You're tall, rich, and still have your own hair. You can get tons of girls on Tinder."

Exhaling deeply, he asks, "Can you show me how?"

Shaking my head yes, "Mike, I've got you covered."

Mike stands up and says, "Thanks for listening, kid." He walks me out and I'm in disbelief. Every one of these guys has a story crazier than the next.

I wonder to myself, will Rob's story top this?

PIZZA AND POKER

One of the best feelings is finishing a paper for school. It's not sexy and probably a sad state of my current affairs, but the jolt I receive after all my homework is done, is unparalleled. Listening to my self-talk makes me realize how badly I need a girlfriend.

Another wonderful thing is the smell of pizza. From my desk upstairs, I can smell my dad walking in with dinner. The past few months he is delivering on his promise of more time together. My mom always made sure that with all the activities, we ate at least three meals together per week. Taco Tuesday was my favorite. With mad cooking skills, she made fresh tortillas with this little press and the guacamole always tasted authentic.

Following my nose like an old school cartoon character, I literally fly down the steps. They are wooden, treacherous, and I forgot to take off my socks.

With no major bruising, I grab two plates and sit down. "Thanks for bringing this home."

Placing two bottles of Coke on the table, he says, "Mexican Coke and pizza. What can be better? How was your day, buddy?"

Staring my dad in his dark eyes, I ask, "Did you meet a girl?"

Laughing, he says, "No. I am getting set up. Maddie has a friend more age-appropriate than her who wants to meet me. The truth is, Maddie stopped with her questions and just told me in harsh language to get it together. Hearing someone say that woke me up. I know I'll never be like mom." And with that, his eyes began to well up. He also did that thing where you look at the ceiling, hoping it sucks up the tears. "But that's okay." Wiping his tears with a napkin, and then blowing his nose like an old man, he continues, "I can still be a dad and a friend. I want you to go to college. You busted your ass and got into every school you applied to. When you insisted on staying home for a year, I should've pushed back. I'm not stupid. I know you felt like you needed to take care of me. And you don't need to do that. Well—not yet."

Since I've cried out most of my tears, I smile. "I'm happy you're in a better place. If you think we've had a crazy life, I have a story for you!"

Sitting at the table, drinking from a glass bottle, eating the best pizza, and talking to my dad feels effortless—and wonderful.

Over the past few years, I forgot how he listens to stories with his hands. So far, I've gotten the sign when you score a field goal, boxing jabs, and the classic hands on the face like in *Home Alone.*

At the end of the tale, he says, "Alex, that's why you need to balance work with fun. Speaking of which—are you playing poker tonight?"

Pointing at him with both hands, "Yes. Don't wait up. These games go late."

With a sincere gaze into my eyes, he says, "I'll be asleep in my bed. If it's super late or you're tired and don't come back, shoot me a text. Driving tired is like driving drunk."

Loading up the dishwasher, I almost want to stay home and hang out with my dad. This was our best dinner in a long time. Turning to him, I ask, "What are you up to tonight?"

Flexing his arms, he says, "I'm going to work out. Thirty minutes per day is all the experts say you need. Well, since they haven't met me, I'm going to walk for thirty minutes and then use those weights in the basement you have."

Now I feel the tears coming back. These are two years of heartache-healing tears. Hugging my dad, he picks me up like when I was a kid. He laughs, "Maybe I don't need to work out. I can still lift you up."

Processing all this love energizes me. My mom insisted that being love drunk was the best high. She would force me to hug her in front of my friends at school and whisper, "I'm love drunk now. Have fun with your friends."

The competitive juices start to take over as I drive to Joe's house. My strategy tonight is to bluff twice early on and then fold until I have a full house or better.

Per Joe's request, I arrive early to thank Jane for connecting me with her dad. The house seems quiet. Jane and I had one class together my junior year where we set the curve. We would study together with the goal of getting a higher score than the other. At least, that's what I was doing.

Joe greets me at the door with this beautiful olive-skinned, sun-kissed girl. She's wearing overalls with a tube top that makes her boobs pop out. Trying not to get nervous, I smile and extend my hand. "I'm Alex."

"Robbie. Nice to meet you, Alex." Oh my god, this is Roberta? Nerves have me confused, and I hope I didn't just utter that question out loud.

Puzzled, I ask, "You're the cook? I had one of your balls today. It was so good."

Laughing, she replies, "Thanks. Oddly, you're the second person to tell me that today."

I can see a light bulb go off in Joe's head and wonder what he's going to say.

"Alex, can you take Robbie home? Jane and her mom had to make a shiva call. You'll be back before the game starts. Or maybe you guys can grab a coffee. You two have a lot in common."

My mind, which consistently overthinks things, goes off course. Is Joe trying to get me out of the game? Is this really Roberta? Could her lips be any fuller?

Smiling at me with huge brown eyes, she asks, "What do you say, Alex? Can I give you a driving tour of campus? This would be good karma for a knife salesman."

Joe definitely told her about me. Feigning confidence, "I could use some good karma."

Ignoring the flirting, Joe adds, "Drive safe, kid."

Junior and senior year a group of friends went to school dances, but I never had a real date. John used to call me "No Balls," because I was so scared to ask anyone out. Too many movies made me think I needed more witty banter, better looks, or money to impress a girl. John thought Jane liked me, but she just used me for my brain, and I did the same. There was another girl, too, but she always had a boyfriend.

Pulling out of Joe's driveway, I head south on Sheridan Road. Robbie grabs my phone and enters her address. I sent you my contact information. It's Robbie Zerlin if you ever need a meal."

"Thanks. If you need some good knives, I'll hook you up." Robbie keeps talking, but all I can think about is whether people say 'hook you up' anymore. Finally dialing back into the conversation, I respond to her comment about my delicious cookies.

"Did Joe tell you about my cookies?"

"Yeah. He said that they were better than mine. Granted, I've branded myself as a healthy cook, but I still want to have the BEST cookies. Can we make them?"

Thanks to my mom, my baking skills are solid. "My mom was a baker. I have a few secrets. I need you to promise me that you won't put this on social media."

As we pull into a grocery store, she puts a hand over her heart and says, "I swear, I'll die with your recipes."

"Okay. Tonight, I will teach you one recipe. There are two other super-secret recipes. If tonight goes south, just know, you're only getting the vanilla pudding secret." I have no idea where my flirt game is coming from but I'm feeling pretty good so far. I cannot believe my mom is helping me on this sort-of date.

Walking over to my side of the car, Robbie goes on her tippy toes and whispers in my ear, "I'll get those other recipes out of you." I can feel my cheeks fill with redness. She grabs my hand and runs to the doors, "Come on."

The store is as you would expect at eight o'clock on a Thursday night: empty. Focusing on the shelves keeps my nerves calm. Grabbing large chocolate chips, grass-fed butter, and organic eggs, I sense Robbie judging me. "I'm not a snob. This butter is amazing. These eggs have this orange yolk that rivals any other, and my mom only used organic flour."

With a head nod, she says, "You are a knife salesman. I get it, baller. It's cool. Organic flour does not impress me. I'm literally cooking my way through college. Customers who ask for organic pay a premium."

Trembling inside, I try to remain cool on the outside. "I want to let you know that I'm buying all this stuff for you, and I expect nothing in return. Except of course, the most intense cookie orgasm of your life."

We both laugh at my ridiculousness. With a straight face, she counters, "I haven't had one of those in a long time." And then she whispers, "I'm looking forward to it."

The drive to her dorm feels like an eternity. The windows are foggy from all the heat we are giving off. If the night ended right now, if she told me she was too tired or had to study, this would still go down as one of the best nights of my life.

Interrupting my thoughts, Robbie says, "This is way better than an Uber, even if the cookies aren't as good as mine."

"Girl, please. These cookies will change your life. And full disclosure, this is better than taking Joe's money. Even though that's fun too."

Leading me into her dorm, my nervousness creeps back in. I can tell she's a little nervous, too. You don't get good at chess without the ability to read people. While unlocking her door, she says, "Joe said you were really good at cards."

Turning on the lights, with a serious look in her eyes, she leans into me. With a whisper, "Do we melt the butter, or does it need to soften." She then locks the door and leans against it. Am I supposed to kiss her?

Placing the grocery bag on the floor. I turn back around, smile, and whisper in her ear, "Soften."

With a laugh, she kisses me. Immediately, I'm hard. Almost embarrassingly so. Robbie doesn't back away. She leans into me, further surprising me.

After kissing for a few minutes, I pick her up and she wraps her legs around me. Her room is getting steamy. I feel the sweat down my back, which I keep to myself. She lets her legs come down and clumsily unzips my pants.

My first thought is whether Joe paid her to do this. That's ridiculous, right? And then she gets on her knees and starts giving me my first sex act. Unsure what the protocol is, I let out, "This feels amazing. I'm going to cum, I'm going to cum." And then she keeps going, and now I understand what all the hype is about. I've been really missing out. "You are amazing."

With a wink, she says, "It's the lips."

Heading over to her bed, she picks up a glass and takes a sip of water. I'm just staring at her and smiling. It's all I can really do at this point. She takes off her clothes and sits on the bed. Her breasts are perfect, softball size and shape. Like a magician, she has a condom in her hand. She's smiling and waves me to her. "Impressive. That's a quick turnaround, Alex."

"It's your boobs. They are amazing."

"With this big butt, I'm glad I've got boobs to even things out a little."

Placing the condom on me, Robbie lays down, ordering, "Get on top of me."

Taking my time, mostly because I have no idea what I'm doing, I assume the pushup position. Carefully sliding inside, I move slowly back and forth. She leans up and whispers, "Just like that."

Maintaining the pace seems to be working, solely based on the moaning. Her back arches and she lets out a scream. Thankfully, this is lasting longer than the quick blowjob. Thankfully, she flips me over because my arms and chest couldn't last much longer.

With her breasts in my face, it does not take long for me to finish.

Glowing, Robbie starts dressing, "That was unexpected. I've never slept with someone I just met before."

Biting my lip, I say, "Full disclosure: I've never done any of that before. I'm not complaining, but how did this happen?"

Sitting next to me in bed, she says, "You performed flawlessly, not that I'm an old pro. There's this sweetness and sadness in your eyes that really attracted me to you. I know that might sound odd. You were just so easy to talk to. Some of these kids are so pretentious. And lastly, you kissed me with this passion against the door. It really turned me on."

Interrupting this odd discussion, my phone buzzes. Joe's texting. I respond back, "With Robbie baking cookies. See you next week."

Watching me, she states the obvious, "You might as well have said we're having sex."

Before I can think of a response, Jane texts Robbie, "How's baking cookies?"

Robbie stands up and snaps a picture of our groceries and adds, "What are you, playing poker?"

First Joe texts me a thumbs up and then Jane writes to Robbie, "I'm taking Alex's place. And nice Hanes."

Pulling up the picture, I see a part of my undies. Shaking my head, I say, "Nice photo work."

Quickly Robbie responds, "Lol. Just messing with you guys."

Jane writes back, "Sure."

Trying to move on, I say, "I think the butter is soft."

Smiling, Robbie says, "And I like your sense of humor. You're funny."

"Thanks, Robbie. You're really funny, too."

The kitchen looks like a professional one. Robbie pulls out a box with all her supplies. As we get going, I try and focus on the cookies. It's almost as if the sex made me want to have more sex. Which is how I think it's supposed to work.

"We need to beat the sugar and butter for four minutes. That helps get some air into them, which makes the cookies light. With every egg, that's another two minutes. Once we add the flour and pudding, we use a spoon, as we don't want to overmix the batter."

Nodding her head yes, she comments, "Damn, Alex. Even your cooking instructions are making me hot." After a kiss, we keep baking.

"Good news. We need to put this in the fridge for thirty minutes. Chill the butter, that way the cookie doesn't just flatten out."

"I am so impressed. You really know your shit. And I really need to know the other two recipes. I think I earned them."

Lifting her up on the metal island, she sandwiches me with her legs. I tell her, "My mom was incredible. Superwoman. After work, she made us dinner and then baked for parties, events, you name it. Never complaining. She was meticulous. Her piping bag handwriting was like calligraphy. As her helper, I learned a few tricks."

Cocking her head to the side, she says, "For real! What are the other recipes? Don't make me get gangster on you." Squeezing me with her thighs, I can't help but laugh.

"Listen, Tupac—I'll get you those recipes. On date number two we can make both the Nutella special and the oatmeal caramel concoction."

With a sweet smile, she asks, "So you want a second date?"

While preheating the oven, I nod my head yes. Removing the dough from the fridge, I begin making quarter-cup balls. I can feel Robbie watching me, but all I can think about is my mom. During the holidays we spent days making cookies. Sue was meticulous. Instead of measuring cups, we used a scale, and she had different scoopers based on the size of the cookie she wanted. Because she wanted each cookie the exact same size, she often busted out a tape measure. I can hear her soft voice saying, "Presentation matters, Alex. People sadly judge things before they even take a bite." And then she would give me a giant smile, "But to me, an ugly cookie can be DELICOUS!"

Looking over my shoulder as I drop the pan in the oven, I catch Robbie videotaping me. "Should I be creeped out or flattered? And did you video anything else tonight? I'm skeptical of your photography for obvious reasons." We both laugh. I haven't felt this at ease in years.

With a hug for no apparent reason, a real tight hug, I start to choke up. It was like the way my mom hugged me. With her arms still around me, I quickly wipe away a few tears. When will a tight hug not trigger a tear? Sensing an odd emotion, she asks, "Are you not a hugger?"

Reaching my arms around Robbie, I hug her and lift her off the ground. "I'm actually one of the best huggers in the country. I just don't like to brag."

With a deep breath, I tell her, "Here's the truth. I'm going to try not to cry. I make no promises. My mom was a great hugger. She was the affectionate one in the family, and she would give tight hugs out of nowhere, like what you gave me." The tears start to flow and I'm fighting the ugly cry face. At this point, Robbie goes in for another hug. Feeling embarrassed, I apologize. "I'm sorry."

"Don't be sorry. I wish I met your mom. She sounds amazing." Continuing to hold me, she says, "I'm sure your mom is looking down right now and thinking, I can't believe my baking skills got my son laid."

I don't think it's possible for me to smile any bigger. "You're ridiculous. Too bad you can't text her the picture with my underwear in it."

With a serious look, she asks, "What's your dad's number?"

I'm now trying to control my laughter. How is the girl so funny and hot?

The timer buzzes, and I carefully remove the cookies from the oven. At this point, a handful of students that were studying are peeking inside the kitchen. One guy walks in and says, "Dude, this shit smells amazing. You got one to spare?"

We both laugh, as this guy is obviously drunk. His breath smells like cheap wine and pizza. Placing four cookies off to the side, I grab plates and put a cookie under a napkin on each plate.

Handing my new BFF a cookie, I warn him, "Be careful! It's hot." I place all the plates on a tray and walk into this open room with students chatting and studying.

All eyes turn to me. Taking a cue from me, Robbie grabs the other tray of plates. We pass out cookies to everyone. Each time I say, "This is from Robbie's kitchen." It's like we're serving food at a toddler's birthday. The smiles on these kids' faces are huge.

As we walk back into the kitchen, Robbie turns to me and says, "You are an excellent businessman. But now I have no idea if these are truly the best cookies. But I have a feeling I'm going to be very popular after tonight."

Pulling out the plate of four, I get a fist in the air. "You are so getting laid again." Watching the enjoyment on Robbie's face is priceless. A little chocolate gets stuck in her dimple, and I snap a picture.

"What do you think? They are even better the next day. I have no idea why."

Giving me the so-so hand gesture, she smiles, "You win. I'm going to get really fat dating you."

Happiness fills me like helium. "So, there is going to be a second date?"

"Sunday night? I'll be in the burbs delivering food. After, maybe we can make the Nutella recipe and grab dinner."

Gazing into her warm eyes, I try not to fall in love yet. "Does this mean I'm sleeping over?"

With no hesitation, she says, "It's midnight, and you're not driving home. And maybe I like to cuddle."

I shoot a quick text to my dad. "Staying over. Thanks again for the best dinner!"

Before we finish cleaning, my phone buzzes. It's Terry King. Robbie peeks at my phone and is impressed. "How do you know Terry?"

Surprised, I tell her, "He coached my summer league ball team. I forgot he played ball here."

We both read the text at the same time. "Are you on campus? My girl just sent me a picture of someone handing out cookies. Looked like you. And cookies looked familiar."

Laughing, I answer, "Yup. I forgot you go here."

Both of us sit in anticipation, waiting for a reply. He's one of their best basketball players, "Dog, did I miss the Nutella Specials??????"

We both bust out laughing, Robbie screams, "Damn! You gave me the B recipe first?"

"TK loves Nutella. Trust me, these are better."

Texting TK, "=) No, BUT I'm making a batch this weekend. I'll hook you up."

He immediately responds, "Much love. Hit me up whenever you're on campus. I know Duke was your goal but Evanston is great."

In total shock, she asks, "Who are you, Alex? Really? Everyone loves Terry on this campus. And he texts you like you two are besties."

"This is as cool as I get. Trust me. I'm as shocked as you are. I made three dozen cookies for the team once. I guess I made an impression."

Looking at me like I farted on our first date, she asks, "You played ball? I thought you were a chess guy."

"Why is everyone so surprised by this? Why can't I play chess and ball? Chess made me a great point guard. This sounds super geeky, but it really helped me with everything. Except girls. But apparently baking helps to get the girls."

Walking out of the kitchen, a student approaches me and asks, "When are you making more cookies? I would pay top dollar for those. Here's my number. Call me. I need this for my party."

"Sure. Robbie and I will discuss and get back to you."

Heading into Robbie's room, my mind wanders. I made a grand last month selling knives. Between prospecting and the meeting, my hourly rate is not so good. However, I would have to sell a lot of cookies to make a grand.

Reading my mind, Robbie asks, "Are you doing the numbers on a cookie business right now?"

"I know, a cookie business is ridiculous. It probably won't buy me a Range Rover."

Sitting down on her bed, staring at me deeply, she says, "Maybe cookies will make you happy. The look on your face while you were baking and then serving those kids was joy. Why not have some joy?"

Sitting next to her, smelling her vanilla lotion—or maybe it's actual vanilla—I ask, "How about a little joy before bed?"

THERAPY

Despite the fact I slept crammed on a twin bed with another person, I feel amazing driving home. The only person in the world I can share this information with is John. He immediately picks up his phone, maybe because it's early on a Friday morning.

With a tone of concern, he asks, "Are you okay?"

"You are not going to believe my night!"

Before I can ramble, he asks, "Did you win more money? Man, you might not need college."

"Even better. I met my wife. Well, that might be premature, but this girl was at the poker game. She makes food for a bunch of the guys. Like meals for the week and then if they have a party, she attends. Her name is Robbie Zirlin. She might just be an angel. I drove her to campus from my friend's house. Since she's a chef, she heard about my cookies and wanted me to make them." As I take a breath, John cuts in.

"I just looked her up. She's pretty, bro! A Minnesota girl. Wonder what brought her to Evanston? What happened?"

Suddenly my self-doubt creeps in. I tell him, "She slept with me. Like, it was all her. And I have no idea why. Why would she want to sleep with me? Is it strange that that's what I'm thinking now?"

Being the most practical person, he tells me, "Because she wanted to have sex. I've been telling you this for years. Chicks dig you. You are nice, you have those puppy dog eyes, and don't forget about the muscle. Sure, you could benefit from a few more pounds, but you are one fit dude."

My confidence begins to rise. "Thanks man. It was amazing. Really. And then TK randomly found out I was on campus and texted me. She was impressed."

"TK! NO WAY! See, you also have serious connections. TK. The Iowa Cubs. Stop selling yourself short."

Again, I would have to thank my mom for introducing me to the Iowa Cubs team. They came to Chicago, and she was hired to cater a dessert party with a sports theme. Sue was not a sports person, so my dad and I helped her with Cubs Cookies, RBI Floats—and Stolen Base Brownies were a huge hit with white chocolate. That pun was not intended.

"Thanks for the ego boost. This girl is like sugary sweet, friendly, and Dave Chapelle funny."

"I get the picture. Put on the brakes. Don't go purposing tomorrow. Just have fun. Send me some pics of you two. I talk about you all the time and with your lack of social media, people think I made you up. Visit?"

Pulling into my house, I realize this is the longest conversation I've had with John since he left. And he's sober for the call, which is also a nice change of pace. "I will. Maybe I can get her to road trip with me after a few more dates."

"That would be epic. You might have more fun without her. Take it slow. See you at Thanksgiving."

Notifications on my phone buzz. I've sold $2,000 in the first half of the month. Checking my computer, I log into my work account. The Google ad I bought is paying off. I'm now getting a few sales from the web. Combined with word of mouth, this is going to be a banner month! The ad I took out on the wedding registry site is also getting me a few sales. If they gamified school a little like this, kids would do so much better. I'll have to mention this to Dave. I text Dave a quick line about gamification and he calls me immediately.

Highly caffeinated, he asks, "Gamification, tell me exactly what you think."

"When I was younger there were a few games you played on a computer in class. They taught basic things like how to build a city. What if the games were more specific and taught skills on how to start a business, how to combat global warming, games that really teach problem solving?"

I can feel Dave agreeing, "Love it. Our software is different, but let's talk through this later."

Without saying goodbye, the line goes dead. With people offering me guidance all the time, it feels good to give some advice.

Speaking of advice, Maddie calls. I answer, "Hello, Maddie. What's going on?"

"I just wanted to check on you. You seemed freaked out about your dad."

Pausing before the word vomit begins, I tell her, "He's great. Your talk worked. It was shocking that he went from boozed-out, depressed dad to attentive. The past few days have been nice. And I met a girl. She's way out of my league. For some reason, she really likes me. Is it weird that I'm slightly obsessed with why she likes me? I mean she could get any guy. I should be ecstatic, not hyper-analytical. Am I incapable of joy? What is the matter with me?"

Interrupting my downward spiral, she says, "Alex. Alex, relax. You are not abnormal. You don't have to obsess over why she likes you. Answer these questions for me. How many medals have you won? How many assists did you average junior year, and what number were you in your class?"

Thinking for a second, I tell her, "I have well over a hundred awards, but many of them are participation awards, I averaged eight assists, but I also played along aside a senior who plays Division I ball. I was number twenty-two in my class, so no Ivy league school for me."

The frustration seeps through the phone in her tone. "BULLSHIT. You are good at everything you do. Go back to therapy. I can't help you in these small doses. You need someone who can delve into your self-worth. And it's okay to be sad even if your dad is happy, even if you have a girlfriend, even if you're an awesome person. But it's okay to be happy. It's okay to enjoy dating and getting a hug from your dad. Here's your homework. Make a list of your top ten accomplishments. Anything you think of: a girl liking you, the buzzer beater against Maine West, getting into Duke. Drop it off with your usual thank you note for the casserole at the end of the day."

Confused, I ask her, "I thought you told me to stop writing you thank you cards? How did you know about the buzzer beater?"

"Let's be honest, your parents raised you right, and I know it's not your dad's handwriting each time. Plus, your picture was in the paper. Get to it."

I take orders like a good soldier:

- *Buzzer beater against Maine West*
- *Acceptance letters from 10 schools*
- *Robbie liking me*
- *Winning almost $1,000 at cards*
- *Doubling my sales goals in half a month!*
- *4th grade chess school champion*
- *7th grade state chess champ*
- *Junior Nationals judo gold medal*
- *Raising $5,000 for Multiple Sclerosis research*
- *Climbing Mount Rainier*

What does this list say about me? Smiling, I think this worked for the moment. With my self-esteem rising, I copy this to my phone. Whenever self-doubt creeps in again, I'll review this list.

I debate whether to text Robbie, but she beats me to it. She sends me a picture of her and TK eating the last two cookies.

"Look who I ran into!!! He insisted Nutella is better."

Nervous energy fills my entire body and I begin to overthink my response. "He's wrong." And I add a kiss emoji.

She responds with an eggplant, which I think is some sort of dick reference. And then, "Excited for Sunday!"

After I respond, "Me too," my phone rings. And while shocked, I answer, "TK, what's up?"

"Dude, I forgot how good your cookies are. I can't wait for the special. Your girl is cool."

A little surprised, I respond, "I have no idea why she's into me, but so far so good. What's up?"

"Don't be a clown. You're smart as hell, a great baller, and not bad-looking for a pale kid. Hey, since you are around, Peter Sims is having a party tomorrow night. You should stop by with Robbie. The dude's house is sick. This will be classy. His folks put in this backyard with a hoop and outdoor bar. He's grilling. Are you up for some burgers?"

Incredibly shocked, I tell him, "I'm seeing Robbie on Sunday and I don't want to overdo it. I would love to hang out, but that's not my scene. Peter was always a dick when he guarded me."

Responding quickly, he says, "That's a true story. Peter sucked. His mom just up and left his dad and moved to St. Louis to date her college love. Those are not my people either, but you know, it would be nice to support Peter."

The mom thing hits me, and I remember Peter's mom was always at school. He was older than me, but she was so nice. The dad was never around, I don't remember seeing him at any game. I reconsider. "It's five minutes from my house. Swoop by and I'll go for a bit."

With a hint of guilt, he adds, "I might have invited Robbie. She didn't want it to be weird, so shoot her a text, but pretend I said nothing. Cool? We'll pick you up."

"That works." Feeling like TK now owes me, I ask, "What if you came early and we played some ball?"

With zero hesitation, he says, "Hell YEAH! Text me your address and I'll see you around six o'clock. Is it cool if I shower at your place?"

"Of course."

The line goes dead, and I can't help but stare at my phone. TK was a high school legend. Our only interaction was basketball related. He was a great coach too. He attended a handful of games my junior year, and our only interactions were him begging me to bake more cookies.

After starting several different text messages, I finally settle on a note to Robbie. "Sat. night, party in the burbs? No pressure, but it would be cool if u join me and TK. We R hooping first, so his gf would drive you out here."

A few minutes go by, but it feels like hours. She finally types, "In class. Sounds good. PS is it weird that I think this makes us cool?"

ROB AND SUSAN BLACK

With class done for the weekend, I have one last sales call to make. Rob told me to stop over at 4:00 because he is working from home and wants some knives.

Since I now compare all houses to Rick's, I'm guessing this one is smaller. Driving through a small forest, I find his house and it feels eerily secluded. The wooden house reminds me of Lincoln Logs—but really, really, big ones. A Range Rover and Silver Tesla are parked in the garage. I park next to a Jeep Wrangler, and head to the front door.

A woman greets me before I can knock. "Hi. I'm Susan. Rob is on a call." She guides me past a mudroom, and I take a seat at this huge island. It has a sink and built-in gas range, in addition to another oven. "Can I get you coffee or tea? I have the best little crispy cookies. They go great with coffee!"

Her enthusiasm sells me. I tell her, "I would love some coffee and maybe one cookie. I did work out today."

Cocking her head toward me, she asks, "Did you spin? I feel like everybody is spinning these days."

"I've done the same workout for five years. I run two miles and then lift weights. On off days, I hit a heavy bag. We have weights and a bag in my basement."

Susan, who looks like she works out daily, flexes for me. Her bicep pops out. She says, "I do yoga, walk, and Pilates twice a week. You've got to try Pilates. It changed my life. I was a little chubby and had a horrible back after I had my kids. A few months after I started this regimen, I felt great."

Walking down to the basement, I see the full Pilates spread. She has machines on the wall, floor, and what I think they call the Cadillac of Reformers in the center of the room. Beaming with pride, she says, "It took me a bunch of years, but I built this up one piece at a time. When the kids started to go to school, I got certified in Pilates. I teach down here. First session is on the house. It's good for your mind, body, and soul. You can bring a friend. Can you tell I'm a hippy?"

Leading me back to kitchen, she asks, "What's your story? Why are you selling knives?"

Trying to match her high level of energy, I tell her, "I want to make money. When I head to college at some point, I want money in the bank. I want to build a good base so one day I can have my own company. I'm not sure what that will be. My plan was to work in investment banking for a few years after college. Get some good contacts, make some money. Then start something of my own."

With a million-dollar smile, she responds, "Ambitious. I like it! Don't forget to have fun."

Smiling back, I say, "Thanks, coach. I appreciate the advice. Do you want to buy some knives? I'm a low-pressure salesman. I've learned that for most people who've been married as long as you and Rob, you still use the knives that you got for a wedding present."

Shaking her head yes, she says, "Shit. Our knives are over twenty years old. I cook all the time. I'm always complaining that these knives are dull. Get me a set. What about flatware? Oh, and I really want copper pots and pans."

Taking notes, I jot down flatware, which it seems like everyone wants, and copper cookware. We don't sell it, but I'll find some.

Looking into Susan's smoky eyes, I tell her, "I'll send you a quote for everything by Tuesday at the latest. Is there a budget you're looking at?"

After a sip of coffee, she says, "I know copper is not cheap. I grew up dirt poor. My mom had one copper pot. Now I'm telling you twenty-five hundred dollars. What a life."

"Done. You really made it! Thanks for making time for me. Tell your husband I'll see him next week at poker."

With her hands in the air, she says, "I can't believe this is my life. I went to college on a track scholarship and met Rob at my first job. We lived in a one bed, one bath for two years. Struggling. Keep hustling."

Running into the kitchen and muting his phone, Rob exclaims, "Roberta! She's nice and a ten! Are you seeing her again?"

Covering my face in embarrassment, I ask, "Does everyone know?" He shakes his head yes.

I admit, "I will see her again. She's pretty awesome."

Susan beams like she set us up. "I only met her a few times, but Rob loves her granola bars. She is the best. She's got great boobs."

"What is the matter with you people? I'll be touch. Maybe Robbie and I will come over for a Pilates session."

Shaking her head yes, repeatedly, she exclaims, "We are totally doing that! I'm so excited!"

Embarrassed, I make my way home. I decide to stop at the store for groceries. Grabbing the ingredients for the Nutella cookies, memories of shopping with my mom play on repeat. The store was her favorite place. When Whole Foods opened, she was in heaven. We walked down every aisle like we were venturing through a secret land, purchasing rare ingredients. Every week she would splurge, and we would try one new item. Celtic sea salt was one of her favorite finds. She would say, "Alex, these thick, salty chunks will make any pastry shine."

Grinning and reminiscing through the store feels good.

"Hey, buddy!" My dad yells through the car as I pull in. He's sweaty, but all I want to do is take a picture of him.

"Great headband dad! Is that from the 1980s?"

Helping me with the groceries, he laughs, "You are a funny guy. Sweat burns the eyes. Hey, are you making the Nutella specials? Did TK ask for some?"

I pause. "That's a great memory. And yes, he's coming over tomorrow and then we are going to a party with his girlfriend and this girl I met."

I feel his magically glowing smile, beaming like a flashlight. "Girl? Oh my God, that's why you stayed out! You little dog. I can't believe it! I'm your dad, so spare the details, but what happened?"

Sitting down at the table, not sure what to tell him, I start rambling, "She cooks for these rich people that play poker with me. Her name is Roberta. I had originally pictured this large old woman, but she's this hot college kid. She is so nice and really likes me, I think. We made cookies in her dorm's kitchen and one of the kids studying was TK's girlfriend. The world is pretty small."

Pride and body odor fully take over my dad. "That is a great story! I'm not going to be weird, but I'm excited to meet her. TK always liked you. I remember your junior year he would come to games and text you tips afterwards. I NEED to go shower, badly!"

FUN?

With all my friends at college, I'm afraid I do not know how to socialize anymore. The only good thing about this party tonight is that I'll know a lot of people. I'm also going with a date which is new for me. With the usual self-doubt creeping in, my personal therapist, Maddie, shoots me a text.

"Like the list. Text me one thing you are grateful for."

"You =)"

Per usual, she responds quickly, "I'll take that."

I fire away, "Is socializing with old friends like riding a bike? Asking for a friend."

A clapping emoji is followed by, "YES! You will be fine. Have a good day!"

Reviewing the library of books in our living room, I see something I was too embarrassed to Google: *The Joy of Sex*. Researching each chapter like I'm studying for an exam, a text interrupts me.

It's Robbie. "What are u doing right now? What's your address?"

I text a picture of the book, as I have no shame. "Just researching =)"

The voice in my mind immediately questions my text. Robbie shoots back, "Um, I'm coming over now. JK. You crack me up. TK said 8:00. Is that cool?"

COOKIES KALE & COFFEE

Breathing a little easier, I write, "Now or then."

My dad walks in as I put the book away, and I feel like I just did something wrong. Without looking my way, he asks, "Do you want to grab some lunch?"

Following him into the kitchen, I say, "Sure. I can also whip something up."

While spreading mustard, turkey, and cheese on chunky sourdough, I say, "Dad, I have no idea if anyone will want to, but is it cool if my friends stay over at our house?"

The full-dimple smile is out. "We have a queen size futon in the basement and a blow-up mattress. I have no idea if I'm supposed to let a girl sleep in your bed. Do I give you condoms? What do you think?"

Swallowing, I say, "I have no idea if anyone is going to stay over, but I wanted to make sure if I offer that you are okay with it. Maybe we will all stay in the basement."

Fully aware when I took health in high school, I was given a box of condoms that I never used. "You are almost nineteen years old. If you went to college like I wanted you to, this would be a nonissue. That's how I'm going to treat this. Have fun and be smart."

Staring into his brown eyes, I say, "Thanks. I will."

The old man cleans up lunch as I finish off some homework. Suddenly, a new text exchange blows up my phone. It's all the poker guys, and Joe's text is the first. "Can anyone teach me stick? I got myself a little birthday present."

None of these old rich guys can drive stick, I muse to myself. I respond, "How is it the youngest guy on the chain can drive stick?"

The responses are similar. "Card shark, lady's man, and race car driver," is Rob's response. He also adds, "Susan loves you."

Joe dials me, "Hey kid. I guess you are my tech support and life instructor. Stop by for a little driving lesson."

Without asking what car he purchased, I agree to stop over at his house. Walking out the door my dad says, "I'm glad you have some friends your own age now."

Carefully, I park next to a silver, two-door, Aston Martin sports car. Joe pops out before I can reach his door. He looks like a kid on his birthday, "Can you believe this is my present? Val surprised me last night. I would never spend this kind of money, but her parents' estate just settled, and she got me this."

"You are like James Bond! This car is amazing. Are you sure you want me driving this? Do you have insurance?"

Grinning ear to ear, like he's 5, he says, "Start it up, kid. Show me how it's done. Maybe we can drive around Edgewood Middle School's lot. It's pretty big."

With my nerves shaking, I take a few deep breaths. My mom had this old Volkswagen that was stick. Of course, her lessons are helping me once again. That clutch was tough. It took me six months before I could drive it without it stalling at some point.

As I start the car, it makes loud noises like a race car. I slowly start to back out of the driveway. I say, "Joe, I cannot believe this is what my life has become."

"Kid, the turns your life will take will surprise the crap out of you. One minute you're a normal guy, and then, suddenly, you're buying a big house near a lake. You're struggling to make ends meet, living on canned tuna, and then you're paying some girl to prepare meals for you. Now, an eighteen-year-old kid is teaching me how to drive a six-figure car."

Beads of sweat form on my back as I fly down Sheridan Road. I have no idea how fast the car is going, but it feels like I'm flying. This car was made for winding roads, and the clutch is like butter. It's so much easier to drive than my mom's old car. Joe is amazed watching me handle the car. We pull into the middle school parking lot doing 60 miles per hour, and it literally feels like I'm going 20. I slow down and explain how to step on the clutch and shift.

Joe practices with an air clutch. We switch seats and I coach him around the lot, then the block. His calmness and focus are impressive. Zipping around the neighborhood, Joe starts poking me about Robbie. Whenever his driving makes me feel like puking, I gaze at the horizon. He's getting better, but still a little jerky.

With a gentle smile, he tells me, "It's impossible not to like either of you. I mean Robbie is so sweet. She told me she would teach me to cook, and I could save more money. It's funny because

I always thought she was a pretty girl, but never put you two to-gether. I thought you would probably go for my daughter. Anyway, this works better for the moment."

I never considered dating Jane, but I had a slight crush on her. She was one of the popular girls. I remember on days there were football games, she would wear her cheerleading outfit and she looked so perfect. The blue in her eyes really shined in her blue shirt. John pressured me hard to ask her to the winter formal, but we were just studying together, and I didn't know how to escape the friend zone.

"Joe, I have no idea what I'm doing with women. Like none. For some reason, I can easily joke around with Robbie, but usually I freeze up."

With his confidence growing, he zips us onto the highway. "The only advice I can offer is to listen to her. Ask her what she likes. That goes for the bedroom, restaurants, and parties. I know kids play games, but I've been a straight shooter my whole life and I did fine with women."

Zipping off the highway to turn around, the car stalls on the incline at Tower Road.

Joe inhales, "Fuck. What I do?"

"Start the car again and keep your foot on the clutch. This sometimes happens. You were doing awesome. Of course, on the highway with no traffic is easy, but hills always suck. Keep going."

The drive back to his place is quick. The jerkiness is gone. "You've got this, Joe. It took me months to get good at it."

Pulling next to my car, he stalls again and turns the car off. "My first car was a stick, but that was like fifty years ago. I needed a refresher course. I really appreciate your help. Was this okay?"

Not holding back, I say, "Are you kidding me? That was AMAZING! I was flying down the street, taking turns way too fast. I felt like we were in a buddy cop movie."

Laughing, he says, "Kid, you crack me up. Thanks for the tips. See you Thursday night."

I drive home in disbelief of the entire situation.

TK waves at me as I pull into the driveway. He's shooting hoops.

It's surreal seeing one of the most popular kids from school waiting for you to come home.

Apologizing, I say, "Sorry. I thought you were going to come in an hour."

"No worries, bro. I stopped in at my house first and my mom was gone, so I got dropped off here. Your pops let me in. He's so nice."

Pulling out my phone, I see the text message from my dad and TK. Excitement quickly takes over as I pull up the picture of the car. I show TK. "Look at this car! I just drove this James Bond car around Highland Park. It's Jane's dad's car. I play poker with him and his buddies, but none of them know how to drive a stick, so I taught him. It was crazy. That car is probably what my college will cost. Well, four years."

Shaking his head in disbelief he says, "Only in Highland Park does some old white dude have enough money to get that car, and need a kid to teach him how to drive it. That's a sweet ride."

With a serious tone, TK peers into my soul. "I need to work on my shot and my handle. Warm up with a game of twenty-one and then shoot, and maybe you can guard me while I dribble two balls?"

Looking at the sky, this is a moment I'm grateful for. The best basketball player to graduate from my school in decades wants to shoot around with me. I didn't even play senior year. Trying to shake the rust off, I do a few shooting drills I learned at basketball camp. My mom found this camp in Los Angeles coached by past and current players. Begrudgingly, I went the summer after she died. I remember my dad yelling at, "SHE WANTED THIS. THIS WILL MAKE HER HAPPY! I PROMISE!"

The camp was amazing. It was two weeks long. I stayed on the campus of a small school and we played ball from sunrise to sunset. My game improved in all facets. Burned out on chess, I focused on hoops and poker. The poker was mostly because the kids would play it on the bus.

Standing almost a head taller than me, TK challenges all my shots. I can see he really wants to block my shot. Eyeing me, he says, "I'm going to block one, kid. I forgot how high your arc is. I need to do that drill you did at the start."

We both dribble two balls up and down the driveway. I can see my dad peeking out from the living room blinds. The glow in his eyes is something I don't think I've seen since I won my first judo trophy. Maybe the old man and I are starting to heal.

Dripping in sweat, TK turns to me, "Water break?"

Heading inside, he asks with a serious tone, "How are things with Robbie? That girl is funny. I'm sitting at a table talking to my girl, and she says, 'I got you, man. Don't go anywhere.' And then she runs away. Ellie, my girl, tells me that's the cookie lady. A minute later, she pops up, hands me a cookie, and tells me the first one is on the house. There we go. She sat down and kicked it with us for a bit."

Trying to stop sweating, I tell him, "I have no idea why she likes me. I mean, she's like really pretty, right?"

In full agreement, he says, "She's hot, dude. She was drilling me for information about you. I told her you were the coolest geek I knew."

Laughing, I say, "Thanks. I appreciate that. But really, why me?"

Checking out my fridge, TK says, "Alex, don't be stupid. You're a good-looking dude, smart as hell, and you can BAKE! Where are my Nutellas?"

Pulling out the freezer row with the Nutella chunks, I say, "I promise we can make some when the girls get here."

My dad, who has been hiding, but probably eavesdropping, pops in the kitchen. "Do you guys want me to order some food? I know you're going to a party, but I can pick up some wings and salad."

Interested, the baller puts a hand on my dad's shoulder. He says, "Maybe?"

"Whatever you want. Just promise me you'll shower while I'm out."

"The old man has some jokes. I don't like spicy, so barbecue would be great. I'm going to shower. Also, I'm in pre-season diet mode, so salad would be awesome if possible. Thank you, sir."

EYE CONTACT

Robbie and Ellie pull up as my dad pulls in with the food. As Robbie gets out of the car, my eyes almost pop out of my head. She's wearing a tube top, her chest is popping out, and the bottom of her flat stomach is just visible. Her jeans are tight, and with what looks like a little make-up, she looks cover girl-ready.

Sensing my nerves, TK interjects, "Just look her in the eyes."

My dad then embarrassingly says what we are all thinking, "DAMN! They both got dolled up for you two." Ellie also looks great, but Robbie is glowing.

Robbie walks in first and after kissing me on the cheek, says, "Hi, Mr. Culp. It's great to meet you. Thanks for having us."

She goes in for a hug and I know immediately that my dad likes her. "It's nice to meet both of you. There's plenty of food in the kitchen. I have to run. I can't even believe I'm saying this, I have my first date in over twenty years. Wish me luck! And kids, feel free to spend the night. If you end up drinking and need a ride home, call an Uber. Have a great night."

Hearing my dad say he has a date is a little freaky. I knew he was getting set up, but it's like he's moving on from mom. I know it's been a long time and he's entitled, but it stings a little. I cover it up with excitement. "Have fun, dad! You'll be great! Thanks for dinner."

In his sportcoat and slacks, my dad heads back to his car. I can sense nervousness in his walk. He looks more uncomfortable than me.

Ellie and TK sit together on the couch and whisper like they're telling secrets.

Robbie backs me into the island where all the food is sitting. Her breasts are pressed against me and the smell of vanilla sugar on her arms is intoxicating. Whispering in my ear, she says, "I love this kitchen. A double oven, big island, two large mixers ... is it weird this is getting me in the mood?"

I can feel my heart beating, or maybe her heart beating, but it's going fast. I'm definitely hard. I have no idea what to say. "Should I ask TK and Ellie to step outside?"

She laughs this belly laugh, and I can feel her stomach push into me. She turns to TK, "You guys, please dig into the food. Alex is going to give me a quick tour."

With her red painted nails, she intertwines our hands and leads me upstairs. The moment we get to my room, she kisses me like I've never been kissed in my life. "Did that kitchen really get you hot and bothered?"

Waving her dark hair behind her, like she's doing a hair commercial, "No, silly. You did. With your arms bulging in that tight polo. And your aftershave." Peeling off my shirt, I try and take meditative breaths like the sex book talked about.

"Robbie, you're beautiful. And I'm not just saying that because you're naked on my bed."

Making the international quiet sign, she adds, "Just be quiet and quick."

Smiling honestly, "That won't be a problem."

As we start kissing, Robbie wraps a leg around me, and rolls. She's now on top of me. Proud of her move, she asks, "Do you like that?" With her breasts covering my face, I continue to take slow, deep breaths. I know she wanted a quickie, but a minute is probably a little too quick.

Slowly riding into her, I use my hands to caress her body. Pressing her body into me, she whispers, "You feel so good." And that's it. I cannot hold it any longer.

Running downstairs like nothing happened, I notice TK and Ellie are still on the couch. Although it seems like we've gone for hours, it's been maybe seven minutes.

Trying to be a good host, I place all the food on plates, and bust out drinks and silverware. Robbie helps, like we're setting the table for our children. Looking toward the couch, with a deep voice, she says, "Kids, the table is ready." We all look at Robbie, as we are a little impressed with how low her voice can go.

With everyone seated, I open the freezer and pull out the Nutella. Turning the oven to 350 degrees, and pulling out chunks of dough, Robbie perks up, "Oh yeah!!! That's my man! You will tell me how the dough is prepared?"

"Of course. I wrote it down for you."

Other than John, my dad, and me, no one has been around this table in a long time. I take a mental snapshot of this moment, as it's my most grateful moment for the day. Age-appropriate friends, good food, and sex with a partner makes for an incredible moment.

Between bites, Robbie asks TK, "Do you have any good basketball stories?"

He explains, "The first time I met Coach K, I was so nervous. I scored fifteen points that night, and he stared into my eyes like he was gazing into my soul. After the game he told me, 'Keep shooting, King.' I was mesmerized. He knows my name? I forgot that it was on my jersey."

Ellie has her hand on his knee while she eats. She has this natural confidence, like she doesn't feel weird in her skin. Dating a school celebrity seems to mean nothing to her. "I know you love these tales, Alex. The truth is, he still can't run a mile. Who do you think helps him out in math? I prep and tutor him before every test."

Robbie is finger deep into her wings. There's no fork or knife, just her own method of splitting the bones to get to the meat. It makes me like her even more. Surprisingly, no one steals a beer from my dad. They all want either Coke or Diet Coke.

With TK still eating, Ellie and Robbie clear the table. Robbie puts her arm around me and asks, "Cookie time?"

After grabbing a giant cookie sheet, I place the frozen hazelnut butter down and put a chunk of dough over it, one by one, until the tray is filled. Robbie helps me with the second tray. We pop them in the oven and Robbie asks, "Why freeze the Nutella?"

"It spreads too much otherwise. Once we tried just mixing it into the batter. That was good, but you really don't get that yummy chunk of sweetness."

Robbie, looking at me puzzled, "Yummy chunk of sweetness. Who says that?"

Ellie, placing a hand in her curly blond hair says, "TK has been talking about cookies nonstop. I really loved the one you handed out the other night. I'm glad you've made them because now he can shut up."

When the timer buzzes, the entire kitchen and family room fills with the smell of chocolate. It's not the vanilla smell from regular cookies; it's better. I pour everyone a glass of milk—not to dunk, but to sip. My mom once threatened to throw a kid out of our house for dunking her cookie. Milk helps balance out the sweetness.

TK gushes, "THESE ARE SO GOOD! They live up to my memory. Alex, you have mad skills."

Out of all my skills, this is the one that builds friendships. My mom is smiling so hard right now. I remember all the variations of this cookie. She spent three days making different types. I loved the cookie with the spread on top. She wanted gooey. This delivers.

Robbie is having a food-gasm, "Oh my God. Oh my God. You are so getting lucky later. You lied. These are better. I could bathe in this stuff."

Of course, my dad walks in at that very moment because what's more awkward than a picture of your underwear on the floor?

Everyone laughs and I join in, but I'm dying a little inside.

Trying to save the day, my dad says, "I need to learn how to bake. I love that smell." I can tell he's thinking of my mom. On Friday nights, the house was filled with some sort of treat, and it smelled amazing. We had to get an extra fridge to store all the sweets. My dad joked that my mom needed a padlock to keep us out.

Robbie turns to my dad, hands him a cookie, and asks matter-of-factly, "How was the date?"

Taking a seat around the island, he explains, "She was fine. Actually, she was really pretty, but super into fitness. I'm all for working out, but this woman was obsessed. She does yoga, Pilates, lifts weights, runs, and something else called Zumba. What the hell is that?"

Ellie cuts in, "I love Zumba. It's like Latin-style dancing to music."

Robbie, talks to my dad like they are old friends, "She might know how to really move."

Biting her lip, like she knows she messed up, Robbie follows up with a question. "Too far?"

Pointing both fingers at Robbie, my dad says, "I love this girl. You are funny, Robbie. When are you kids going out? I thought for sure I would come home to an empty house."

Answering for the group, I tell him, "They wanted cookies. We are leaving shortly."

Getting up, my dad hugs everyone like he has four kids. He walks upstairs, purposely giving us privacy. I immediately turn to Robbie, "What is the matter with you? You told a sex joke to my dad."

With her hand on her head, she says, "I know. I'm sorry, and when I said the 'You're getting lucky' comment, I had no idea he was home. I promise I won't send him the picture."

Ellie, who has been mostly quiet cuts in, "What picture? You guys are kinky."

While my cheeks fill with embarrassment, Robbie responds, "Long story."

Driving to Peter's house, TK tells the story about how Peter's mom left and about how the dad's a mess. Peter has one more year at school, but since he's at Lake Forest, he sees his parents all the time.

Walking into Peter's house with TK, I feel like I'm friends with a celebrity. All these frat boys greet TK with high fives, fist bumps, and hugs, like he's in the NBA. I recognize most of them from high school. Most of the guys are close to my age. They probably only know me because I played ball. Bobby Smalls comes up and gives me a hug. I took his starting point guard job. He always joked, "I could crush you at chess." I thought he would hate me, but he was nice enough. His friends used to give him shit that a junior took his spot. Kids can be cruel. Because my mom passed away, it brought me some peace at school. You must be a real dick to make fun of a kid who lost him mom.

"How's college, Smalls? You still hooping?"

Completely ignoring me, and staring at Robbie, he extends his hand, "They call me Smalls."

Smalls continues, "We played ball together. Don't let this guy fool you. He's a stone-cold killer on the court."

Without missing a beat, Robbie says, "You should see him the bedroom. Nice to meet you, Smalls."

Beer shoots out of his nose as he laughs. "She's a keeper, Alex. I play intramural ball, but I stole your pump fake. I could probably take you now."

At this point, TK walks up and laughs, "Shut up, Smalls. I have twenty dollars that says you couldn't get three shots."

Beer courage keeps Smalls talking, "Fuck you, TK. I'll take both of you, Wildkat."

Shaking her head, Robbie cuts in, "What is the matter with you guys? But my money is also on the stone-cold killer."

Observing this conversation feels like high school. Trash talk was never my thing, but I would beat that kid. Removing myself from the conversation, I say, "I'm going to grab a drink. Feel free to continue this discussion."

Smalls starts yelling as I walk off, "I would WHIP you at chess."

What is the matter with him? Grabbing a Coke, I try to ignore him. Whenever I was in a match and someone started talking smack, I completely ignored them. That always irritated them because they all want to get a rise and a response. When I lost, I would always shake their hand and say, "Good game," and made sure the following game, I would crush them. No one likes a trash talking chess-head.

Sitting back down, stupidly, I figured the conversation ended. Peter then rolls a chess/checkers table next to me. "Will you please shut Smalls up once and for all?"

"You really want to have a party where lame kids play chess?"

Responding, he screams, "HELL YEAH! I just remember when you took over Smalls spot, his only defense was how good he was at chess."

"FINE!" Turning to Robbie, "I'm sorry. This is officially the weirdest party."

Kissing me on the cheek, "This is actually super fun for me. I'm having a blast. I go to school with a bunch of geeks, so nothing like this has ever happened. But maybe it should."

Quickly setting the table, I see Smalls bouncing his knee up and down. He's already nervous. Now I feel bad because I took his spot on the court and now, I will beat him at chess. Robbie whispers, "He's a jerk. Just smoke him."

My confidence and ego are now boosted. Who knows, maybe he's good. Maybe he played two hours of chess a day as a kid, like me. I let Smalls go first. He makes a rookie mistake by leaving his queen open on the first move. Maybe he likes to attack with his knights.

TK is commentating like this is Monday Night Football. More than half the kids are watching us play.

Three moves later, I scream, "SMALLS!!!! Why did you make me do this? Checkmate."

TK announces, "And it's over. Have a good night, ladies and gentlemen."

He stares up at the sky like he just lost an Olympic gold. "Best out of three?"

I can't stop laughing because I have no idea if he's serious or kidding. Robbie sits down in his seat. "How about me?"

With Robbie sitting next to me, I assume more people would watch, but I'm wrong. The group moves onto the ping-pong table. Starting out with her pawns, Robbie carefully attacks me. Allowing the game to move slowly, I ask, "Tell me about your family?"

Intensely gazing into my eyes, she says, "Check."

"Robbie, that's not check. That's my queen."

"I knew that. My family is the best. They are Minnesota nice. My sister is a senior in high school and hopefully going to the University of Wisconsin in Madison. We talk or text throughout the day. I did not send her the picture, but I told her about you. My mom and dad are barely married. They are complete opposites. My dad is a serious CPA, focused, and an intense sports fanatic. He warned me that I could not become a Chicago Bears fan. My mom is sweet, loving, and goofy. I'm her child for sure. She can also cook! Everything I learned is from her or from cooking shows."

With most of her pieces gone, she says, "I give up. Thanks for not embarrassing me."

Robbie moves onto my lap. I softly kiss her cheek. "How did this happen?"

Her one drink is starting to kick in, "I mean Alex, you're like boy band pretty. How did you get all those muscles?"

I think that's a compliment, "I spent ten years working out intensely when I did judo. The workout is no joke. Comparatively, basketball was a walk in the park. Now, I have nothing to do but homework, sell knives, and lift weights."

"Why did you quit? Are you a ninja?"

Kissing her feels so natural. After a sweet kiss, I explain, "I went to class two to four times a week for over an hour. I loved the matches, as they felt like chess. But I got burned out. Basketball was more fun. I liked chess, but I really enjoyed the camaraderie of a team sport. What was your thing?"

Her entire face lights up, "Dance. I wanted to be a dancer. My mom has legs for days, she was a ballerina growing up and that's all I wanted. But I'm built more like my dad's family. I didn't have the height. Hip hop was my jam."

Taking a quick picture of us, I send it to Maddie and write, "Grateful for her."

Looking at me, she asks, "Who's Maddie? And I'm glad you feel that way."

Getting lost in her warm brown eyes, I tell her about my neighbor. "She's a therapist friend. In two years, she's dropped off a dozen casseroles. I think my dad asked her to stop by because I hated all the shrinks he sent me to. A few days ago, she asked me to write this list, and tell her what I'm grateful for."

Somehow, looking deeper into my eyes, "Are her visits helping?"

Shaking my head yes, I say, "I feel great!"

Music starts to pour out of speakers and Robbie stands up and starts dancing like she's in a music video. I comment, "You can dance!"

Standing up, just trying to bounce to the beat, Robbie gets close, "Hey, did you really read that sex book?"

With a perverse grin, "Of course! I'm a researcher."

Leaning in and standing on her tip toes, she asks, "What are we going to try tonight?"

Laughing, because I know she's serious, I say, "I have some tips for long strokes and circular motion."

With a confused look, "Are we talking about oral sex?"

A little embarrassed, I tell her, "It's actually for both, but there was an entire section on oral sex."

With a serious look, she exclaims, "That's what I'm talking about." We both burst into laughter.

TK and Ellie are sitting down near us. I thought he would be talking to everyone, but he's just relaxing with his girl. Robbie leans toward him, "TK, are you ready to go?"

Shaking his head to the beat, "I think we are going to hangout for a while. See you guys on campus." With hugs, Robbie and I head out.

Instead of taking a ride with a possibly sober kid, we call for a ride. Somehow the driver arrives in no time.

Heading straight to my basement, I have questions. "You're really good at fooling around and you attacked me on our first date. How many boyfriends have you had?"

Sitting on the couch, Robbie waves me next to her. "True story, first time I ever attacked a boy was you. I've had three boyfriends. Miles was my high school boyfriend. All he wanted was to have sex and I was not ready, so he dumped me. Freshman year of college, I dated this MBA student. We met at a bookstore. You should know that I like bookstores. Anyway, we dated for six months, but it took him two months to sleep with me. Boyfriend three, I met at a bar. He went to Loyola and we just hit it off. We dated for about six months. It took him five dates, and a lot of White Claw. Okay, maybe it was two dates, drinking puts me in the mood. And you?"

"I've been practicing a lot, but not so much with a real person."

Pulling me on top of her, we make out. She takes off her pants. "Let's see what you learned."

Focusing like I'm doing surgery, I do as the book says and listen for hints of what she likes. The moaning indicates I'm doing a good job. Panting, she says, "Stop. Stop! You did it. Oh my God did you do it!"

Because I need confirmation, I ask, "Really, was it that good?"

Smiling, she says, "Are you kidding me? That was amazing. Are you sure you've never done that before? You better hurry up with that condom!"

While sitting down, Robbie sits on top of me, facing away. Placing two yoga blocks under her feet, she goes to work. Her amazing butt bounces on me, and I'm trying to think of anything else, hoping that will buy me more time. She grabs my arms and puts one hand on her breasts and the other down low.

Cleaning up afterwards, I ask, "How did you get the idea for the yoga blocks?"

"I saw them and thought that might help me get a little more leverage." Giggling, "Next, we use that suspension trainer."

COOKING

Sleeping in the basement just felt awkward. I set up Robbie with sheets and pillows, but I stayed in my room. With my dad on his new workout kick, I hear his door open and I don't want him to wake Robbie.

Surprised to see me alone, he asks, "Where are your friends?"

With a yawn, "TK and Ellie headed home last night. Robbie is sleeping downstairs. Do you care if we use the kitchen for her meal preparation? She has clients out this way."

Drinking water so cold he is forced to slow down, my dad holds up a finger to buy him some time. "Of course. It's not like I cook." Raising both his hands in the air like he has the best idea ever, "You need to make her the blueberry pancakes for breakfast!" He pauses. "But then she might never leave you. Those are powerful pancakes."

Baking with my dad feels funny. Sometimes he would help my mom, but that was really my job. She even paid me on the weekends when I would spend hours in the kitchen with her.

My dad throws me a lemon so much harder than my mom. "It's not a baseball, dad."

"Sorry. Baseball was really your best sport. Why did you quit?"

"I hated getting hit. Why did I always get hit?"

Laughing, "I thought you did that on purpose to get on base. Now I get why you hated it."

Zesting the lemon into the batter, I hear the pitter patter of feet walking up the stairs. Even with bed head, wearing an old Five Star Camp shirt of mine, and shorts that almost go to her feet, she looks beautiful. With a smile, she says, "Good morning, guys."

Before I can pour the first oversized pancake on the gridle, she yells, "I FREAKING LOVE PANCAKES. Man, this house is good to me!"

My dad inappropriately cuts in, "I do not want to know, but these pancakes will blow your mind."

The sweet smell of blueberries and hint of lemon fills the air. My dad brings her a cup of coffee and I serve them both giant pancakes. Warming the syrup in hot water, I place it in the center of the table. Robbie digs in before getting the syrup. "DAMN! These are AMAZING! You two should open a bed and breakfast."

With a cheesy grin on his face, I know my dad already loves her. "Robbie, do you like cream or sugar?"

Without a missing a beat, she says, "I like my coffee like I like my men: strong and black!"

I haven't seen my dad laugh like this in a long time. Robbie adds, "'I'm kidding. Some milk would be perfect."

As awkward as it could be having my girlfriend of a few days staying over and eating breakfast with us, it feels like we've been doing this for years.

Sitting down with half of a pancake and chicken patties, I feel them both ready to pounce on me. Robbie starts first, "Portion control—*that's* how you keep the six-pack."

My dad turns to Robbie, "Right? This guy is so regimented. It's ridiculous. He takes thirty minutes during the week to brainstorm how to sell more knives. That's at seven o'clock, after his fasted workout. Today, he's going to take you to the gardens for a ninety-minute walk. Then, he will eat a salad with chicken for lunch."

Interrupting their moment, I interject, "I'm a creature of habit. Get off my back, slackers. I'm on track to sell a ton of knives and copper pots. Don't ask. And Robbie, Susan wants us to do Pilates with her."

Robbie, turning to my dad, "Be honest, sir. Is this how he gets the girls—cookies and trampoline sized pancakes?"

Taking his plate to the sink, "Yes. I do love the cookies, but the cinnamon scone—that's my favorite thing. Oh, and the banana bread."

Giving us some privacy, my dad heads downstairs. Robbie is still working on her pancake. "I never thought to zest lemon into a pancake. That's genius. Are we really going to go to the Botanic Garden?"

"Baking often equals sampling sugary treats. To offset that, my mom walked and walked. On the weekends, we went to the gardens before cooking. We don't have to do that. I know you have a lot of meals to prep. We can do it here, and I'm happy to help. If you want."

"The gardens are awesome. We have to hit the Japanese gardens because it's my favorite part."

"The first six months after my mom died, my dad took me to the gardens. I never wanted to go and we said nothing to each other the entire time. It was awful and peaceful at the same time. Once he started drinking, I went alone. This is my meditation, and I always start with that part."

With a serious look, she says, "I don't want to interrupt your meditation. I can run to the store and get my food."

Taking her hand, I tell her, "I would love if you joined me. It's so quiet when you go there early. I think you'll like it."

The crisp fall air is colder than I want it to be. Robbie, wearing one of my hoodies, an old school Chicago Bull's hat, and a pair of my sweatpants rolled up, gives off a homeless chic style. We hold hands and walk mostly in silence. The frost on the grass looks picturesque. After an hour, I can tell Robbie is fading.

Pulling her towards a bench, we sit down. Huddled, because it's cold when you stop moving, she asks, "Did I ruin your meditation? We have spent a lot of time together—not on purpose."

Looking out at the pond as the ducks decide it's too cold for a swim, I turn to my new girlfriend. "This was nice. Why don't you take my car and go to the grocery store? It will still be empty, and I'll meet you at my house. We can cook together and drop off some meals. I can help with whatever you need to do."

Robbie sounds a little confused, "Wait you're trusting me with your car and your house? Are you sure?"

Nodding my head yes, "That car is old. Drive safe. My dad will be gone anyway. Just don't steal anything."

"I'm stealing some recipes. I can't stop thinking about those pancakes. Are there more in the fridge?"

I'm 8-year-old-with-a-new-toy happy right now. "Of course. Help yourself. I can share a few recipes with you."

Whispering in my ear, she says, "I'll earn them, don't you worry." Then she reaches down my pants and I don't know what to do. Are we going to fool around at the gardens?

Still in my ear, she says, "Man you get hard easy. I'm going to stand up now. You should probably wait a few minutes before getting up." She's laughing so hard, tears are rolling down her cheeks, and I love it.

Confused, she points at me, "How will you get home? Do you want me to swing by after I go to the store?"

"I'm cool. I'll walk. I live two miles from here."

Looking at me like I'm crazy, "Are you sure?"

"I like to walk."

After a kiss on the cheek, I'm alone again. My sadness is melting. I can feel the smile on my face, people probably think there's something a matter with me. All these thoughts flood my mind. I mutter out loud, "It's okay to be happy." A few warm and therapeutic tears run down my cheeks. I think about how happy my mom would be. Her pancakes were a hit. Towards the end, whenever we went walking, she would wear one of my hoodies with the hood up, to keep her bald head warm. With her arm around my shoulders, at a snail's pace, we would take in the scenery. She never once complained. At least once a week, she sat on this very bench, and asked me if I would walk home to give her some time to sit. Today, I just wanted a longer walk, but I knew Robbie was done.

Returning home, the house smells like onions, and I hope it's not me. Robbie is in full-on preparation mode. As I close the garage door, she looks up with a grin, "Hi, babe. I'm about halfway done with my prep! How was the walk back? Thanks for giving me an out. Man, I'm out of shape."

No one has ever called me babe. "I'm great. I ran back. I didn't feel like walking for another hour to get home. I'm going to shower. Do you need help?"

Intensely reading and checking things off a list, she says, "I'm cool. I have this down to a science. Where's your dad? No family time today?"

Drinking some water, I tell her, "This may sound really weird, but my dad goes to a sweat lodge. He leaves early and then comes home around noon. I think he also sits and reads at a coffee shop."

While chopping red peppers with speed, she says, "I don't think much would surprise me about your dad. He's just, like, out there, in the best possible way. And I know I just met him, but I feel very comfortable with him."

Sitting at the kitchen island, watching her work, I say, "One of the things I like most about him is that he does not care what people think. A few weeks ago, before he had his epiphany, I was really worried about him. I once said, 'Dad if a friend comes over and you're sleeping in your underwear on the couch with booze out, it's going to be weird.'"

Peeling an apple so the skin is one big line, she replies, "What did he say? What was his epiphany?"

Since I have not had many friends in the past few months, it feels good to talk about life. "He told me to cover him and ask my friend if she wants to cuddle."

Laughing and swinging her hair back like in a commercial, she says, "I could see him saying that."

Between chewing, I explain, "He told me someone said he didn't have to be sad anymore and that he needs to be a dad and quit wallowing."

Nodding her head yes, "That's a friend. I'm glad he's in a good place. Why don't you shower—hint, hint—and then do some homework? I need about an hour and a half to finish and then we can relax before making deliveries. Is that cool?"

"You're so bossy when you work. I like it."

Smiling even bigger, "I'm one hundred-percent that bitch."

"Alright, Lizzo. Keep up the cooking."

Watching Robbie cook is amazing. It's like she's dancing, bouncing back from one dish to the next, adding an extra hint of spice and then tasting it. And she looks so cute, with a pencil holding her hair in a bun. I had to go into another room because all I wanted to do was ravage her.

Since I do most of my homework after class, today I will study. Reviewing the notes I take in class and researching anything I didn't understand goes by quickly. If I keep up my GPA, maybe I can get into an even better school.

My knife business is also distracting me. Between my online ads and sales calls, business increases every week. With all the requests for silverware, and now pots and pans, I decide it's time to build a business plan. I've learned a few things dealing with the wealthier clients. They want high-end equipment, and they want to feel like they are getting a deal. Sales is a serious balancing act.

My phone buzzes, and it's my dad telling me he'll be home in an hour. Yelling into the kitchen, I ask, "Robbie, do you want anything special for lunch? My dad is going to pick up food from a deli in Skokie."

"I would love some matzo ball soup! Would you split that and a lox sandwich with me?"

With her smiling at me, I respond, "We are food compatible. It's a deal breaker if you don't like sushi."

Emphatically, "HELL YEAH! Let's eat our weight in sushi on our next date. I know this cool place near campus."

Waving Robbie to the chair I'm sitting on, "We have one hour, that really means forty-five minutes until my dad gets home."

With a devilish grin, Robbie asks, "You want to fool around?"

"You look so hot with your hair up and in that sleeveless shirt and my shorts."

Running back into the kitchen, she says, "Hold that thought. I have to turn the oven off and let everything cool before packaging."

Popping out of the kitchen with nothing on but some whip cream, Robbie smiles at me. "Do you need a snack?"

Making sure the blinds are down in the living room, we start to have fun. "Robbie, I need to get a condom."

Pushing me down on the couch, she hops on top of me. "I like how much of a boy scout you are."

She whispers in my ear, "Don't worry. I'm on the pill and clean."

Remembering the sex tip about lasting longer in a condom, I go back to deep breathing. The feeling of her melting into me is amazing. I know this is just the infatuation stage, but I'm smitten.

Slowly rocking on top of me and grabbing my arms, she leans close. "God, you feel good, Alex."

Trying to be a little aggressive, mostly because I need a break, so I don't finish early, "Why don't you bend over the couch?"

Internally, I debate how fast I should go, and whether I should spank her. As if she's reading my mind, she says, "Faster! Fuck me hard."

I obey her orders the best I can, but start to lose control, "OH MY GOD!"

She yells, "Hold it!" She turns around and pulls me close to her chest. My only thought is: How is this my life? It's better than any dream I've had.

"Robbie, that was amazing."

Cleaning herself off and smiling, "Well you did your research, so I did mine. I read that guys want to finish on boobs or a girl's face. Option number two is not going to happen. Even I have some limits."

LONELINESS

The first delivery is Joe's house. He's getting out of his fancy ride as we pull up.

With a friendly hug for Robbie and a handshake for me, Joe walks us inside. I can tell he's proud of having introduced us. "I knew you two would like each other. You're both really nice kids."

Placing the food on his kitchen table, Robbie gives him the menu. Joe asks, "No cookies?"

Turning to me, "How about two dozen for Thursday night? I'll pay you. How does fifty dollars sound?"

Robbie interrupts, "Seventy-five dollars. Those are seriously amazing cookies."

Turning to Joe, "You don't have to pay me, Joe. It's my pleasure."

Joe responds, "Sixty dollars, and it's settled. Thank you. Val wants a dozen because she plays cards Friday afternoon."

Mike's house is next. Turning to Robbie, I say, "I wonder if he'll be in a robe. He told me the story."

Robbie yawns, "It's awful. She was always a bitch, but he's pretty gruff. She should've said she wanted a divorce instead of cheating on him. She's high maintenance. Mike's been an easier client with her gone. Also, he gets lunch and dinner five days a week now."

Robbie asks, "Is that Mike painting his front door?"

Deepening my gaze, "I think so. Figured he would hire someone for that."

Walking to greet Mike with all his food, he turns to us and smiles. "Nice undies, kid."

With her business face, Robbie says, "Thanks for paying me online. Here's your lunches and dinners. Let me know if you want some snacks. I tossed a few granola bars in there. Dave loves them. Keep them in your freezer."

Taking a long inhale, Mike asks, "You two love birds want some coffee, wine, or ice cream? Halo Top cookies n' cream is pretty good."

Giving him a needed hug, Robbie answers, "I would love some, but we need to get these deliveries done. What if we bring dinner next week for the three of us?"

With a sincere look in his eyes, Mike says, "That would be nice Robbie. Wish my kids were that thoughtful." To me, he says, "See you on Thursday night, kid."

"Sounds good, Mike."

Robbie turns to me as I back out, "I hope he's okay." Her phone rings and it says "Mom."

Holding up a finger to her mouth, silently asking me to be quiet, she puts the phone up to her ear. "Hi, mom!"

Since her mom is practically yelling, I can hear everything. She speaks in a high-pitched voice, "Where have you been? I called your room last night and this morning. That boy is really taking up a lot of your time."

"Oh, Mom. Things are going well with Alex. He helped me with my deliveries today."

I can tell Robbie is tensing up as her mom continues, "Has your dad called you? You know, you can work less, and he can send you some money. Are you ready for Italy?"

My heart stops. I feel it crumbling. She's going abroad.

"Mom, I have over three months. My counselor is helping. Everything is on track."

With a considerate tone, she asks, "How are you holding up, mom?"

"Robbie, these divorced women tell the worst stories. They're so mean. One woman told me that I have to swallow."

Controlling our laughter, Robbie cuts in, "Mom, I'm glad you feel that comfortable with me, but you shouldn't talk to your daughter about that. Save it for your therapist. You're still young, leggy, hot, and nice. You'll meet someone."

With a deep breath she says, "Thanks, Robbie. Oh, your sister is calling, I should go. I love you."

The moment the call is over, Robbie places a hand on my leg. "That was a lot to unpack. I'm going to start with Italy." With a smile, she says, "I really like you a lot. Hopefully, you feel the same, and if we are together before I leave, we will be together when I get back."

My heart begins to settle back together. I'm not sure what to say. "You should have fun in Italy and not have to worry when some guy with a Vespa wants to take you for a spin."

"Alex, I'm not going there for international ass. I could not care less about that. I want to cook, see the sights, learn Italian, and shop. Based on our first date, you might have the wrong impression. I'm not everyone's ho." With a smile, "Just yours."

Feeling more at ease, I tell her, "We are going to live it up until you leave! I'm sorry about your parents. I thought you said they were married."

Holding back tears, she explains, "I just wasn't ready to talk about it because they are not officially divorced yet, only separated. My mom is in our childhood home and my dad rented a house not far away. Being twenty years old, I thought I would be fine with this, but it sucks. I had a great childhood. It's just sad."

"I'm sorry. It's never easy. Have you talked to anyone about it?"

"I've been talking to my RA. Her parents got divorced a few years ago. I'm going to miss holidays, and now I will have to divide them in two. That's another reason I'm staying here this summer."

Sitting in silence for the rest of ride, I don't know what to say. We just met, but I'm hooked already. I think she feels the same way.

Turning to me, she says, "I'm still kind of in awe that we hung out with TK. I feel like we were with a celebrity. He really likes you."

"Honestly, I have no idea why he likes me so much. It's like from day one when he coached our summer team, we just hit it off. We went to this place called the Hoagie Hutt together, and all my friends were so jealous."

With this smirk, like she knows something, she says, "He told me about his nickname and how you got guys to stop calling him Token. He really appreciated it."

Again, my mom helped me make friends. I told her that they called this guy Token. Right away, she turned to me and said, "That's racist. Kids don't mean anything, but you should put a stop to it."

With no idea what to do, I went to the coach. I asked if he could tell the kids the nickname is not cool. He was a sociology teacher and never sold me out. Turning to Robbie, I ask, "How did he know it was me?"

"Your coach said, 'All I can say is that it was a freshman.' TK knew right away it was you."

After all these years, I had no idea why he'd looked out for me. Continuing, she says, "Another reason is that you're pretty amazing."

With a passionate kiss, Robbie pleads, "Stay with me a few days. Come on. This week I have all these papers due, so I'm not sure when I'll see you."

The truth is that I want to stay, but I don't want her to get sick of me. She should learn about my neuroses in bite-sized increments.

With a smile, I ask, "What if I just come over with dinner on Wednesday night? I'll spend the night and then we can do something Saturday night."

With a huge grin, "Two Saturday nights in a row! Wow. That's serious, Alex."

I give her one more kiss and head home.

PROFESSIONAL KITCHEN

Pulling into to my driveway, I see Maddie's car. I also get a text from Robbie. "Thx again for everything!" followed by a kiss emoji and "I left a few meals for you in fridge!"

I already know what happened. My dad thought the food was from Maddie, so he called her. Maddie looks striking. She's wearing workout pants that really hug her body, and a sleeveless blue shirt that shows off her arms and really makes her blue eyes pop. Why did she try and set my dad up?

Looking guilty, my dad starts, "I'm an idiot. I thought the food was from Maddie. Robbie cleaned up so well, I forgot she was here cooking."

Maddie turns to me, smiling, "He tells me it was the best meal ever. I was about to hit the gym, but curiosity got the best of me."

Setting the table for two, "Since you started eating, sit down."

Maddie gives me a confused look, "What about you, Alex? I need to hear more about Robbie. Your dad said she's amazing."

"She really is. I have a lot of work to make up. Since she was over all day, I didn't get my studying done. I also have a group meeting about this project in Lake Forest. I'll be home by ten."

I do not understand adults. It's obvious that Maddie likes my dad. Again I wonder: Why did she set him up with a friend?

I'm very curious about what's going to happen while I'm gone. Will two years of celibacy come to a crashing halt?

Driving around Lake Forest trying to figure out how I'm going to kill two hours leads me to Sushi Kushi. Sitting at the bar, I start working on my business plan.

The ads I bought online are paying off! I have $4,000 in online sales, and with the traditional sales it's going to be a banner month. I need to spend more time formulating an online strategy. Reviewing all the face-to-face sales, these people also want other silverware and copper pans. What if I offer high-end equipment with a nice discount? Maybe I can sell plates, bowls and kitchen tools.

Researching different vendors takes me down a two-hour rabbit hole. Building a chart in Excel, I input price, contact information, and various ratings for each company. Interrupting my research, I receive a call from my dad.

"You didn't have to leave, Alex."

"Please tell me you made a move?"

Pausing, "She's thirty-eight years old. I thought for sure she was thirty. What's ten years, right? Also, she was married once. I had no idea. She doesn't have any kids though."

I start to pay my bill while listening to my dad justify his new love interest. "Did you ask her why she set you up?"

Laughing, "I did. She said that I never made a move in two years, so she figured I was not interested or needed more time."

"I'll be home in thirty seconds."

The first thing that I notice is that none of the pillows are on the couch and the cushions are all a little disjointed. "Oh my god—you had sex on the couch!"

With an embarrassed smile, "Alex, did I ask you about your girlfriend?"

"Sorry, dad. I don't know why I just blurted that out. Did you have fun?"

Sitting down at the kitchen table, my dad pours us some water. "You did not have to leave. That was a smooth move, except you grabbed a computer and an empty bag. I don't think she noticed. Where the hell have you been?"

Swallowing, "I can't believe I didn't take any books. Whoops. I went to Sushi Kushi to work on a business plan. Online sales are going well. I'm working on selling other stuff. I think if I can market it right, I could make about eight to twelve thousand a month. It would cost me about two thousand dollars to advertise, but I will make good profits."

Beaming with pride, "Alex, that's amazing. How are you doing it?"

"That's not important. I'm just applying what I learned in my business classes and some research. If I stop taking classes, I could do some serious research and make bank!"

Shaking his head, "No—stay in school. You can still make money, trust me. Just have fun with this. How's Robbie?"

The sadness begins to creep in. "She's going to Italy next semester. I'm not sure I can take that kind of heartache."

Putting his hand on my arm, "Buddy, you're already smitten. That was fast. I'm the same way. It was love at first sight with your mom. Our moms knew each other and introduced us at temple during the High Holidays. It was slightly embarrassing. Your mom had on this black dress that was borderline too short and low cut for temple. Later, she told me her mom bought it for her and made her wear it."

"That's hilarious. I forgot that story. What did she whisper to you?"

Shaking his head up and down, "That was when I fell for her. She whispered right after we met to ask her for her phone number or her mom's going to make her wear this dress at Yom Kippur. When she stepped away after our awkward hug, I casually said, 'Would you like to grab coffee tomorrow?' I could hear her mom loudly whisper, 'I told you this dress would work.'"

Grabbing more water, my dad continues. "Don't worry about Robbie. That girl is into you. I've never seen anyone look at you like she does. This is in the infatuation phase, where everything seems great. If she lasts another month, even if she goes away, you can make it work. Life is too short to worry about things that are out of your control."

Tossing away some garbage, I see a used condom in the bag. I knew it! Good for him. I have no idea what she said to him to get him out of his funk, but it worked. Two years of being super nice can't be faked. Before I can comment further to my dad, my phone rings.

"Hi, Maddie." My dad turns to me with a slightly shocked face.

"Alex, I want to tell you that whatever happens with me and your dad, I'm still here for you. I don't want you to think our texting and talks are going to stop."

My dad is sitting right next to me, listening to our conversation. "Maddie, unlike my dad, I never found a therapist I liked. I felt like they weren't listening and didn't understand me. You did. I really appreciate that. I'm happy for you and my dad. I hope you're cool with an old man."

At this point, my dad is laughing and says, "You're so funny. Tell her I'll call her tomorrow and I'm sorry I said that Robbie's meal was the best food she's ever made."

Hanging up the phone, I turn to my dad, "Isn't it funny that my girlfriend cooks better than yours?"

With a hand on my shoulder, he says, "I cannot believe I didn't realize it was Robbie. She was in our kitchen for hours. I'm so stupid, but it all worked out, and I kind of owe Robbie. That girl can cook! Are you heading up to bed?"

Pulling out my laptop, "I have a few more ideas for my kitchen supply company that I want to work on right now."

Confused, but proud, he tells me, "Keep making that money, but don't get too obsessed. You are going to college next year!"

Hugging the old man as he walks by, I decide to further build my business plan. There are so many brands and equipment out there. Using my mom's *Consumer Reports* login, I spend a few hours researching top brands.

BALANCING ACT

The high I get from being with Robbie is something I've never felt before. Her sense of humor and warmth are intoxicating. While we both study in her dorm room, I can't help but steal glances at her.

Catching my gaze, she wonders, "What are you looking at? I need to finish this assignment before you can rock my world."

"Who says, 'Rock my world?'"

Pointing at herself, "Michael Jackson," and with a long pause, "BITCH!"

My hands shoot out, like I'm trying to stop a car, "You got my dad some action. No joke. My dad thought your food was our friend's, who leaves us casseroles. He called her to say it's the best she's ever made."

We are both laughing, "She came over to see what he was talking about. I walked in and I could feel the tension between them. She's been trying to get my dad's attention forever. Anyway, after I left, they hooked up!"

With a huge grin on her face, she says, "Look at that. Cookies work for you and prepackaged meals work for your old man. I love you, but you need to shut up so I can finish this."

Realizing she just told me she loves me, her eyes sparkle, and she gives off this facial expression like she made a mistake by saying that. I think she really meant it, though. Smiling back at her, I say, "Do you want me to shut up, or answer?"

"Don't keep me in suspense."

"It's probably way too early to admit this, but I'm crazy about you. I love you, too."

Standing up, we meet in the middle and kiss and it's a deep passionate embrace. I feel like I'm wrapped in a fleece blanket. Staring into her beautiful big, brown eyes, "Now finish your work, so we can have sex."

She agrees with me, "Okay, but we'll be making sweet love. P.S. I'll never use that expression again."

Watching Robbie study, I start to process what just happened. I've never told anyone I love them, other than my parents. No one else has told me they loved me, either. Glowing with warmth inside feels amazing. My mind starts wandering, and I think I am with my wife right now. We would have super cute kids.

Robbie stands up, as I remain on the floor. She whispers in my ear, "Help me take my clothes off." Immediately standing up, I slowly take off her clothes. She does the same for me. The sex feels more intimate this time and there's less laughing. With Robbie pressed on top of me, she whispers, "I love you." Trying to not to come, I take my hands and pull her closer into me. She lets out an "Oh my God," and squeezes my shoulders tightly. When she's done, this angelic smile forms on her face.

And then it hits me: I'm really going to miss her. We fall asleep in her dorm room and wake up the next morning to her room-mate opening the door. This is the first time I've met Nicky. While yawning, she introduces us. "Nicky, this is my boyfriend, Alex. Alex, this is Nicky."

Looking down on me, figuratively and literally, she says, "Hi, Alex. Don't get up. I just have to grab my books." The mean look she gives me is like we live in a caste system, and I'm out of place. Robbie was right—she's a bitch.

Holding in my disdain, I say, "It's nice to meet you, Nicky. I would shake your hand, but I'm not wearing any underwear." She shakes her head and I add, "I'm just kidding. Have a good day."

With no class until 11, we fool around a little and bake muffins. The entire large study room outside the kitchen smells like blueberries. I hide one for Rick, and then Robbie and I split one. The smile on her face says it all. With a mouth full of muffin, she says, "This is good! I can't even tell they are frozen berries." I text TK and Ellie to stop by but only Ellie can make it.

With her hair in a French braid and in a brown leather jacket, Ellie oozes coolness. "You guys are the best. TK does not want one. He's trying to cut his sugar intake during the season. But I'll take another if that's cool. My roommate's pretty cool, and she'll love this."

Ellie and Robbie talk excitedly to each other as I clean up. It's funny how they live a few doors away, but never spoke until we made cookies. Realizing the time, I say, "I have to go guys. Tell TK I say Hi."

The fact that Rick agrees to meet with me is huge. All his experience in investing and growing businesses is bound to help me out.

Robbie told me he's a muffin man, so hopefully he likes this one.

Parking next to a Porsche, I walk excitedly to his front door. Through the windows, I can see the lake is choppy today. Despite the cold and the wind, it's toasty warm in his house.

He greets me with a guy hug, and then we sit down in his kitchen. I take out my laptop and hand him the bag with the muffin. A huge grin forms on his face. "Man, Robbie really knows me." His face lights up. "It's still warm!"

Spreading a little butter on the muffin, I look at him, insulted. "You think my muffins need butter? What the fuck, Rick?"

Laughing, "You sound like my wife. These are amazing. Can you send me the recipe?"

I nod my head yes. "No problem. The real key is that you need to turn the oven to four hundred twenty-five degrees and then drop it down to three hundred fifty after five minutes."

Pouring me some coffee, he asks, "Do you need any milk, sugar, or cream? Tell me about your business. I want to know the sales, costs, and your long- or short-term goals."

Watching Rick dig through my notes is like watching a chess master—no details are too small. He asks, "How much time do you spend increasing sales, optimizing, meeting with prospects, and researching?"

"I don't track hours, but I spend about four to six hours every day on it. I'm not trying to brag, but that's probably someone else's eight-hour day. I really focus. I only take breaks to use the restroom."

With a serious look, he asks, "So eight hours, seven days a week, to make almost two grand per week? That's not horrible. Can you automate things? Work less? Create other products where you can pull in another few grand?"

Nodding my head in agreement, "I have been spending a lot of time thinking about that. A lot of people have been asking for flatware and pots, so I sell them, too. Rob's wife wanted copper pots, so I'm working on finding the best price. I have several leads and just need to verify the quality. They have a higher margin, so if I can replicate that with the knives, I can probably increase my revenue."

With his eyes scanning my sales portals, he says, "Excellent. If you can double your revenue without doubling your time working, fuck college. You're giving yourself an MBA."

Hearing this from a guy who is worth millions is like a bolt of caffeine shooting through me. "Thanks. I really appreciate your time and thoughts."

Turning to me and looking deep in my eyes, he adds, "You should go to college anyway and do an entrepreneurial program somewhere. Have fun, make friends, date. I mean, I love Roberta, but who knows?"

Drinking the last of my coffee, I say, "Thanks for the advice. Things are going great with Robbie. She's warm, loving, and so funny. I've never met anyone like her. How are your kids?"

He replies, "And she's gorgeous—what a smile on her! My daughter is kicking ass at vet school. She met a nice guy, and my son graduates in the spring. That guy is living the dream. He's never coming back to Chicago. He already has a job working with one of Joe's boys. It's all about connections."

Placing my cup in the giant sink, "One more question: Is your daughter's boyfriend Jewish?"

Laughing, he says, "Good memory, kid. Yes, she's smart and went to Jewish overnight camp for a decade. This was bound to happen even if my dad didn't try to pay the kids off."

While standing in the doorway, Rick drops another business bomb. "Kid, if you make up to five thousand dollars a week, I'll help you sell this company for a few million."

Replaying the sentence in my head, I ask, "Are you messing with me?"

Smiling, he says, "I want five percent and I will hand you the deal."

Cocksure, I tell him, "Two percent and you have a deal."

Pointing at me, he says, "Now you're a fucking businessman. I love it. Always negotiate!"

When I won at chess, my parents had a rule to celebrate the wins and take the next day off. If I lost, I could practice for a few hours. One time, this kid beat me with his pawns. I had never seen anyone do that before. I let him take my queen because I was so curious about his plan. My parents watched me lose, and knew I let him win.

The car ride home, my mom turned to me and said, "Why did you let that boy take your queen?"

Now the truth was, I wanted to spend hours studying how to effectively strategize with pawns. If I won, we would have dinner and watch a movie. I couldn't tell my mom this, but I didn't lie. "I wanted to see what would happen. I thought I could get the queen back."

That night, I spent hours watching videos and playing simulated games. For the next few weeks, it was my obsession. I feel the same way right now. I will figure out how to double my sales.

GAMBLING GUILT

With Thanksgiving approaching, schoolwork is slowing down. This allows me to dive in deep into the world of search engine optimization, social media advertising, and how to improve my website.

While preparing food for the guys, Robbie says, "Don't work all day and night when I'm gone. It's not good for anybody. Keep playing hoops with TK and maybe visit your friend at Madison."

Logging off my site, "I will pick up a hobby. Guys seem to really like jujitsu. I think with my judo background I would be decent. Let's be real, I'll be working. Can I use you in my videos and other media?"

At this point, my dad walks into the kitchen and grossly comments, "I don't think girls want to be on video. What's the matter with your generation?"

Shaking with embarrassment, "Dad, I'm talking about cooking stuff. I have some product samples coming in. I want Robbie to test them out and then use images of her cutting, dicing, and cooking for ads."

Exhaling deeply, "Son, I was joking. Come on. Lighten up. Robbie, that smells amazing. What are you cooking?"

With a smile, "Thanks, Jerry! I'm baking blondies and I have some guacamole here. I roasted carrots and cauliflower and made this dip that's basically cheese and beef."

Watching Robbie spoon my dad some queso dip is just about the cutest thing. They get along as if she's his daughter. Tonight, he's driving her to campus while I play poker. With my anxiety, I worry that if we break up, he's going to be mad at me.

With totally sincerity, "This is the best thing I've had in a long time. Robbie, can you leave the recipe for us? It tastes like you roasted a pepper with that meat."

Nodding her head yes, "You have great taste buds. I totally did that! I just roasted a few peppers and blended them with melted cheddar. I left you some with jicama chips."

She's even helping him with his healthy eating—except for the cheese and meat. My dad adds, "Robbie you are the best."

Pointing at him, "You have no idea. I doubled the blondie recipe. They are made with chickpeas, so they are healthy and also delicious."

Intervening, mostly because I feel left out, "You guys need to get a room. This is a serious love fest. Are you almost done cooking, Robbie?"

With a big kiss on the cheek, Robbie adds, "We both love you the most, don't worry. I just want the dessert to cool a little bit."

My dad is excited to meet Joe. I told Joe that my dad is driving Robbie home, and he told me I had to bring my dad inside. I'm curious to see how they interact. Joe is like grandpa-friendly, and my dad is very easygoing as well. Part of me wishes I was a little more easygoing. He's also taking Jane home, who I have not seen since I started dating Robbie. Joe helped her get an internship with Goldman Sachs, so she's always working when she's not in school.

Nerves for some reason get the best of me. It's something about introducing my dad to my unofficial mentor, Joe. Watching my dad's facial expression as he pulls into Joe's driveway, I can tell he's impressed. It's hard not to be in awe of this house. "Dad, you should see this guy Rick's house. It's crazy big and right on the lake."

"I like this place. It's big, but still has a homey feel." Walking inside, Joe greets us.

Hugging Robbie and me, and then shaking my dad's hand, "Great to meet you, Jerry. You've raised one amazing kid. Come to the basement while the kids set up."

Disappearing down the stairs, I help Robbie carry the food into the kitchen. Jane scares us both. "Hi, guys!"

Jane is gorgeous. I don't remember her being this leggy or beautiful. Dressed in yoga pants and a sleeveless blue hoodie, her sky-blue eyes pop. Her blond locks are braided to the side. She hugs Robbie and then gives me what feels like an extra tight hug.

"Damn Alex, when did you get those muscles? You're buff."

I can feel my cheeks flush. "Thanks, Jane. I lost weight dating Robbie. I think I'm eating healthier snacks, but the only thing I do consistently is lift weights."

Robbie starts setting up the food and is probably jealous and annoyed we are not helping. Jane has laid out the serving plates but is gazing deeply into my soul. "Are you okay? The last time I saw you was right after."

Smiling nervously, "Much better. You were sweet when I was falling apart. Junior year was rough. Luckily, I don't cry while studying anymore."

Turning to Robbie, Jane asks, "Can we help you?"

Without looking our way, she says, "No, you guys catch up. I'm almost done."

Sitting next to each other on high stools, our legs accidentally touch. Nervously, I scoot back. "How's your job?"

Her eyes light up. "I love It! I'm learning about analyzing stocks, market trends, different vehicles, like ETFs. It's interesting. How's the knife business? Can you make some banana bread for my old man?"

The first time we studied together, I made a banana bread. John insisted that girls are suckers for banana bread. With nothing to back up his claims, I made it anyway and she loved it. Finished setting up, Robbie stands behind me with her arms around my shoulders.

"I thought you were being polite! You ate the smallest piece ever and brought some home for your dad."

Giggling, Jane adds, "I didn't want to seem like a pig. I ate the rest of that piece the second I got in my car."

Robbie cuts in, "I want some banana bread!"

"How about on Saturday night when I pick you up? I can bring you one."

More curious than jealous, Robbie looks Jane in the eye, "How did you pick each other for study partners?"

With a smile, "Well, I knew Alex was smart, and he met the criteria. The teacher wanted us to partner with someone in a different grade and gender if possible. The theory was different genders have different strengths, and I'm not sure about the younger–older thing."

"I was shy talking to girls; I really think it helped me get over that. I spent more time on schoolwork, so I didn't have to deal with my life."

Laughing, Jane adds, "You made me feel at ease from day one. I remember my eyes were all puffy from crying. Some guy made a rude comment on a picture of me online and it garnered a ton of comments. You told me not to worry about it. And who doesn't cry? From that moment on, you were my new best friend."

That is another moment I owe to my mom. When she started to lose her hair, I lost it. She came home from treatment and between her coloring and hair loss, I couldn't suck the tears back. My shirt was soaked. With a hug, when I should've been consoling her, she told me, "I cry all the time. Who cares? It's cathartic."

Joe and my dad pop up from the basement laughing the way little kids laugh when someone farts. Joe puts his hand on my dad's shoulder, like he's his son. "Your dad is great. You need to bring him to play cards."

Shaking his head, my dad answers, "You probably would love that, but I'm awful at cards. No idea where Alex got his gaming skills—maybe from his mom. That women could bluff and had laser focus."

Watching my dad interact with everyone, I zone out. My mom was the warm and fuzzy one. She was also curious and asked everyone a million questions. I remember her checking out a laundry bag's worth of cookbooks from the library and spending hours looking at every single page. My dad, on the other hand, is gregarious. It's been a while since I've watched him work a room. My friends' dads always wanted to hang out with him. It only took me 19 years, but I think his personality has finally rubbed off on me.

"I would hang out here all night and just drink a few beers, but I need to get these kids to campus. I also might or might not have a date tonight."

Robbie cuts in, "Have you properly thanked me for hooking you up?"

Jane and Joe stare at my dad, wanting an explanation. With his left dimple showing, "This is funny. For more than two years, this woman brings us casseroles. They are fine. Being deep in depression, I thought nothing of her gesture. She's younger and pretty, so this must just be a pity plate. Anyway, Robbie left a few meals for us. I think I was eating zucchini lasagna. It was delicious. I called our friend Maddie, who dropped off the other meals, and went on about how this is the best thing she's ever made. I couldn't stop eating. She came over and looked me right in the eye. She says, 'You fucker, I didn't make that.'" At this point, everyone is laughing. My dad continues, "Now I'm the asshole. She's shaking her head and I feel awful. I looked at her workout outfit and complimented her. I'm not joking, she turned around and told me she finally has a butt. I had no idea what to say because it seemed extremely flirty. I told her, If I was ten years younger, I would not be able to take my hands off you." At this point, my dad is gauging how much detail he should tell us.

Robbie cuts in, "Don't keep us in suspense! What happened after that?"

Pointing his finger at Robbie, "You've got it. It gets better. She leaned in a little too close to me and said, 'You couldn't handle this.' Again, my flirt game is off, but I know she's flirting. So, I just asked her if she wanted to have dinner with me." Pausing for effect, the old man takes a break.

Joe jumps in, "And then what?"

"She told me I'm old fashioned and plants one on me. Then she asked me for Robbie's contact information. She wants to order a few meals."

Robbie is glowing. "You have no idea, Jerry, how good that story makes me feel."

With that, Robbie, Jane, and my old man head out. I have not seen Jerry the entertainer in years. My sophomore year, he told John and another friend about meeting these German girls on the beach in Florida, and how frisky they were. The moral of the story is that there's nothing a little Penicillin can't clear up. I was mortified, but John still talks about that story.

A few minutes after Joe and I start snacking, the others arrive. Mike walks in first, unshaven, solemn, and uses a nod to say hi. I offer up a hug, and he pulls me in tight. I think he just needs some company.

Joe hands him a beer. "How are you holding up?"

With a deliberate exhale, "I'm okay. Therapy is helping. The kids have been kind. I apologized to them for being an absent father. They are both fucked up but turning their life around. This has been the worst time, but we are all becoming better people."

Silence is my friend as I watch Joe and Mike talk. Dave walks in with energy and a smile. "What's up, Knife Man? What up, Joe and Mike?"

I answer, "All is well, Dave. How are your kids?"

Grabbing a few mini sandwiches, "Baseball and soccer are my life right now. We also shot a commercial for my company at my house!"

Patting him on the back, "That is awesome! I want to shoot a bunch of short cooking demonstrations, but I need to rent some cameras. Who did you use?"

Pointing at me, "I've got you covered. I bought lights, a tripod, and a camera. It was cheaper to do that than hire a company to bring all that shit in. Plus, we will use this for other stuff. Jessica is good with a camera and we want to have a library of images for the site."

"Can I rent them from you?"

Smiling and shaking his head no, "Are you kidding me? Just don't break anything. Jess and I will come over and show you what to do."

Mike cuts in, "It's been a while since you took all our money. Did you get bored?"

Smiling, "I just missed your beautiful face."

Rick then cuts in, "How are knife sales?"

While Joe starts to deal, I answer Rick. "It's going well. Once I get some videos up there and a recipe blog, I think I'll get a lot more hits."

Watching these guys make bets is interesting. No one spends too much time making their bets unless they have good hands. I usually fold when I see someone really thinking about how much to bet.

Conversation flows around the stock market, politics, and tax avoidance strategies. I stay quiet and just play cards.

Rob is in the minority when he says, "I'm okay paying more in taxes if we can help the impoverished. We all have enough money."

Joe cuts in, "Hey, I'm retired, and I don't want to give all my savings away, but I'm okay paying some taxes."

After quite a bit of Donald Trump bashing, I find myself ahead by $725. I can tell Mike is starting to get pissed.

Looking at me, "Girls, baking, sales, cards, what aren't you good at kid?"

Sensing his angst, I throw my hand. He wins back a few hundred bucks. I'm still up $500, but I can tell he feels better with a few dollars in his pocket.

When I take a bathroom break, Joe follows me. Before walking into the bathroom, Joe grabs my arm. "Kid. Don't throw a game. Eventually, you'll lose. Streaks end, so you should just enjoy it. Fuck Mike. He's one of the top litigators at his company. Do you think he needs two hundred more dollars? You can offer to help someone, but sometimes you make a tough deal and win. Win that money back."

Shaking my head yes, "I get it and I will do that. I had a moment of pity. Gamblers should not feel guilt for winning."

"Exactly. You're a smart kid who works his ass off and my guess is that you've read way more about poker than all of us combined."

Getting back to the game, I ignore the chit chat and focus on the cards, reactions, and bets. After folding a bunch of times, the cards are starting to fall in my favor. I have a pair of aces, a full house and then end my night with a straight.

Handing me his pile of chips, Rob asks, "Do you want to come with me with me to Vegas, kid? I'm going on a work trip, and you can stay in my room. It will be a suite. You can gamble all day and night. I'll throw in a few dinners."

Aside from Joe, Rob is the best gambler. He wins a lot of hands and seems to stick to whatever rules he has for himself. He also plays on Friday nights where thousands of dollars go in and out of pockets. "I would love to, but I'm only nineteen."

Shaking his head yes, "I forgot. In a few years. You look twenty-one, so you might be able to sneak in some games."

Joe interrupts, "No, you need to visit colleges. Where are you going to be next year? Your dad said Duke was his bet but now Northwestern."

Duke basketball games always played in the background while I studied. "I wanted to play ball there and the job placement is top notch after graduation. But now I'm a little confused. I'm making good money with my knife and flatware business. This term I am taking web design, computer analytics, and social media marketing. Maybe I can get an associate's degree and keep building my business?"

Rick, shaking his head no, speaks first. "Go to college and have fun. You should spend some time figuring out who you are."

Mike cuts in, "Drink a few beers, sleep with some sorority girls, live it up. Don't rush this shit."

Dave raises his hand to speak next, like we're in grade school. "Alex, these guys might think I'm crazy, but fuck that. You can go to school in a year or two. Blow this business up! You love researching, making sales, and figuring out how to grow your business. Don't stop learning but ride it out until you're ready for the next challenge."

I look at Joe because for some reason I trust his opinion the most. He cuts in, "I couldn't tell my boys anything. Everything for them was the hard way. Jane asks for advice, listens, and then makes an educated decision. I say listen to yourself. Follow your own path."

Walking out, my mind goes to selling knives and kitchenware. I need to get Robbie to cook for some videos. I also need to start a blog and Instagram needs to be filled with recipes, cutting up different items, and finding a cheaper knife without losing quality. That will really increase my revenue. I decide that I am going to ride this business out.

The only messages on my phone are from Robbie and John. Robbie is long asleep, but I'm sure John is still up drinking with his buddies.

"Yo, Alex! What's up?" His words are slightly slurred.

"Not much, man. I just finished playing cards. I saw Jane tonight and she was flirty with a capital F. I could tell Robbie was jealous. It was so odd."

"Damn, dog. You're in a love triangle. I told you Jane liked you. That's why she never hangs around with you two."

Ignoring his ridiculousness, "What's up with you? Any girls?"

Laughing, "I'm actually with a girl right now. Say hi to Aubrey."

Awkwardly, "Hi, Alex. Your friend is slightly intoxicated. He cannot handle shots."

The phone drops and I hear John yell, "SHIT! Sorry about that, my man. Aubrey is this super-hot redhead that's about to take advantage of me. Visit soon!"

"How about tomorrow?" With Robbie heading home to help her parents, it's the perfect time to get away if John is cool with it.

Aubrey and John's excitement are over the top, "OH YEAH!!" And then the phone goes dead.

Quietly opening the front door, a surprise greets me. Robbie is laying on the couch in only a blanket. She's out cold, lightly snoring, in the cutest way possible. I turn off the television and carry her to the basement. Placing her on the futon, she wakes up all smiles.

"I meant to stay up. Man, I'm a shitty college student. I can't even make it until twelve o'clock."

She begings kissing me, and I pull away. "This is a nice surprise. I thought my dad took you home."

Quickly flashing her naked body, she covers up again. "I told your dad I was getting an Uber to O'Hare in the morning, and he said that you could drive me because you don't have class tomorrow.

Feeling guilty, I ask, "Would it bother you if I visited John without you this weekend?"

Pulling me on top of her, she says, "Have fun! Maybe you'll want to go to The University of Wisconsin. My sister wants to go there. I almost went there, but when I got into Northwestern my dad said I had to go."

ROAD TRIP

Most kids jump at the chance to visit their friends in college, but I hoped my dad would say not to go. His face lights up when I tell him.

"That sounds like fun, Alex! I always had such a blast visiting my friends at school. You should take a nap and then drive up there."

Yawning, "That's a good idea. I'm beat. I'm going to work out, do some work, and then nap. If I leave here at one o'clock, I'll miss rush hour on both ends."

With a serious look, and hand on my shoulder, "I really like Robbie. She's great. And I'm not suggesting you sleep with another girl, but it's okay to flirt and have some fun."

I have no idea what to do with this advice. "Noted. John is quite the partier now. He used to be so straight-laced, so it will be fun to just watch him."

With a hug and kiss on the forehead, "I'm off to work. Text me when you leave and get there. Drive safely."

Before heading into the basement, I check my sales. With the optimization, new website, and advertising, I still can't top $3,000 a week. Hopefully when I start shooting videos and have all the cooking demonstrations, I can sell a lot more.

Driving to Madison, I am filled with apprehension. Maybe Maddie can help ease my nerves. I decide to call her. "Hey, Maddie, do you have a minute for me?"

I can feel her smile through the phone. "For you, kid, I have exactly seventeen minutes. What's up?"

"I'm driving to see my best friend from high school at his college. I think that I told you about him. He's the only one that sends me texts. He loves school, getting drunk, and hooking up with girls. That's just not where I am."

"That's okay. You don't have to get drunk or sleep with a co-ed to have fun, right?"

Agreeing with her, "True, but then what am I going to do? Just watch everyone get drunk?"

I hear a deep exhale, "What would be fun for you to do there?"

With no hesitation, "Check out the campus, see the sites, eat on campus, see what a fraternity party is like, and check out the gym. This is dorky, but—maybe hit the library?"

Laughing, "My guess is that John wants to take you out and get you drunk. I would tell him you want to do a few things and then you'll head out for drinks. Then hold a beer all night or something. Here's a tip. Buy him a shot and ask for one tequila and one shot of water."

Feeling better about this, "You solved my problems in six minutes! Enjoy your eleven remaining minutes."

"Enjoy your weekend." With a pause, Maddie adds, "I know I will!"

"You are so nasty. That's so wrong. I know you're talking about my dad."

Trying not to laugh, she says, "Sorry—I can't help myself."

Blazing old school rap and singing along, I don't hear my phone ring. I have three missed calls from Robbie. I knew this weekend with her parents was going to be difficult, but she's only been home for a few hours.

While putting gas in the car, I call her back. She's sobbing, "They just hate each other so much. My dad says nothing about her, but I feel the disdain every time my sister or I mutter mom.

My mom holds nothing back. She thinks just because we are older that she can word-vomit hate." Only taking a few seconds to blow her nose, "Why would she tell me he just wanted to take Viagra and bang for an hour or two?"

Trying to hold back laughter is impossible. "I'm sorry. Hearing you talk about Viagra and banging is something I wasn't expecting."

Taking a few calming breaths, "You have no idea what she was talking about. My dad is a freak, and my mom thinks he's boring."

Sitting in my car at the gas station, I tell her, "Lean on your sister, but I think she might need you more than you need her."

"You're right. She really needs me. I wish I could take her back to school with me. I'm off to dinner. Wish me luck. Have fun, but not too much."

Starting up my car, I tell her, "Good luck, and I won't." As she hangs up the phone, I can hear her yelling at her mom. I feel guilty I didn't go with her, but that would've been awkward.

Parking is much easier than I had anticipated. According to Waze, I'm 200 feet from my destination. The campus looks picturesque, as it is covered in snow. I can't believe how huge it is! John's dorm sits close to an area with restaurants and shops. Pulling up his text, I read, "Park near my dorm, walk to the Union, and text me when you get inside."

Shivering a little, I speed-walk to the Union. There are kids walking in small groups or alone. The smell of weed blows past me as a dude with dreadlocks walks by and says, "It's fucking cold, even if you're high."

The minute I step inside the Union, I'm overwhelmed because it's packed. Before I can text John, I hear, "ALEX! ALEX!"

John, looking a little buzzed, hugs me like I just got back from a tour in Afghanistan. Taking a step back, he stares at me for a second, "Dude, are you in jail or Juco? You're like prison jacked." Shaking my head, I say, "Thanks, I think. There's nothing else to do but work, work out, and study."

Still patting me on the back, he says, "Bro, it's so good to see you. Follow me."

John snakes his way through the packed space. I can't believe how many kids are hanging out here. Claustrophobia and anxiety kick in while we make our way to his friends. Flashbacks of my mom's funeral and then my house flood my mind. My house was filled with kids and friends of my parents.

Taking deep breaths, I pretend I'm merely a spectator and there's an exit right near his friends' table. His three friends stand up to greet me and offer up handshakes and hugs at the same time. It's one of those bro-hugs where you pat the other on the back so hard to prove you're manly.

Jack, Jordy, and Toby are all rushing the same Jewish fraternity with John. "John, I had no idea you were Jewish."

Smiling, he says, "Well, my mom's dad is Jewish. But the truth is that I grew up in Highland Park, and I've probably had more matzo ball soup than most of the kids here."

All four of them are drinking beer from water bottles. It's not even 5 p.m. I should think this is cool, but having spent the past two years watching someone drink their life away, I'm not impressed.

Toby asks how John and I met. The college John is way more affectionate, and he's got his hand on my shoulder. "We go way back, but really from high school chess club. This guy was a master. His mind works like a fucking supercomputer. I joined because my parents said if I wasn't going out for sports, I needed to do something. This guy taught me everything. He was the coolest geek. He played varsity ball, has a black belt in judo, and now he has this smoking hot girlfriend and sells knives."

All the compliments make me nervous. Jack, looking at me like I'm a puzzle, and asks, "Knives?"

John speaks for me like a proud dad. "He's killing it. He is setting records and he's still in school."

Cutting John off, I say, "I'm in junior college this year. I had a few rough years. I'm trying to figure out what my next move is going to be."

Jack, who looks like a movie star with his slicked back dark hair and olive skin, shakes his head yes. "Good for you! I love it here, but I have no idea what my next move is, either. Are you hungry?"

"STARVING!"

While we walk to a sandwich spot, Robbie sends me an odd text that I read aloud. "Rose has huge boobs now. I would normally save this to discuss with my mom, but she's too fucked up."

The guys all beg for a picture. I reply, "Do you have a picture of you two?"

While waiting on our waitress, the guys gawk at Robbie and her sister. Rose is shorter than Robbie and has blond hair and blue eyes. They have a similar nose but look very different than each other. I reciprocate with a picture of my crew for the night.

Robbie writes me back seconds later with a request. "This is completely superficial, but Rose would like to know if the guy on your right is single."

Of course, she is referring to Jack. He has this charming smile and confidence when he says, "Call her."

I do a video call, and her sister is in the middle of the screen. She's pretty, and as hard as we look, we cannot tell that her boobs are huge. I introduce myself first. "Hi Rose! I've heard a lot about you. This is Jack, John, Tobey, and Jordy."

Jack takes the phone from me. "When are you going to visit me?"

With a flirtation and slightly nervous laugh, she tells him, "I'm actually coming down next week. Do you know Julia Fink? She's in a sorority house, but I can't remember which one."

With a big smile, "Sure. She's good people. We have an ugly sweater party next weekend. You should bring her and anyone else you want. I'll send her a note."

Robbie says, "Don't take advantage of my sister, Prince Charming. You see that guy next to you? He will find you."

Jack is still smiling. "I see, muscle man. Don't worry, I have nothing but respect for people from Minnesota."

The other guys are ordering drinks and fries and Jack continues to chat. It's as if they've seen this movie before, and Jack usually gets the girls.

Jordy, who hasn't said much since I met everyone cuts in, "Damn, Jack, you even have FaceTime game. Can you teach me, Master Yoda?"

John seems so happy. He was always cracking me up at school but was very quiet in class. College has helped him get out of his shell.

When the food arrives, Jack looks at my salad and I can just tell he's going to give me shit for it. "A salad? Really, how are you going to maintain those pecs with a salad?"

Feeling comfortable, I say, "Fuck you. I love a good chopped salad. Why do you look so familiar?"

Before he can answer Tobey chimes in. "I see the beginning of a beautiful bromance over there."

Jack puts his arm around me. "Maybe you're right, Tobey." Removing his arm, "I went to Glenbrook North. We played you guys junior year. You had a great game, ten dimes, a dozen or so points, and at least three steals. I didn't see you last year on the court."

John interrupts, "Dimes?"

Jordy answers, "Assists, dude. You need to turn off the porn and watch ESPN occasionally."

Facing Jack, "I'm sure John told you that I had a rough time in high school. I had a solid junior year, but I was a basket case. What position did you play? Shooting guard? Swing?"

Wiping up a little burger juice running down his chin, "Sorry about that. I played mostly small forward and a little guard. I just needed to grow about six more inches to play in college. You want to hoop in the morning?"

Shaking my head yes, "That would be awesome. Thanks!"

When the check comes, I grab it like a parent. "You guys are hosting me. The least I can do is pay for a few meals."

After a few "Thanks, dads," we head to their frat house to find me a fake ID.

A row of similar-looking houses sits near each other on the street. Some look charming, others huge, but their house is average. It's not dirty from the outside, but it just looks well worn. Ivy is wrapped around the front of the white house. Once inside, the smell of beer, pizza, and weed immediately greets me. There's a light fog filling the hall upstairs.

Turning to John, "They smoke a lot of weed here."

Bopping his head up and down, "That's for sure. Most guys smoke, but a handful of dudes have a problem. You want some?"

Trying not to sound ungracious, "Not my thing. Thanks."

All the doors are open, and I think John is just looking for someone that looks like me. The third room does the trick. I walk in, and it's looks like a room from the 1990s. There are posters of Nirvana, Pulp Fiction, and Dave Mathews Band. Old school rap pours through two tiny speakers, and the television is muted.

John and these guys do their handshake. "Hey, Cy. This is my buddy, Alex. Do you have an ID he can borrow? We are just hitting a few spots tonight. Tomorrow we'll be at the party of course."

Extending his massive, calloused hand, "Nice to meet you, Alex. Take it and have fun."

"Nice to meet you. Thanks for helping me out. I'll give it back to you tomorrow."

John and Cy share an awkward hug and then search around for the other guys. Tobey and Jordy are smoking pot from this huge blue bong. Tobey exhales for what seems to be two straight minutes. He has some serious lung capacity. Looking at him, I ask, "Were you a high school swimmer?"

Still exhaling, he shakes his head yes. Jordy either can't get up or doesn't want to. His eyes are already red and glassy. Yawning, he says, "I'm staying in boys. See you at breakfast."

Downstairs, we run into Jack, who's drinking a beer and watching these guys throw darts. Tipping the beer bottle upside down in three sips, he finishes it. With Tobey walking in slow motion, Jack close to drunk, and John bouncing around with energy, this is going to be an interesting evening.

All bundled up, we walk three blocks to a small bar. Having never broken a law, I'm a little nervous handing this ID to the bouncer. John walks in first and gives the bouncer a fist bump. "What's up, Shakes? This is a friend from growing up." He glances at the driver's license for two seconds and lets me in.

"Nice to meet you. Where are you in school?"

A little embarrassed, I tell him, "Community college back in Chicago. I'll probably go away next year."

The others head to a table. Shakes, standing about a foot over me, keeps chatting me up. "Man, I wish I did that. I would have been able to save some money and get the B.S. classes out of the way. Any idea where you want to go?"

Taking a sip of his beer, he looks at a few more IDs and then turns back to listen to me. "Honestly, I have no idea. I'm doing pretty well selling knives, and I know this sounds ridiculous, but do I need to go anywhere?"

Placing a ginormous hand on my shoulder, "Just get that degree from somewhere. You might not want to sell knives for another forty-five years. That's my two cents. Grab a drink and relax."

Jack looks at my smile, "Why are you so happy, bro?"

Laughing, "I never imagined that walking into my first bar the bouncer would give me life advice. I'm not sure how to take that."

John, halfway through a mixed drink, says, "When Shakes is giving you advice, you listen."

As I slide into the booth, he continues. "I got you a Long Island Iced Tea. No pressure, but it's sweet and easy to drink."

All three of them are staring at me, so I say, "Fuck it!" After a sip, I realize, "This is awful. I'll drink it, but then I'm done."

Tobey, speaking slowly, yells, "WELCOME TO COLLEGE!"

The bar is dimly lit and a little seedy. There's a golf video game, dart boards, and a small bar opposite a handful of tables and booths. Our waitress is a tiny blond with light blue eyes. She seems to know the guys. With a voluminous smile, she asks, "Can I get you anything, cutie?"

I can feel my cheeks get a little flushed. She's gazing into my eyes and has her manicured hand on my shoulder. Already feeling the drink, I can't help but smile, probably a little too big. "Water would be great."

Still staring into my soul, she says, "You have the best smile. I'm Shari."

Trying to dial back my hormones, I respond, "Thank you, Shari. I'm Alex. I went to high school with John."

Shari leans in and whispers in my ear, "He's trouble." I can feel her lips brush against me and I'm 14 all over again. There's no way

I can stand up now. I have a girlfriend, so how is this girl turning me on so much? She's very good at her job.

As she walks away, I can't help but notice her perfectly round butt. Jack laughs, "Eyes over here buddy. You see, college life is not so bad."

I turn to John, "She said you were trouble."

Banging his fist against his head. "Stupid drunk John. I was a little drunk last time, and I asked her if she could give me a piggyback ride home. She laughed and brought me a water."

The bar slowly fills up and I see a few familiar faces from high school. We exchange nods, but no one really talks to me except for Epstein. This guy had the biggest ego for no reason. He was average looking, had decent grades, was a swimmer, but was mostly a jerk.

After an initial "HELLO" yelled across the bar, he approaches our table. Jack is talking to a cute red head, Tobey is eating nachos, and John is in the bathroom. Epstein pushes a few people out of the way and sticks out his hand.

With a weird handshake, I ask, "How are you, Epstein?"

Smiling, he reveals his tiny teeth and a sinister grin, like he's about to tell a dirty joke. "I'm great. College is awesome. I'm crushing it! It has been unbelievable."

As Epstein continues to brag about his life, the waitress and I make eye contact. I mouth, "Save me."

Shari puts her hand on Epstein's plaid shirt, "Excuse me, I need a word with Alex." She hops in my lap like we are old friends.

"Keep crushing it, Epstein. Good to see you."

He walks away surprised and jealous. In the meantime, the drink is really hitting me. I feel good and a little buzzed. John walks back and stumbles while staring at us.

Shari has this huge grin on her face, as if she's really enjoying flirting with us. Before I can thank her, she says, "That guy is a huge douche. I would even sit in John's lap if he was bothering him."

John has his hands out to the side like he's really insulted. "Really, Shari? I thought we had something. I saw sparks, maybe a few kids. Your eyes, my coloring, maybe a dog?"

At this point, Shari is off my lap. I'm watching John flirt, and I feel like a proud parent. This guy could barely talk to female teachers, but now he's a pro.

I look across the bar and spot Jack. He has moved on and is now doing shots with some tall brunette. Tobey is playing video golf with a friend. There's nacho cheese on his sleeves, but I don't think he cares.

John sits across from me and orders us another drink. I slam my water, trying to sober up a little. Shari says, "I'll get you a refill."

"Wait. You are really good at this."

She smiles, "Thank you."

While holding her gaze, "You want to make more money?"

John and Shari look confused. Shari responds, "Yes, do you have a job for me?"

Confident, I tell her, "Yes. Can we talk tomorrow? It will be less hours, more money, and a resume builder."

Pointing at me, "You have a deal, Alex. Jack has my number."

John and I smile at each other and say at the same time, "Of course he does."

The bar continues to fill up. Taking in the crowd, I make eye contact with a Latino girl. John waves her over to our table. She stops by with another girl.

After he hugs both girls, he introduces us. "Alex, this is Sam and Liz." They hug me like I've known them for years and sit down with us.

Liz is the one I noticed from across the bar. She's tiny and has this huge smile. Even a little drunk, Robbie is the one for me, but I'm glad Liz came by. Is this normal?

"Where are you from, Alex? I haven't seen you around."

Taking a sip of water, I tell her, "I went to high school with John in Chicago. What about you?"

"I'm from Minnesota."

Without hesitating, I tell her, "That's where my girlfriend is from. Do you know Robbie Zirlin?" Now I'm starting to feel a little guilty. Guilty that I stared so hard at this girl and guilty that I didn't go home with Robbie. What's the matter with me?

With a surprised look on her face, "You're the cookie man? I've seen pictures of you. I went to high school with Robbie. I'm closer with her sister, Rose. She is visiting me next week."

We take a picture on Liz's phone and send it to Robbie and her sister. Within a second, they reply with happy face emojis. Robbie adds, "Small world! Make sure my man doesn't drink too much."

Putting down the phone and taking a long gulp of water, I ask, "What was Robbie like in school?"

Taking a long sip of a fizzy drink that smelled like fresh berries, she explains, "She's super smart. She was at the top of her class, an overachiever, a great dancer, and she can sing. She's shy about it, but it's her hidden talent." Scratching her head as if that will jog her memory, "She wasn't that into boys in high school, but she's always been gorgeous. Her sister, who looks just like her dad, is similar but sillier and more laid back."

"It's funny, I never really thought about what she was like before. She's amazing. I'm not sure what she's doing with me."

Liz and I are now sitting face to face with our legs touching because it's so loud that we are having a difficult time hearing each other. Nervously, she smiles at me, looks away and says, "You're like, really hot, Cookie Man."

Laughter fills up inside of me, as I've never been referred to as hot. She can tell I'm embarrassed. "Really. If I didn't love your girlfriend ..." She then leans in and softly says in my ear, "I would've totally made out with you."

Between the compliments, liquor, and Liz's warm hand on my shoulder, I kiss her on the cheek. "Thank you for the compliment." I stand up to walk away and her hand is inside my back pocket, against my butt.

I look back at Liz with a guilty look on her face, as if she was just caught stealing candy as child. "Sorry, but not that sorry."

John stands up and grabs my shoulder as I start walking away. "Wait, you can't just leave. We're grabbing pizza with these girls."

"John, she's one of the girls Robbie's sister is visiting. She just grabbed my butt. I want you to hook up with Sam, but you don't need me. I'll find Jack and he'll let me in the room. Have fun."

Trying to turn me around, he says, "Alex, please. You are a great wingman. You don't have to hook up with her friend, but Sam is like a unicorn. She is always studying or playing tennis. I might never get this chance again. It's just pizza."

"How about Tobey? He can be your wingman."

Laughing, he asks, "Did you see that kid? He's so high he's playing video golf but without money."

We both laugh so hard, the girls give us a weird look.

Giving in, I wave the girls toward me. "Are you girls hungry?"

Sam answers first. "Always. Let's get some chow."

Despite the cold temperature outside, I do not feel it. Liz has zero body fat, so she is shivering. Despite her long winter coat covering everything but her calves, she leans next to me, seemingly expecting me to put an arm around her. Trying not to be overly handsy, I take out my massive knit scarf and wrap it around her.

When my mom was sick, she taught herself to knit. The only thing she made were scarves and hats because she was always so cold, and the patterns were simple and beautiful.

With a huge grin, Liz looks up to me, "THANKS! This is amazing! I feel like I'm being hugged."

Gritting my teeth together and trying to suck the tears back into my eyes, I look up at the sky. When my mom handed me this scarf, she tied it around me tight and said, "When you're cold, put this on, and feel me hugging you." Then she hugged me and whispered, "Since the moment I knew you were inside of me, I have loved you and always will."

Using my gloves like tissue, I wipe my eyes. Liz catches me in the act and asks, "Are you okay?"

"The cold makes my eyes run."

Enjoying a break from routine feels good. I'm not going to eat any food at midnight, but being on this campus with kids pouring into the street feels comforting. Since John ordered the food ahead of time, he skips the line and picks up our order.

As if they planned to meet here, Jack pops out of nowhere. I momentarily forgot about text messaging. "What's up, boys?

Sammy, Lizzie. It's always a pleasure. I was at the front of the bar, looked back, and you guys magically disappeared."

Walking back to John and Jack's place, they describe the quad they live in. The concept is odd to me because there's a room with a television, desks, and a bathroom. Then there are two separate rooms, and each has two beds.

Walking in, I totally get it. It's like a two-bedroom apartment, but with no kitchen. Tobey's room is opposite their room, and his roommate is a local who's usually at home on the weekends. Their place smells like beer, pizza, and nacho chips. I'm not sure if that's what it always smells like, or if it's because we bought a pizza, and everyone is drinking beers except me.

I wish Robbie were here because sharing this experience with her would be fun. Northwestern is such a different campus than this and I'm a little bit lonely.

The moment Jack appeared, Liz changed. He makes her nervous. You can tell in the way she laughs at almost anything he says. Jack, on the other hand, is totally calm and is enjoying flirting with her. He's a natural.

John and Sam look like they've hooked up with each other before. They have little inside jokes, and she cannot keep her hands off him. She's leaning into him while they sit on the floor eating pizza, not like she's trying to prop herself up, but in the way new lovers can't keep away from each other. As he wipes sauce off her cheek, she kisses him a little too long with all of us watching.

I have no idea what I'm supposed to do. Business ideas start to creep into my mind. Ignoring Jack as he comments, "Listen, the rules are simple. We don't touch, but we give Lizzie a night she can't forget." At this point, John and Sam are in the other room.

Buried deep in notes, I look up to see Liz in a bra and shorts that are folded so they don't fall down. She has great abs. I say, "Liz, that's a solid four pack!"

Standing in front of me with Jack's shorts on her, feels like I'm in a porno movie. She's smiling, and now I'm starting to think Jack's offer was maybe a little serious. With a dirty grin, Liz inches closer to me. "You can touch them. I worked hard for those," then, placing her other hand on her butt, "And for this. It's never going to be J. Lo."

Jack picks up Liz as if he's carrying her over the altar. With a laugh, he asks, "Are you coming?"

"I think you're kidding, but honestly, I can't tell. I'm fine and this couch will do."

Putting someone's headphones on, I put on a rain app from my phone and quickly drift off.

FOOTBALL FIGHTS AND FUN

My mouth is incredibly dry in the morning. I look at my phone and it's 8:00. I haven't slept that late in years. No one else seems to be up yet. With a quick trip to the bathroom, I pee and brush my teeth. There's a set of exercise bands and dumbbells on the floor that I did not notice last night.

Trying to be quiet, I use the bands and weights to work out. When the clock hits 9:00, I'm drenched in sweat, and I feel much better. A few more glasses of water and I'm ready to get some food.

I hear a door open just as I take off my shirt. It's Liz, wearing a U.W. shirt that's long enough to be a dress. She looks at me like we've never met. "Alex, you've got the two I'm missing and maybe more."

I close one eye and scratch my head, as if that will help my brain figure out what she's talking about. She runs her hands over my abs, "Impressive." A huge yawn crosses her face. "How long have you been lifting this morning?"

She bends over to pick up her clothes from the night before, and she's wearing no underwear. She has a cute little butt. I don't want her to feel self-conscious, so I keep my mouth shut.

Jack on the other hand, doesn't keep quiet. He walks out of the room in sweatpants and no shirt. "Would you look at that cute butt?" Liz's cheeks fill with color. She dashes into the bathroom and gets dressed.

Jack puts his hand on my shoulder and asks, "Do you want to play some ball?"

"Done. Just remember, I'm a point guard and you're a shooter. This is not a fair match."

Shaking his head, he says, "Already with the excuses. You don't even remember playing me. I can't be that good. Besides, this is a school with over forty thousand kids. We'll get in a game with people that can school both of us."

"Really?"

With a big cocky grin, "Are you kidding me? We are going to put on a clinic."

The gym is empty as we start shooting around. Jack can shoot and he's quicker than I would've imagined, but I think I could take him. He's thin, so I push him around on the inside. A few guys start shooting around near us and Jack knows most of them. He asks, "You guys get your beauty sleep? Ready for a game?"

Our team is winning. Jack is hitting shots all over the floor, and when he occasionally misses, this guy on our team, who's, like, giraffe tall, picks up the ball and lays it in. I hit a few shots, but mostly spread the ball around. If TK were here, we would put on a show. The other player on our team, Bobby, is scrappy. He's diving for loose balls, taking charges, and rarely shooting.

After five games in a row of winning, we lose the sixth. I'm sort of happy we lost because I needed a break. The last time I played this much ball was a while ago and my stomach is a little queasy from drinking. Jack, barely sweating, turns to me, "One more?"

"How about breakfast?"

Laughing, Jack responds, "I'm so glad you said that. I'm beat."

In the basement of his dorm, there's a huge cafeteria. Using his meal card, he takes me to breakfast. "This is the least I could do. You bought the drinks last night, and dinner. All I remember from last night is asking you if you wanted to fool around with Liz and me."

"Is every night that great?"

FOOTBALL FIGHTS AND FUN

Thinking about my question like it's an oral exam, he says, "Well, not always. I dated the same girl off and on throughout high school, so I just want to have fun this year. Some nights I go home alone. I'm a big flirt, but my game plan is simple. I smile at a girl, but I make them come to me."

Sensing my confused look, "It's easier if they start off as the aggressor. That way I know they are single, and I know they want to talk. Worst case scenario: I just have a good time with my buddies." Looking at his phone, Jack continues, "I texted Shari for you, and we are meeting up tomorrow at eleven o'clock for brunch. Is that cool?"

"Thanks. I have some ideas for you guys to make money. I have a serious question for you. Did you hook up with Shari? There's something real sexy about her."

Adding some hot sauce to his eggs, "She's hot. When I first got to campus, I met her in the library. She waved me over to her table and asked if I had a charger she could use. We started hanging out a little bit. I liked her, but she got back together with her boyfriend from home."

Out of nowhere, John and Tobey sit down with us. With a little guilt in his face, "Sorry I didn't join you guys this morning. I heard you leave and felt bad, but I was alone with Liz and Sam. I guess I didn't feel that bad."

Jack cuts in first. "Did you have a threesome!? What happened, big player?"

Laughing, "I wish. Liz left a few minutes after you guys. Sam was a lot of fun. I'm not sure if she's my girlfriend, but I would be cool with that."

Sitting back in my chair, I watch kids file in and out of the cafeteria. Almost everyone is decked out in Badger clothes. Catching me gazing at students wearing head to toe University of Wisconsin gear, John says, "Game DAY! Are you ready? I got us tickets and it's going to be fun. Ohio State. They'll probably win, but it will still be fun. The fans are annoying though. I thought we drank a lot, but I heard those kids get stupid drunk."

I turn to Tobey, who looks like he's been up all night. "What happened to you? Have you been to bed yet?"

Clearing his throat for what feels like an eternity, he grumbles, "I went for a burrito, as I was not in the mood for pizza. Fraiser and Shaggy were there." Looking at me, "They are two guys that live in the fraternity house. They were throwing a small party with some girls I did not know. Jell-O shots were had, and then I woke up on Shaggy's floor. I need a nap."

John looks at Tobey and shakes his head like a parent judging a kid that misbehaved. "Those are the two craziest mother fuckers in the house. Don't hang out with them. What happened to Jordy? I texted him about breakfast and heard nothing back."

Tobey laughs, "He was out cold when I got there. They drew a dick on his face." Taking out his phone, Tobey shows pictures of two girls next to him. One is pretending to pull down his pants, and the other one pretends to kiss him on the lips.

Jack cuts in, "Hashtag me too."

Tobey is still giggling. "Wait until you see the next picture. The same girl that pretended to kiss him has her boobs out, almost in his face.

John is shocked. "What the fuck? Where did you guys find those girls?"

Tobey says with a guilty smile, "She's a stripper. Shaggy met her at a bachelor party for a friend of his that lives here."

Jack asks, "He's dating a stripper?"

Tobey quickly answers, "Not dating, necessarily."

Listening to this story, I'm less sold on college. Not that I have anything against boobs, but I can't help but wonder, how many knives did I sell last night? Are people going to register for my flatware? More importantly—have I hit 4K in sales for the week?

While everyone naps, I turn on my laptop and check my sales. $3,475 for sales and a profit of almost $3,000. Next, I Google college plates, college gift baskets, college confection, hangover supplements, and beer-of-the-month clubs. I jot down a bunch of notes on what college kids want. A cluster of thoughts fall from my head to the paper. Five pages later, I feel like I have some good ideas.

Between the mellow music in the background and the lack of sleep, my eyes forcibly close. I hope no one draws on my face while I conk out.

On Saturdays, college football was on at my house. No one really watched it, but my dad had it on in the background. I knew it was a big deal but walking to Camp Randall Stadium is cool. Thousands of kids line the streets and the houses along the way are crammed with kids and adults drinking and grilling. It seems like someone is handing out beers because everyone has a drink in their hand. Since John loaned me a college sweatshirt, I fit in. All the fandom rubs off on me and I buy a hat on the way into the stadium.

Depending on your seat, you wear either red or white so they can have this striped effect in the stands. It's cool, and the place is packed. The handful of Ohio State fans are hard to spot amongst all the Badger fans. John and Jack are on their second drinks, and the game has not even started yet.

Like a kid, I'm sipping hot chocolate and perfectly happy. It's a little cold out and I'm not into day drinking. The moment the ball is kicked off, everyone stands. A junior high kid, sitting with older kids, starts yelling, "Fuck you, Ohio State!" The ferocity in his voice is like they killed his mother.

Jack whispers, "Poor kid doesn't he know they are fourteen-point favorites."

Watching everyone interact is almost more exciting than the game. I literally have no idea what's going to happen in the stands. Between verbal jabs, puking, and drunk fans, I'm not sure what to pay attention to.

Down by 12, Jack and John decide it's time for the post game party at their fraternity. Weaving between crowds takes us thirty minutes, and it's only a mile walk.

A drunk Ohio State fan yells a pleasantry to us as we cross the street in front of the house. Jack does not take kindly to this and stands an inch from the pale guy's nose. "Get the FUCK out of here!"

Two more Ohio State fans appear from behind a tree. These are big boys, each standing a head taller than Jack, and they are thick.

I'm waiting for guys from the house to pop outside. I say, "John, go get some of your buddies to come out here."

He walks away and this pudgy tall kid tosses a beer at his back. Adrenaline takes over and the twitches and nerves I used to get from judo matches start up. I slip a foot behind this guy and push both his shoulders. He falls on ass and his head slams into the cold grass.

The other big guy takes a swing at me, but he's a little too slow and he leans forward. I grab his jacket and use his momentum to toss him forward. The other guy looks scared. The one closest to me says, "Sorry. We're just a little too drunk."

At this point, there are 30 fraternity brothers staring down these kids. I help both kids up as one of John's friends comes closer with a bat. This friend of John's is raging, "GET THE FUCK OUT OF HERE! COME ON!"

When we walk inside, I receive a combination of fist bumps and pats on the back from every single guy. John is beaming with pride, as if he taught me everything I know. I spent a decade fighting in matches, but I've never been in a situation like that. My left arm keeps shaking, but I try and play it off like I'm just cold.

A tall skinny kid with a beard and hair like Jesus sits next to me. "Want a gummy? It will calm you down without getting you too high. That was bad ass. That third guy, he was so scared of you, it was funny."

Finally calm, I notice my phone buzzing. "Hey, babe."

As if she's rapping, she asks, "Are you okay? What happened? I saw you throw down these two giants like they were nothing and then you picked them back up. You really did do karate."

"That was literally not even fifteen minutes ago. How did you already see that online?"

Responding quickly, "My sister is already friends with Jack on Facebook. Someone posted it and tagged him. She saw it and said, 'I think that's Alex.'"

Laughing, I tell her, "That is crazy. Good thing I didn't hit either of them. Man, last thing I need is to get arrested. Those guys were just drunk assholes."

Before I can ask her how she's doing, she asks, "Are you sure you're okay? Those guys were big."

"I promise you. I'm fine. They were drunk and stupid. How are you?"

With a sad deep breath, "I'm okay. This is a lot more emotional than I thought. Rose is a trooper. She's getting me through it. I thought it would be the other way around. I can't wait to see you. I thought I would have to worry about girls hitting on you, not guys trying to hit you."

With a smile, "Thanks, Robbie. You have nothing to worry about. Have a great night. I'll see you tomorrow night."

"I love you." Then she hangs up. It feels so good to hear that.

Hanging up the phone, I get a text from my old judo teacher. "Well done! Next time kick his leg out more. Don't get sloppy. You mixed in some Aikido. Love it. Be safe."

"Thx. Man! I'm not even tagged, but you found it."

"Say hi to Logan Gold. He's in the fraternity house you're staying at. He took the video. He was three years older than you ..."

Music starts blaring from the room in front of me, and girls from a sorority next door start walking in. A herd of yoga pants-wearing girls march in with crockpots. A few are dressed like cowboys. I wondered what all the tables and extension cords were for. According to the flier John hands me, it's a crockpot and crawfish hoedown—whatever that means.

John sits down next to me, waving at girls that walk by. "Hey, that was awesome, Alex. Thanks for being you. You've upped my social standings."

Tobey and Jordy are now standing in front of us, bowing. Jordy makes eye contact first, "Where did you learn that? Are you a ninja? Or can you not talk about it?"

"Thanks for putting me at ease, Jordy. I took judo for years. It's not a big deal. They were drunk."

Getting up to grab more water, I'm greeted by a gaggle of girls. This short brunette wearing a tube top that barely holds her huge chest stares up at me, waiting for me to say something. The other three girls just shyly say, "Hi."

"Hello, I'm Alex. You guys know John. He's my buddy from school."

One girl, who's almost my height, wearing black boots up to her knees, answers. "I'm Shelly. We love John. Nice moves out there. Can you teach us that stuff?"

The shorter one hugs me. With her chest grinding into me, she smiles and looks me in the eye. "I'm also a ninja." With a pause, she adds, "Natalie." She steps back and I really have no idea what to say.

"Natalie the ninja. I can't forget that." With John grabbing some food, there is no one to save me. I see Jack out of the corner of my eye, so I wave him over.

He hugs all the girls and gives them kisses on the cheek. I'm in awe of his confidence and charm. "Alex my boy, I see you've met the stunning Natalie. This is the equally dangerous Julie, Shelly, and Rachel."

I put a hand on Jack's shoulder. "Jack and I would love to teach you guys some self-defense."

Jack puts his arm around Shelly. "I'll show you some moves tonight. Let's grab a drink. Ladies, do you want to get some punch?"

Like the pied piper, they all follow Jack except Natalie. She reaches around behind me, grabs my belt, and pulls me down on the couch. After an awkward wink, she walks away.

Confused, I just sit there for a minute, waiting for John or one of his friends to talk to me. Of course, my new best friend Natalie is back with a drink for me. Handing me a bright red drink, she explains, "Sorry I threw you down, Alex. I went to the game and have yet to sober up. I got back to the house and only had time for a quick shower before this shindig."

Making herself more comfortable, she takes off her shoes and lays in the corner of the couch and puts her legs over mine. "That's better. So how long did you do judo—or was it wrestling?"

The punch tastes like fruit punch Gatorade with a hint of alcohol. I take a small sip. "I have done judo for ten years. What about you?"

"Six years of flipping and getting flipped was enough for me. I was doing dance and gymnastics, too. Then a friend took me to a tennis court, and it was over. I quit everything and went all in on tennis. I thought I was going to be a professional. Then I played kids from Florida and got crushed. It wasn't even close. It totally sucked."

Natalie yawns and then closes her eyes. Standing up, I tell her, "I'm going to get you some water."

I lift her legs and look for one of the three girls that seem to be her friends. The tall one is still talking to Jack.

"Hey—Shelly, right?" She nods her head yes. I continue, "Where does Natalie live? I think she needs to get home. She might be sleeping right now."

Walking with me, Shelly looks disgusted staring at her friend. I scoop her up, and we walk half a block before running into their house. Shelly unlocks the door and guides us upstairs. Jack helps me place Natalie in her bed. Motherly, Shelly covers a blanket over her, and we walk back to the party.

Tobey, holding a giant mug and standing on the porch, enthusiastically waves to us as we approach the front door. "Man, Alex, this is one banner weekend. Break up a fight, carry a hottie home, what's next? Threesome with Jack?"

Without smiling, I say, "That was last night, in your room."

Shelly looks at us both confused. "I thought that was going to happen tonight. Right?"

Jack responds, "Of course."

Shelly smacks my butt hard as we walk in. "Alex, I have to give it to you. Natalie would've rocked your world if you didn't let her fall asleep. Despite what Jack's been telling me, you're a good guy."

I try to rein in my ego. "Wait, I would've rocked *her* world! Actually, I wouldn't because I have a girlfriend."

Pointing at me like I insulted her, she says, "Oh, Natalie? That bitch could care less about your girlfriend."

Jack laughs. "It's true. That girl is tenacious. I'm impressed that she kept her boobs from popping out tonight."

Taking Jack's hand, Shelly adds, "Me, too. Play your cards right and you might see some others."

Jack looks at me shocked and offers up a fist bump.

The house is now officially bumping. The country western band is jamming, and most of the girls are dancing with about half the guys from the house.

John is dancing. Pride swells up watching him. He was so shy before, and now he's swing dancing with two different girls. The smile on his face is priceless. All I want to do, like Natalie, is sleep. It's been a long day. Not wanting to rain on John's parade, I head to the kitchen and pour myself a coffee. My facial expression says it all, as this lumberjack of a guy says, "I know it's awful. I have some great cold brew in my fridge if you're into that, Alex."

Pausing, I ask, "Logan?"

He nods his head yes. "Yup, Nice to meet you. That was a messy take down, but pretty good considering how big those cats were."

I follow Logan upstairs. His long, thin, blond hair is pulled back in a ponytail. He's wearing denim overalls and a black T-shirt. Even the veins in his arms are big.

We walk into his room, and that's when it hits me. This guy wrestled for my coach. That's why I never had him in class with me. "Coach sent me a text about a minute after the fight."

Walking into his room, he pulls out a fancy bottle of cold brew coffee. "Sit down, kid. One warning: This will keep you up for at least another six hours."

Taking a sip, I immediately wake up. "I'll drink half. I could pass out right now, but John has his dancing shoes on, so this might be a late night."

"Half is a good call. Are you thinking about coming to school here? I'm not sure what type of shape you're in, but you could probably walk on here. Coach said you were good. I redshirted my freshmen year. I'm working on my MBA and finishing out my last year of eligibility."

I haven't been on a mat for a few years. "Thanks, but I'm rusty. I'm just visiting John. This might sound odd, but I have this business idea. I might get my associate degree and focus on business."

With a serious tone, he says, "Make your business happen, but I think you should still get a four-year degree. It might be easier to get venture capital."

Walking back downstairs, all these ideas flood through my mind as the caffeine spins the dials of my brain. With the raucous party on the main floor, I head to the basement to jot down notes in my phone. I turn on a light, and it's just one huge concrete room with a few couches. I do not want to even imagine what happens down here. I'm pleasantly surprised no one is making out on one of these gross couches.

Since it's dark and not so loud, I hammer out a few pages of ideas. I feel the energy flowing through me. I quickly text Maddie: "Is it odd that I'm jotting down notes for business while everyone is getting drunk around me?"

I feel a little bad for just dropping my crazy on her when it hits, but she's always welcomed it. Before I can walk upstairs, she responds. "You do you. You have this business building and it's exciting. There's nothing wrong with that. Make sure to have some fun, too! Be safe. Your dad says Hi!"

"Thx. Hi dad! P.S. Being safe."

Walking back upstairs, it's pleasantly quiet. I see John sitting on the couch, where I was earlier talking to Jordy. "What's up, guys! Why is it so quiet?"

Jordy asks accusatorily, "Where did you disappear to? The band is on a break."

"Logan kidnapped me. That guy is intense!"

John is smiling like he's been overserved. "That guy is INTENSE! I told him I used to work out with you, so he dragged me to the gym with him. It hurt to walk for a week. I could only use the handicap stalls to poop. Do you want to get some food?"

Jordy shoots up from the couch like someone shot a gun. "Food! Jack?"

Jordy looks annoyed. "Finding Jack is our life story. Actually, finding Tobey is much harder."

"Jack was with this girl named Shelly. Judging on my short knowledge of Jack, he's probably gone with her."

Jordy puts a hand on my shoulder like a proud dad. "You're a smart kid, but Shelly is too classy to go home with Jack. He's tried before and failed. She's wants an actual date. Jack has been considering it for a while, but you know—so many girls and only one Jack."

John, relying on technology, hunts down Jack with an actual phone call. "Ian's Pizza, asshole. Bring Shelly and maybe a few for the rest of us?"

Wind smashes into us as we step outside. Three steps out the door and Jack yells, "Hold up, dicks!"

Shelly, Julie and Rachel follow him. He slaps my butt, like we scored a touchdown. He adds, "See, I share. I'm a very philanthropic guy. You guys were about to give up on me."

Listening and watching everyone drag their feet I wonder aloud, "Am I the only sober one here?"

Jordy answers first. "Yes, on this entire campus. Don't be such a stick in the mud."

Julie, with no hesitation, puts her arm around me. "Perfect. Now I know who can help me walk. Thanks, ninja Alex. I love how you carried Natalie home. Her goal tonight was to take you home, so in some way, she succeeded."

The idea that this girl's single goal was to take me home is beyond flattering. Less than a year ago, women wouldn't return my text messages. Now, they want to hook up with me. It's all so odd. My crowning achievement has been graduating from high school. I wish I knew a world like this existed when I was playing Xbox with John instead of going to school dances.

The pizza place is packed. The people watching is incredible. There's a handful of college kids in front of us. One is a transvestite who stands a head taller than me with a short stocky dude next to them, and a bunch of high school kids wearing letterman jackets are behind us. What a night. You don't get this diversity back home.

WAKE UP CALL

A cold rush hits me as someone runs past at 4:30 a.m. I only know this because the microwave is in my line of sight from the couch. All I can see is the outline of Tobey speed walking into John's room. Then, I hear the sound of rain.

"What the FUCK, Tobey?" I can hear the confusion and anger in John's voice. He doesn't get upset often.

Tobey says nonchalantly, "I had to pee."

Jack laughs. "You just pissed in our closet."

Tobey responds, "Classic. Sorry. I'll clean it up. How about using baking soda tonight and tomorrow I'll bleach it?"

John answers, "Fine. You are banned from boozing and smoking up."

Tobey fires back, "Yes, dad."

I'm just laughing. "Good thing you didn't bring Shelly here."

A girl's voice emerges. "I'm here, Alex. I just could not stop crying and laughing. You guys are like sitcom funny."

John seems annoyed. "Okay, let's all get back to bed."

Shelly surprises everyone. "John, do you need me to cuddle you?"

With a happy tone he says, "Yes, please!"

Within minutes we all somehow fade back into a deep sleep. However, at 8:30 a.m. I'm the only one up. With a big yawn, I start organizing my notes for Jack and Shari. I want to make sure my broad idea is coherent.

A little bored, I start lifting weights and watching ESPN with the television muted. Shelly pops out first. She's wearing one of Jack's T-shirts with boxers that are folded over to keep from falling down. She catches me glancing at her outfit.

With a hand on my shoulder, she explains, "I tried on several bottoms. These are John's because he's skinnier than Jack, and because John just seems like someone who does laundry."

Taking a break from lifting, "I don't judge unless you put pineapple on your pizza."

With a shocked look, she asks, "How did you remember that? You really were sober. You're like a boy scout. Now tell me, did any part of you want to knock one of those assholes out?"

Now sitting on my bed/couch, with her perfect long legs dangling on the edge, I turn to face her. "Honestly, I've never gotten in a fight that wasn't part of a match. I had sobriety, luck, and some training on my side. But yes, I did want to knock that first dude out. Why did you decide to sleep over?"

"Jack has been flirting with me since the first week of college. I've resisted him for months, which has not been easy. Last night before Natalie took a nap, she told me to stop thinking so much. He also paid for the pizza."

Laughing, I tell her, "That was actually me."

Shifting her legs around, she wraps them around my legs and smiles with all her teeth. "Then I guess I owe *you*."

Trying not to blush, I say, "It's okay. A thank you will suffice."

Pulling me closer with her legs, "I like messing with you."

Surprised, I ask, "Why? Didn't' you just hook up with Jack?"

She shakes her head. "Jack fell asleep before me, so I just spooned him. You get so nervous like I'm going to attack you or something."

With my hands on her legs, I tell her, "This is definitely an attack. Remember—I'm the fighter."

Releasing the leg lock and standing up, she stares at me with her light eyes. "I like you, Alex. Come to school here. We have fun and get a great education."

Still standing toe to toe with me, Shelly leans in closer and kisses me on the cheek. With her arms around me tight, I can feel her chest melt into mine. Before I have any idea what to do, she smacks my butt and heads to the bathroom.

She should go into recruiting. I have the sudden urge to transfer here. This has been the most fun I've had in a while. However, between the fight and Tobey peeing in the closet, I'm not sure this is what I want.

The door to the bathroom is now ajar, and a hand waves at me. Curious, I walk in and see the most perfect naked body I've ever seen. Her hourglass figure is flawless. She's lean but has curves, and her abs are completely flat.

"I'm never going to have the courage to do this again, so do you want to join Jack and me in the shower? You don't have to touch anyone or anything."

Smiling, I turn her down. "That's the nicest offer I've had in a long time. If I didn't have a girlfriend or know how much Jack really liked you, I would jump in there."

Cocking her head to the side, she says, "I respect that, Alex. You're a good guy. Jack said you would decline." Walking a little too close to me, she continues, "I just really like nice guys. Maybe next time you visit."

Walking out of the bathroom, I bump into Jack. Looking up at me with sleepy eyes, I wonder what he just heard.

Leaning in, Jack hugs me. "Bros for life."

The only thing I can think of: "Don't drop the soap."

Jack opens the door and walks in. Avoiding the urge to eavesdrop, I pick up the dumbbells and work off some nervous energy. I play the scenario over and over again in my mind. Flirting is fine, but I love Robbie and couldn't do that to her.

Working out, listening to a book on my phone, and watching SportsCenter takes my mind off whatever is happening in the shower. Tobey and John are still sleeping and I'm feeling a little more awake.

When Jack and Shelly leave the bathroom, Shelly stares at my shirtless body. "Not bad, Alex."

Looking at them, I ask, "Is this normal? Does this shit happen every weekend?"

Shelly answers first. "I've only slept with two boyfriends. To be honest, this is not normal for me. I was really turned on this morning. Maybe it was sleeping next to Jack and being around all you guys. This situation is an anomaly. At least for me."

Jack grins ear to ear. "This has been an epic weekend. We always have fun. Other times it's video games until we pass out on the couch. Let me get dressed, we'll get some breakfast, drop off Shelly, and then meet Shari at the library."

John wakes up after my shower and joins us for breakfast.

We head to a breakfast place near Shelly's apartment. The conversation bounces between classes, going abroad, and Tobey peeing on the floor. I mostly listen. Internally, I'm debating if college life is for me. John comes with us to the library ready to study. I invite him to talk with us about my job. He says, "Sorry dude, I have no desire to work. Projects I can handle. Let me know when you get rolling."

Shari greets Jack and me with a hug and kiss on the cheek. It feels unnatural, but I just go with it. Shari is a ball of energy, and she hammers us with questions. "Did you guys have fun yesterday? Alex, do you like it here? Did you meet a girl? What happened with that fight?"

"You're a lot more caffeinated than me. I had the best time. Really, this place is awesome. I have a girlfriend but met lots of girls. The fight wasn't really a fight. What about you? How was your night?"

Running her hand through her blond hair, she says, "I worked and made some good money. A few coworkers went to an after party. Pretty lame. There were a lot of dudes just smoking pot. What do you have for us?"

Feeling empowered, I explain, "Follow me through this rant and hopefully you'll figure out what I want to do and join me. I think this would be great for your resumes and the experience would be something you can talk about in an interview."

I take a few breaths, smile, and carry on, "There are over forty thousand students here. The University of Texas is even bigger.

We know people at big schools like Indiana University, University of Illinois, Ohio State University, the University of Michigan, Michigan State, and Alabama. I could go on. Parents want to send their kids care packages, but many of them are too lazy to make them. What if we had a directory of local places that deliver care packages to kids? It could be like Yelp or Amazon for college kids and college towns. We can also list places kids love."

I look at Jack and Shari, and they are listening. Shari is taking notes. "What if we start off with a general website selling college gifts? I can put together a general site where we make money based on the products people order. As we spread the word about this site, we will start to get local partners. Unlike Groupon, we don't ask for discounts and a cut, we just price the item to include a five percent fee for us. Mom and pop shops get business, kids get what they want, and we make some money. We could possibly get small discounts, but let's tackle one thing at a time. What are your thoughts?"

Jack speaks first. "What do we do exactly? Is this a paid internship?"

Pointing at Jack, I explain, "You get paid. I'm making some money from my other business, so to start I could pay you each two hundred dollars a month and once we start making money, we can do a profit-sharing system. Your first job is to spread the word and find friends at other campuses to do the same. Once we have a web presence, you'll start finding us potential local vendors."

Shari is looking at me, confused. "I love this, but why me?"

Staring into her light blue eyes, I tell her, "You are a natural salesperson. The way you worked all the other tables for a big tip was magic. I wanted to tip you double the bill. You have this way of making people feel special. Jack has that, too, but looser morals."

He shakes his head in agreement, and we all laugh. He adds, "Those are all true statements. This is a great idea. My parents sent me a huge vat of shitty baked goods. If the cookies were awesome, that would be one thing, but how much crap can I eat? Hook me up with a hoodie, some winter gear, a gift card for some food, and maybe a beer of the month club. Now we are talking."

Shari cuts in, "College guys do love their beer. That could totally be a thing. We just have to worry about laws around sending booze. People ship wine all the time, though. I'm in. What about you, Jack?"

Jack extends his hand. "My lazy ass needs some job experience. Count me in!"

Endorphins pulse throughout my body. As thrilling as it was to see a naked coed, this high is much better. This business fills a need and hopefully can make lots of money.

Jack and Shari give me a hug and we head out of the library. John walks me out and starts talking. "I wanted to show you a great weekend, but man, you showed *me* a great weekend. I'm cooler now because of you. Seriously, these older guys from the house that never talked to me are now texting me. Best weekend of my life!"

I hug John. "Thank you, man. This weekend was beyond amazing. I needed a weekend of socializing. I'll be back."

John hugs me one more time. "I hope so."

WORK AND PAIN

The drive back home is quick. My lunch of beef jerky and nasty gas station coffee fills me up until I get home. Business ideas continue to bounce around in my brain as I drive.

The smile on my dad's face is so large, it's as if he knows everything that happened the last two days. "Dad, you wouldn't believe my weekend even if I told you."

He puts down his book and sits up. "John did text me before you left, promising you would come back a Badger."

Taking a long exhalation, I tell him, "I had an awesome time. Women were trying to hook up with me, some drunk guys tried to fight me, and I went to the football game on Saturday. This weekend was awesome. If you're wondering, I did not cheat on Robbie. I did have an epiphany, though."

Leaving my dad in suspense, I pour myself some real coffee and join him back on the couch. He looks confused. "So, you are not going to enroll at Madison?"

"No. I want to focus on this business idea, College Comforts. I already have two employees! Long story short: I want to start a website where people buy stuff for their kids in college. There aren't any companies yet that are really dedicated to that. Then, I want to build a repository of companies at each school that sell stuff kids want. I would sell books, hoodies, baked goods, and more. I want to connect local businesses with parents, grandparents, and friends. Does that make sense?"

Shaking his head in agreement, he says, "That sounds great, but you'll need to either rely on Yelp or find kids at every college."

"That's right. At first, I'm just listing companies that will give me affiliate deals until I build a better site and then an app where companies can eventually add themselves. First, I will need to garner interest, get a lot of hits, and then it will be easier to grow. There's one thing I wanted to ask you, though."

With his arms raised like he's directing planes, he asks, "What?"

Forcing a large smile, I explain, "I want to stop taking classes. It will take two years to get this thing off the ground. If it's moving nicely, then I can finish school and hire someone to manage or sell it. What do you think?"

With no hesitation, he says, "Do it!"

I was not prepared for this response. "Who tells their kid to drop out of school? Why did you make this so easy for me? With all of my AP classes and summer school, I have twelve classes left to get my associate's degree. Shouldn't I keep working on that? Is this reverse psychology?"

Laughing, he says, "Your mom and I would've had a huge fight over this. I told you the answer you really wanted. I see how hard you worked with the knife business. Do I think you should at least get your associate's degree? Of course, but you are already making close to six figures. I know you're going to sink all that money into this company. Worst-case scenario: You lose some cash and gain this incredible story. You should talk to Robbie, too. She's a smart girl."

Looking at my phone, I glance at a recent text message from her. "Legend, Gentleman, Boss. Who's the girl?"

Since I read the message out loud, my dad solved the question. "She's talking about Instagram. Your friend John posted two pictures and a video. In one, you are throwing a giant on the ground, then you carry some cute tiny girl with huge boobs, and then you're at the library. The caption is Legend, Gentlemen, Boss."

Annoyed, I say, "I only set up social media accounts for business. Why would John do this? What should I tell her?"

With a hand on my shoulder he tells me, "You did nothing wrong. Just tell her what happened. I love Robbie, too, but some people get jealous."

Looking at the picture of me and Natalie, it doesn't look good. She's asleep, I look a little annoyed, and Jack and Shelly are each on one side of me with drunk grins.

I text her back. "Did you land? I thought you were getting in at five o'clock. I can get u. Just pictures on IG. Fun weekend."

Before I can turn back to my dad, my phone rings. "Hello. How are you and your sister doing?"

Wasting no time, a grumpy voice answers, "This weekend sucked. I'm glad you had fun. It's just hard when you have one of the worst weekends of your life while your boyfriend is carrying drunk girls around. I wanted you to have fun, but not carry big boobs around drunk. What the fuck, Alex?"

Having never been in this position before, I have no idea what to say. "The truth is, I had fun. Your sister is going to have a great time. I'm sorry you had a crappy weekend, but nothing happened. Really, this girl passed out on the couch I was sitting on. I didn't want some drunk fraternity boy to take her to his room, so I carried her home. Her girlfriend put her to bed, and that was it."

I can hear her crying in the background. "Part of me wanted you to go to Madison and have fun. You would be close and could keep an eye on my sister. But I'm not sure I can handle long distance. My mind just goes to you sleeping with that girl in your arms."

Using the calming tone my mom used on my when I was upset, I ask, "How about I pick you up and we grab a bite and talk?"

"It's okay. Jane is home and she'll take me back."

Concern starts to build in my heart. "Don't you want to see me?"

Wasting no time, she answers, "Not right now." I feel like someone punched me in the gut.

"Okay. When you're ready. Bye." Without waiting for a response, I hang up. My dad puts his arm around me.

Holding in the tears, I tell him, "I think I have to puke."

I run to bathroom and throw up coffee. "I feel better."

After brushing my teeth, I pop back downstairs with my notebook, ready to work. My dad hands me a cup of water. "Love is hard. She might just be going through something."

Trying to block the pain, I tell him, "I'm just going to work."

Searching through Facebook, I look for people I knew in high school that go to different big schools.

First, I jot down contacts at Midwestern schools: Iowa, Illinois, Indiana, Kansas, Michigan, and Michigan State. Jasper and Ellie are at UT in Austin, so I add that to list too. Ellie was also my first crush. I see that my new Madison friends have followed and friended me. I'm not sure what to do with Natalie's request. She sent a message, too. "Sorry I was so drunk and tired. You're my hero."

Tracking my activity sounds like a good step. Using Excel, I list my new hires, emails I send, and possible next moves. Jotting notes on a legal pad, I start building my business plan.

Working through dinner, I already have a skeleton website and a list of affiliate companies to put down. I need to start somewhere.

Fatigue sets in just as I get a text from Robbie. "Sorry. I'm a mess right now. Can you come over to my place tomorrow?"

"Sure. Nighty night!"

After brushing my teeth, she sends a kiss emoji and a heart. Love is a rollercoaster.

QUESTION, DISCUSS, REWORK

Using the basic web training I learned in high school, I have a simple website up and running. Shari and Jack have already sent me some spots in Madison to list. I decided to list all the places they recommend and make a list of possible advertisers.

My next list is all the people I can reach out to. It's amazing how many schools I can reach. Before I get too deep, I call Dave from poker. He runs sales for a tech company.

"Dave, hey. It's Alex. Do you have a minute to discuss a business I'm starting?"

I can't tell if his exhale is one of aggravation or a centering breath. "Sure, kid. Let's hear it. Give me a second, I'm closing my door."

I hear a door shut. "Okay, Alex. Shoot."

"I'm starting a college website where parents and others can buy items from either the town their loved one is in, or from a favorite place from home. I'll charge a fee of some sort on the sale. They can run specials. Once they see a lot of sales from the site, they'll want to advertise."

He interrupts me. "Ads are where you make your money. Don't get caught up with a fee. That's a huge pain in the ass because it requires a lot of staff. Look at Yelp and Groupon. They have all these kids making code calls. You want people calling you because it's so much easier. With all the things on the tech end, and building some content, you can bring a lot of visitors. This will then attract advertisers."

"Dave, what do you mean when you say content?"

Dave laughs. "Articles about college life. Why not post articles like short blogs or videos or reviews? People like reviews. You could divide it into town, food, fun, and clothes. I'm just spitballing."

I'm typing his suggestions as fast as he tosses them out. These are all great ideas. I have a lot of work ahead of me.

"Dave, I don't want to take up anymore of your time. Thank you so much. If you have other ideas, can you shoot me an email or text?"

Excited, he says, "Of course! This was fun. We can sit and talk more later. I'm going to email contact information for this kid that recently graduated and does great website work. He interned for me and lives out here. His name is Josh Fine. Also talk to Rob because he works in sales."

"Thanks, Dave! I'll reach out to Josh."

Before I hang up, he adds, "Think about including your baking recipes, and then you can sell and mail the dough. That's when you hit them with, 'Check out this company if you don't have time to bake.' List the top five fuzzy pajamas. Have your college kids write some articles."

"Great ideas!" In case Dave has more, I wait a few seconds before hanging up. Jotting down notes and organizing them takes me past lunch. Grabbing a protein bar, I sit down and look at my knife business. Sales started dipping last week. Judging by my analytics, Google and Instagram are giving me the best results.

Thoughts of Robbie start to creep back into my mind. What does she want to talk about? Are we still together?

Pushing visions of Robbie out of my head, I focus on work. I fire off emails to Shari and Jack, asking for content. Next up, I need to contact kids at other schools. Ideas start to flood my brain. Instead of running around crazy, I continue organizing my thoughts on a spreadsheet. Ignoring texts, emails, and phone calls, I form pages of action items.

Interrupting my prioritizing, Maddie pops in, grinning with a handful of groceries. "Want to help a girl out?"

Saving my files, I ask, "You have a key already?"

Hugging me, she explains, "Your dad doesn't move that fast, but I know the garage code. He said you were going to Robbie's for the night. I thought I could stop by early to talk. How are you?"

With no ability to control my emotions, words vomit out of me. "I don't know what's going on. She was so mad and cold, but I did nothing. Yes, it looked bad that I had some drunk girl in my arms, but she was sleeping. I literally carried her home. All that girl wanted was for me to sleep with her. Then another girl asked me to shower with her. It was like something out of a dream."

With a serious look, she asks, "What do you want, Alex? Is Robbie the one? At nineteen years old, with no prior relationships, and this intense desire for business success, can you tell me Robbie is your future wife?"

I search my brain for the answer. "I don't know." Thinking more, I add, "I love her. I've never felt this way about anyone. The one thing I learned with my mom's death is that I can get through heartache. I don't want to, but I can."

With a serious look, she says, "You're resilient and you recently learned that girls like you. Do you want to explore that?"

Thinking back to the first girl I liked, I tell her, "My freshmen year, my mom told me if I like a girl, don't stress. Ask her out for coffee, but if she says no, move on to the next. I had no confidence, but I asked this one girl out, Ellie. She told me she danced every day and worked on the weekends, but we could do lunch. So, we had lunch and merged friends. Nothing ever happened, though."

Inquisitive, she asks, "Whatever happened to her? Where is she in school?"

With a smile, I tell her, "The summer after sophomore year, Ellie came back to school with big boobs, and became very popular with the senior boys. She's at UT. We haven't spoken since she left for school."

Cocking her head to the side, she asks, "Is that a school you'll be visiting?"

Laughing, "It's on my list, but if Robbie wants to make things work, I'll reach out to another friend there."

Maddie pats me on the shoulder and heads to the kitchen. "Remember, you have a say in this relationship. Either way, you'll be okay."

Logging back onto my computer, I list almost 100 ideas and possible revenue streams. I remember when I first met with Rick, he mentioned that multiple revenue sources are the key to success.

This process feels like when I started playing chess. After learning the basics, you're taught how to attack, defend, and then you start forming a strategy. I had these tricks to throw people off their game, like changing the pace. I would methodically make a move, taking all the time I had, and then I would just make two quick moves. How do I apply that to business?

The smell of onions frying with garlic fills the air and kills my concentration. Peering into the kitchen, I watch Maddie browning vegetables. She tosses in spices lightly, and I'm not sure whether to comment.

Catching my gaze, she asks, "What are looking at? Am I doing something wrong?"

Tossing my hands up in the air, I respond, "Do you really want my advice?"

With no hesitation, she says, "Hell yeah. Get over here, my little chef."

I laugh because Maddie is almost a head shorter than me. "I would go a little heavier on the spices. Don't flip these steaks yet. Let them get a good sear on each side and then finish them in the oven."

"What else?"

"If you want your potatoes to be crispy, but not overcooked, wait until my dad walks in. Then turn up the heat for a few minutes. Add a little more salt before you take them out of the pan. Last thing: Use the salad spinner."

With a hug, she says, "It's funny, I made you guys casseroles thinking you didn't know how to cook. It turns out that you are so much better at this than me."

"My mom always had a pie in the oven, cupcakes to decorate, or dough resting on the dryer. While that was happening, she had me cook. With her usual sweet tone, she would tell me that I must caramelize the veggies. She taught me to toast the seasoning before adding the meat to a pan. I loved spending time in the kitchen with her. Each of my parents had a role. My dad would work with me for hours on the weekends, shooting hoops, and then I spent the night cooking and baking. I was lucky."

With a warm smile she says, "You were lucky, and you still are. Now hit the showers, maybe throw on some nice jeans and a plaid shirt. Wear your dad's winter vest."

"Maddie, maybe you'll make me cool."

She yells as I head upstairs, "You *are* cool!"

HELP AND HUGS

Nerves bubble up as I park near Robbie's place. I know I want to be with her, but I'm prepared if she wants to break up.

Greeting me at the dorm's front desk, she's glowing. She has a white waffle shirt on and black leggings that hug her butt perfectly. She hugs me tightly and I can smell vanilla lotion. She's really trying to seduce me.

Walking to her room, she holds my hand. "I'm sorry, Alex. I got so jealous. I've never been like that before. I know that nothing happened. Rose's friend said you're a great wingman."

Four candles are lit inside the room and Robbie leads me to her bed. She unzips my jacket, unbuttons my shirt, and pulls off my jeans. The ambience, music, and smell quickly soothe my nerves. Pushing me on the bed, Robbie takes off her top and pants.

Gazing into her puppy dog eyes, I say, "You're not wearing any undergarments! You think I'm so easy."

With a smile, Robbie adds, "You *are* that easy."

Make-up sex is intense. The room is thick with sex. I don't think I've heard Robbie ever make those noises or twitch like that.

While lying in the crook of my arm, she says, "I've been thinking about my trip. I'm gone for almost five months. I don't want to lose you over those months, but I feel like I can't handle seeing and hearing stories about your adventures. And you need to have those adventures." She pauses and then wipes tears from her eyes. "Is it crazy if we take a break and then get back together when I get back? Is that a gamble? Would you want that?"

Turning so we are face to face, I say, "I love you. I want you to have the best time overseas. If that's what you really want, I'll be here when you get back."

With a kiss, she continues. "You are the best. I'm going to miss you like crazy. Without suffocating you, can we spend a lot of time together until I leave?"

Kissing her, I say, "Of course. It's you, my business, and school. By the way, I still haven't told you about my new business."

Placing her hands on my chest, and laying on top of me, she apologizes. "I'm sorry. I want to hear about your new venture. Maybe I can help."

"The Cliffs Notes version is that I'm building a Yelp-type site for people to send baskets, treats, drinks, and other items to college kids. I'm piloting it at a few schools around here like the University of Wisconsin, University of Illinois, Indiana University, and the University of Michigan. If it goes well, I'll add the University of Texas and a few other schools."

She whispers in my ear, "You are so smart that it makes me wet."

Laughing, I say, "You are such a dirty girl."

After another round of sex, we both pass out. I'm not sure what's going to happen, but I'm not going to think about the future. As much as I like to plan, I'll have fun with Robbie and put her semester abroad out of my head.

Driving back to my house, my phone rings. I see that it's a Wisconsin number, but it's not Jack or Shari. I answer. "Hi, this is Alex."

"Alex, this is Judd. I own the bar where Shari works. She told me about your business, and I love it. I want to advertise this new business I'm starting after winter break. I want to launch a food delivery company with healthy prepared meals. Lot of kids struggle to stay in shape in college. What do you think? Can you help me with social media too?"

Surprised, I tell him, "Well that's not my focus, but I can help. I can get a good social media plan and SEO. It's really about getting the word out with lots of pictures. Do you want to set up a call later this week?"

Judd talks fast. "Yes, Let's talk. Ten o'clock is usually the best time for me. Figure out what you would charge for some social work and for listing me on your site."

Trying to control my excitement, I tell him, "Great! I will send you a contract and we'll go from there."

The minute I get home I research contracts, advertising costs, banner ads, coupons, promotions, and videos. It's overwhelming. I need to set a structure and amend things when people reach back out to me.

With no experience to pull from, I form a list of questions. Never afraid to ask for help, I'll ask my poker buddies. They are all successful businessmen.

When I was struggling to understand how to best use my knights, my mom suggested I ask a friend. None of my friends or my teacher had adequate knight skills, according to me. With help from Google, Jim Kim popped up as an upcoming chess star in Milwaukee. I asked my mom if I could watch him play. Two weeks later, we were at a library in Wisconsin, watching this teen master in action. He was decisive and used his knights to slay kings. My mom was bored to death, but I was entranced. Nervous, I slowly approached Jim. He was so nice, and we sat talking for over an hour. It was a free education. On the ride back, we stopped at the Mars Cheese Castle and my mom reinforced the lesson to always ask for help.

As my phone starts buzzing, I put my work aside. I answer, "How is my new best friend?"

Jack replies, "Great, my man. How are you?"

"All is well. I spoke with a web designer and am working on a layout and business plan. I could go on and on. What's up? How's Shelly?"

Wasting no time, he says, "Shelly, doesn't want to go out with me. I asked her out, and she said no. I think she's into you. It's cool,

I've been texting with Rose. Anyway, I have a buddy looking for an internship at the University of Illinois. Can you hook him up? He doesn't care about the money, although he needs to make some scratch. His plan is to move to Silicon Valley after he graduates but needs some experience."

Without thinking too hard, I say, "Sure. I'll interview him. Have him send me a resume. Is he a smart guy?"

I can sense the smile over the phone. "Alex, I'm not going to send you a dud. This dude, Steve Marks, is smart as hell. He could've gone Ivy league, but didn't want the loans. He's got close to a full ride at Illinois. He's a fun guy and reminds me of you."

"Thanks, man. Sounds like I have employee number four. Have a few drinks for me. I have some more work to do. Be nice to Rose!"

"Of course! Maybe take a break and sleep. It's getting late."

"Alright, Jack. Have a good night."

MONEY IN AND MONEY OUT

"Dad, will you read my notes for tonight?"

Looking at me confused, he asks, "Notes? Giving a speech at school?"

I shake my head. "No, I put together some notes to talk to the poker guys about my business."

The smile on my dad's face is priceless. I can see all of his teeth. Putting his hand on my shoulder, he reads through my three pages. "Looks good. My only suggestion is to let it happen naturally. Tell them about your new company and just ask for tips."

"Thanks, old man. I wanted to get my thoughts down on paper, pick out a few nuggets, and then throw them out throughout the night."

He hugs me. "Alex, I love how you prepare for everything. That's going to help you become successful. What else are you up to today?"

I look at my phone calendar. "I have phone calls with my new web designer, a friend of a poker guy, and I'm getting TK to start working with me. He needs an internship for a graduate class, and then I'm uploading a bunch of places. Man, I put one post online, and I keep getting spots to upload. I'm overwhelmed."

Pouring coffee for us, my dad points to a chair. "Sit down, buddy. Take it one step at a time. Building anything takes time, divide into small steps. I will be free labor. Make a list of things I can do for you."

"Thanks, dad."

He holds up his index finger. "More importantly, what happened with Robbie?"

"She wants to date but take a break when she's abroad. She was very jealous of my trip and doesn't want to always be wondering what I'm doing. Hopefully we will get back together when she returns."

Putting his hand on mine, he asks, "Are you okay with that?"

I can feel myself getting sad. "I can wait and be a good boyfriend while she's gone. I am focused on work, but I'll have fun, too. When I was in Madison and flirting with other girls, it was fun. I also have some trips planned."

Reading through me, my dad looks at me. "I know where you are going. University of Texas."

I smile like I've done something bad. "It's on the list. It's a big school with a lot of opportunity."

"And Ellie."

Playing coy, I respond, "Oh yea—and Ellie."

Looking at the clock, realizing he has to go to work, he says, "Have fun and be safe. Get it out of your system."

When the coffee buzz hits me, I hit the basement gym and start my day. In between sets, I jot down more notes. My mind is overwhelmed with ideas. My cell phone cuts into my workout time.

"Hello, this is Alex."

"Alex, I'm Steve, Jack's friend. Is this a good time to talk?"

Putting down a dumbbell, I say, "Sure, Steve. Jack spoke highly of you. Did he tell you what I'm trying to build?"

Wasting no time, he says, "Yes, and I think I can help. I have experience with web design, coding, security, and CRM systems. I'll email you projects that I've worked on."

He's literally emailing me while we're talking, and I start reading these amazing projects. He's developed 20 websites, sold software, worked as an IT tech, and the list goes on. Without thinking, I tell him, "I'm not sure I can afford you. You have amazing experience."

"Alex, I don't care about the money. I want to help grow a start-up. That's missing from my resume. Seriously, I have a full ride and I make good money with web design. I can help you with structure on the technical end."

I decide to tell him, "You're hired! Look at my site and I'll send you my plan for growing the business. You can advise me. Does that work? I'll come to your campus in a few weeks. I have a few friends sending me listings and I'm trying to spread the word."

With an excited voice, he says, "THANKS! That sounds great! We will make this take off. I really like the concept and I've seen your site. People are spreading the word. I'm going to pick apart the site, but I'll help you improve it. Send me your other designers' information. I have to run. Thanks for this opportunity."

I take a quick shower and I'm back online. TK calls me as I send more places to list online to my new web designer. I'm getting emails from schools all over the place. Drilling down deep, I can see most orders come from businesses around here—which makes sense as most kids I know grew up here.

I can hear TK yawn, "Yo, Alex, love the site. Part of my entrepreneurial program is working on a startup. Thanks for helping me out. I've been spreading the word. I got some other ball players interested. I also have two buddies in Europe that really miss stuff from the States. You got them?"

Unsure of the answer, I say, "Maybe. I mean if they want to pay for shipping, why not? Did you learn anything in your classes that will help me?"

I can feel the excitement through the phone. "MAN! I have so many books to recommend to you. There are some easy things you need to do today to help yourself out. I know this sounds like B.S., but you need to write a mission statement, define your principles, and all these small steps, so when employees start, they know what you're all about. What are your various revenue streams? You need to define them. They can and will change. When we meet, we can

COOKIES KALE & COFFEE

talk financial structure, too. I'll work for free. You just need to fill out some paperwork for my professor ..."

Not meaning to cut him off, I explain, "I have some revenue streams. Maybe you can help better define them and develop a code of conduct. You can also do some human resource work. I have a friend offering some law advice but could use people management advice."

"I'm on it, bro. How about we hoop later in the week and talk more face to face?" TK hangs up before I can thank him. Circling back to my email inbox, TK has already sent me a list of books to read. Whenever I exercise, I'll start listening to audio books.

My company now has 11 employees. Luckily, many of them are working for school credit. With all of the attention I'm paying to this business, my knife sales are dropping, and I'm draining my bank account. It's lucky I'm a good saver.

While answering Joe's call, I watch my inbox blow up. "Hi, Joe. Poker tonight?"

A warm "Hello" greets me. "Kid, I heard about your business, and I love it. We might not get a chance to talk tonight. I figure you've helped me with my computer and driving a stick, maybe I can help you."

Shocked, I tell him, "That would be amazing. I have all these questions for the guys. You could probably answer most of them."

Laughing, he says, "Come over now. Whatever I can't answer, we'll ask the others. You can try my new coffee machine that I got from Italy. It's amazing. My friend runs the company and wants me to invest, so he gave me this machine. It's used in high-end cafes across Europe."

"You had me at coffee. Give me a few minutes to pack up."

Grabbing my notes and computer, I head right over. Parking next to his fancy car, I have two thoughts: He must be really bored, and it's nice to have a coach.

With a hug, I follow Joe into his kitchen. The coffee smells fresh, strong, and a little sweet. The monstrosity of a coffee machine sits on his island. It looks expensive.

Staring at it, I ask, "They just gave you this?"

Smiling like he got a new toy, he says, "I know. It's like thousands of dollars. I almost feel like I need to invest in the company. I'm also a little bored. My sons are starting to FaceTime with the grandkids, so hopefully they'll let me visit, but with Jane at school and my wife at work, I have time on my hands. Tell me about your business."

Sitting at the kitchen table, I sip my coffee. Which tastes amazing. "I'm building a company that connects college kids to either their new home or where they grew up. I thought it would be all about gifts from their college home, but I pivoted a little."

Clicking around on my computer, he says, "Man you're blowing through money pretty fast." Then he clicks on the revenue tab. "The knife business is still your bread and butter. What's this optimization project?"

"A few bars and restaurants want me to help them with their website and social media."

He nods his head yes. "You have a few streams of income. Nice. How are you doing all this?"

With a smile, I explain, "I don't sleep anymore. I mostly dropped out of college. I take night classes. Then, all I do is work."

Looking at my eyes, like a doctor, "You look tired. You're going to kill yourself at this pace. Hire some more people."

Confused, I say, "You just said I'm blowing through money."

Pointing out numbers, he explains, "You still have thirty thousand dollars. The kitchenware business pulls in almost eight thousand per month. I would concentrate on your consulting with these bars and restaurants. Is it that hard?"

Shaking my head yes, "For me, yes. I'm sure there are systems, AI or something, that will make it easier. If I can get a few more people working on the site, that would free up my time."

Three more cups of coffee and three hours later I have an updated business plan, legal documents started, and a tax consultant. I feel like I'm getting my MBA.

As I'm walking out the door, I can hear Joe calling Rob. "Rob, can you drop off cameras, lights and a tripod to Alex before tonight's game?" Joe is convinced pictures of Robbie cooking will sell more knives and pans. He's not wrong.

COOKING AND CUDDLES

When YouTube became a thing, my mom put a few demos online. Sue read up on lighting, angles, and food photography tricks— like using glue in place of cheese. That was not her style. All she wanted was a few cooking and baking tips posted, so instead of telling people her secrets a million times, she could point them to a video. My dad held up some sort of light reflector, I shot the scene, and my mom was both star and director. Since we didn't have money for lights, we did everything when the sun hit the kitchen. When she first died, I remember sitting on the bus watching the outtakes on my phone. My favorite video was her wearing swimming goggles. That was her trick to not cry while cutting onions. The only problem was that watching it made *me* cry.

A warm hand on my back interrupts my thoughts. With her sweet tone, Robbie asks, "You're thinking about your mom, aren't you?"

Falling into Robbie's deep brown eyes, "How did you know?"

With a smile and kiss on the cheek, "You have this deep gaze when you think of her. What were you thinking about?"

Pulling up Sue's YouTube station, I show her. "This."

Robbie sits down in my lap and patiently watches the video. "She's so pretty. That wide smile is like Julia Roberts."

As my dad walks in the room, I feel like I should be embarrassed with my girlfriend on my lap, but I'm not. "Robbie, I was the worst. As every shot started, I laughed. Alex kept shooting me death glares, but it was funny. I don't know how she did it. She smiled and cut. One time she was looking at the camera and didn't notice a kitchen towel was on fire."

Shaking my head, "That was so funny. She was so focused, she thought you said she was on fire, like a compliment."

Robbie pops off my lap and my dad—not in a gross old man way—compliments her. "Robbie you look great! You are going to shine on the camera."

With serious concern, "Should I not wear jeans? I thought this brown shirt would bring out my eyes. Seriously, is this too much cleavage?"

My dad's cheeks blush. "I think you're okay."

While filming the scenes, all I can think of is how wonderful Robbie is. Her electric smile and dimple are so cute, and her sweet laugh is what I'm going to miss most when she's abroad.

The smell of onions and browning meat fills the room. Robbie comments, "If you could smell the amazing aroma of veggies caramelizing, you would want these pans even more."

Next, she pulls out cookies baking on a ceramic sheet. She flashes her pearly whites. "You see how the corners are brown, but the middle is not over cooked? Perfect."

Wasting no time, she slowly removes a pizza from the oven. "The reason you want to use ceramic is how it cooks the crust." She lifts up the pizza with a spatula. "It's not burnt or mushy. Restaurant-quality. I can't wait to eat this."

My dad, who's stuck around to help, claps as I yell, "That's a wrap!"

Our cheerleader and dad exclaims, "You were great!"

We all clean up as the files load to my computer. We package up the food for the poker game, minus dinner and dessert for my dad and Maddie.

My old man packs up the food and heads to Maddie's with wine. He hugs both of us. "Thanks for letting me be a part of this. I had so much fun. I think I'm going to take film classes."

When the door closes, Robbie asks with a smile, "Do you feel like doing some other stuff on camera?"

Jamming a cookie into my mouth, I nod yes. She rubs a little chocolate on both sides of her neck, like perfume. Kissing it off, I lift her up on the kitchen island.

Working hard to thank her for her services, she comments, "We need to do this more often!" She has this new confidence that's alluring. The passion is also heightened because we both know that in a few weeks she'll be an ocean away.

Leaning on my shoulder, she asks, "You never really turned those cameras on, right?"

With a wink I answer, "Maybe I did, maybe I didn't."

Borrowing my car, Robbie heads to Joe's house. I skip out on poker to edit the videos. With one class in high school, this will take a while.

Robbie binges reality TV while resting her head on my shoulder. Even though she's with me, I already miss her.

REAL MONEY

Sipping my morning coffee, I review all my statistics. I've only released two videos and sales are way up. Money is also starting to come in from College Comforts. The number of views increases every day. The kitchen products bring in more revenue, but I'm getting far more hits on the other site. My payroll continues to skyrocket. Between web designers, ambassadors, and content creators, I can't believe how much money goes to staff.

Interrupting my analysis, a text message startles me. "I still owe you for carrying me home."

Ignoring the text, I focus back on work. Another text comes through. "Maybe a few pictures."

Wasting no time, I respond, "No. Not necessary. Be careful!"

She sends a smiley face emoji. "I'm kidding. It's Shelly. When are you coming back to Madison?"

"So funny. After break. How R U? Is Jack still in the picture?"

"We are just friends. He's into your girl's sister. She came to visit a few weeks ago."

Putting my phone down, I dive into emails, analytics, and calls. My influencers, like Jack, are driving a lot of action to the website. I need to figure out a way to thank them more. Since my generation loves hoodies, I order a bunch with the College Comforts logo printed on them. How can I keep them happy with less cash? I fire off that question to Jack and get back to work.

My favorite call of the day is my 9 a.m. "Hey John, how are you doing? What's new with your side of the business? I don't want it to cut into your schoolwork."

I can feel John's happiness over the phone. "Listen, Dad, I've got it. Seriously, I'm only spending about fifteen hours a week and most of those are Fridays when I only have one class. You are paying me anyway. How are you? How's Robbie? When is she leaving?"

Trying not to read my emails and be present, I tell him, "I'm tired man. This is a lot. The good news is that we get more business every day. I'm sad about Robbie. We spend time together and it's great, but for some reason I miss her already. She leaves next week." Thinking of her for a moment I pause, and then refocus, "We have three more clients. Can you take one of them? What type of support do you need?"

Laughing over the phone, he says, "It's funny. I have two guys working for me. They are both seniors and way smarter than me, so it's hilarious telling them what to do, but it's working. I could use a little more help, or I can cut my course load."

Stern, I tell him, "John, your parents would kill me. I'll get some more help. My network is growing. I think I have some good leads to help us with this. TK has a friend, Mitch, that's been working in this field for a few years. I bet we could nab him. He's not growing in his current role, and he's a bright guy."

"Alex, I'm happy to get him up to speed. There's a huge need to teach companies about marketing with social media, and just helping them grow their online personality. I think that might be your biggest money maker one day."

Anxiety over my email inbox pulls me away. "John, I have to go. You are right. I think that focusing on marketing to a younger population with money is the niche, along with parents. Maybe we will focus on the Latin market next."

While John says goodbye, I'm knee deep in emails. My eye starts to twitch, and I have no idea if it's from looking at this screen too much or nerves. While taking a few deep breaths, I text

Maddie and set up time to talk with her. Now that she's dating my dad, I don't feel so bad word vomiting all my issues to her.

While sitting at my desk, a sporty, gold, two-seater BMW catches my eye. Whoever owns the car just parked it in my driveway. Peeking out the window, I see Rick walking to the front door.

Rick is dressed in jeans, cushy running shoes, and a thin parka. I open the door as he walks up. "Hey Rick, to what do I owe the visit?"

With a guy hug, he walks in and asks, "Shoes on or off? There's a little snow out there."

"Off, please. Do you want coffee?"

Showing me his aluminum coffee mug, he walks right in and heads to the kitchen. "Maybe some ice, too, kid. This thing keeps the coffee too hot. Sorry to stop by unannounced, but I figured you might be home."

While he sits down at the kitchen, I start yapping. "Mitch seems like a good guy. Northwestern, sales experience, he's a friend of a friend. Solid resume. Are you here to vouch for him?"

He grins. "He's a great kid. You should hire him. That's not why I'm here. I told him to name drop me, though."

Scanning the kitchen, I catch him eyeing muffins. "Did Robbie make those for you?"

I shake my head no. "They have too much sugar to be a Robbie recipe."

With a huge smile, he asks, "Perfect. Can you spare one?" While I grab a plate and a fork, Rick's face turns serious. "I thought you were going to tell me when you hit four thousand a week in sales!"

Like in chess, I carefully weigh my next move. "What am I supposed to say in this situation?" I'm hoping by hitting him with a question, I'll learn more about his intent.

With both hands up in the air, he says, "The NUMBERS! I'm here to help you, kid. I wasn't joking when I said I could find you investors."

Taking a long exhale, "The videos of Robbie pushed me up to four thousand, but that's only been for a few weeks. With the other businesses bringing in three thousand combined, I'm looking at seven thousand per week. I don't really know how to forecast, but with the help of a friend, he thinks we can end the year at five hundred thousand in sales. My costs, which are mostly salary and software, are around five thousand a week. If Mitch takes the job, I will break even."

As if he was struck by lightning, Rick shoots up. "Shit! You are doing it. This is amazing! What can I do?"

Rick sits down and tears apart the muffin as if he's deprived of sugar. I dive right in, "One, don't feel guilty you're not using a fork. Two, I have no idea how these things have taken off. I mean, one of the two businesses happened organically, and I think I'm filling a void in the market. I lost ten pounds because my workouts are running and listening to business books. Am I making a huge mistake breaking even?"

Brushing his graying hair with a hand, he tells me, "Keep doing what you are doing. This is great. Break even. Once all the videos are out, your sales will peak a little more, and then plateau, unless you start a cooking show. The other businesses will hopefully keep growing. Don't quote me, but I could easily see you getting five hundred to a million dollars with investors. If you could sell more knives and pots, maybe that business will get bought." Grabbing my shirt sleeve, he continues, "I'm so proud of you, kid. This is great. I'm going to send you a presentation that I loved. I'll cover up the numbers and company name, but the women who put it together did a great job of showing the numbers, forecasting, the mission of the business, and the culture. That was two years ago, and then Google bought her business. She's now rich and started a foundation to give out money."

"I would cure cancer if that happened to me."

Standing up again, he says, "One step at a time, Alex." Walking himself out, he says, "Say hi to Mitch for me."

A 100% self-funded business has worked fine, but with extra cash I would hire three leaders for each company, and start sleeping more.

LOVE TALK

The best move I've made so far is hiring Mitch. I have no idea what Rick said to him, but he agreed to work commission only for the first year. I handed him a client, so that helped, but after a few weeks, he brought some of his old clients on board. Since he was so junior at his company, he never signed a non-compete clause. Lucky for me, Mitch has a car and has been driving out to my home office at least once a week.

I never realized how much I missed human interaction. I've been going weeks without seeing people other than my dad, Maddie, and Robbie. Mitch, aside from bringing in money, is fun to work with. He's funny and charismatic, so it's no wonder he's doing well with sales.

Wearing what has become his uniform—dark jeans, white collared shirt, and a blazer with elbow patches—Mitch pops in. "Hey, Alex! How are you doing, buddy?"

Pouring him some hot water, I tell him, "I can't believe you don't drink coffee. I would've bought you tea. You didn't have to ship it. How are you?"

Sitting at the kitchen table next to me, with a comfortable smile on his face, he asks, "Can you believe this is corporate headquarters?"

I'm not sure if that's a compliment or complaint. With no emotion, I answer, "It could be worse. Low overhead is key."

A few minutes of silence escapes, which is unusual for Mitch. With my call to John over for the morning, I'm checking all the data. I have no idea if I should be doing this every day, but it takes thirty minutes to review site analytics and sales. It's part of my routine.

Mitch disappears into the dining room to make a few calls. Unintentionally, I eavesdrop as he sets up a meeting with a prospect. I wish I had his carefree demeanor. "I can come down to the University of Illinois. Let me know what works best for you, Joe. I know you have the pitch from Shari. We are a team, Joe. I'm not stealing you away. Once she graduates, she can have you back." He pauses and laughs. "I mean, I can already tell you're difficult. She's all yours." After a few more laughs, he says, "Sure, a Zoom call works for me. You're saving me a trip."

Walking back in the kitchen, he says, "You found a star in Shari. Her contacts are really interested."

Sipping my coffee, I tell him, "The funny thing is, I had no idea that's what she would be doing. Jack is also great at sales. You remind me of him." Holding his head up like a dog, Mitch smells the air.

"YOU BAKED!!!" The smile on his face is so big, I'm glad I saved him a treat.

Sauntering over to the oven, I say, "Robbie leaves tomorrow. I'm cooking up a nice dinner and made dessert already. You're smelling chocolate lava cake."

I see his smile vanish. Trying to fake my own smile, I add, "Don't be sad, man. You're smelling your soufflé. When you drive out my way, this is how I take care of you."

Sticking out his non-existent belly, he says, "I'm so EXCITED! Thank you. And you two will be fine."

TK said Mitch was one of the smartest people he knew, and coming from a Northwestern student, that carries serious weight. I find Mitch to be smart, but his social smarts are off the charts. He reads a room well and is great at absorbing facts.

Waving his hands up in the air like my old man, he asks, "What else? I want to know the rest of the menu."

Turning away from my computer, I tell him, "Grouper tacos with a little mango, cauliflower rice with salsa, guacamole, and chips. She's bringing an appetizer, too."

Shaking his head yes, he confirms, "That's a solid menu."

With a little sarcasm, I tell him, "Thanks for your approval. Can we get to work? Did you bring your project list? I have the prospects and proposals set up."

"Yes, I'm blanking on our web guy's name. I found you someone new."

"Why did you find me a new Josh? He is super cheap and a wiz."

Looking at me like I'm an idiot, he explains, "He quit and is moving to Austin. He got a job with some big tech firm."

Throwing my hands up in the air, I ask, "What the fuck? Why didn't anyone tell me?"

Laughing, he says, "I love it when you get mad. You're like the nicest mad person ever. He quit yesterday and said he can give us three weeks. He also sent me a few friends of his. One is a rock star. He worked on President Obama's campaign when he was in middle school. Not as the main guy, of course."

"Do the first round of interviews and then send them my way. I would love to talk to at least three people."

Pointing at me, he says, "You got it, boss."

Taking a conference call while cooking, I wave goodbye to Mitch as he walks out, and focus on Jack speaking. He's now my head of influencers. I had no idea how creative he was. Jack's designed a program to encourage hashtags and posts, giving away fun swag, and saving me from hiring more influencers.

While multi-tasking, I've done everything but cook the fish. The table is set in style with candles, fancy plates with a fun design, flowers, and my parents' silver. For some reason, I'm nervous. If this is the last time I see Robbie, I want to give her a night she will never forget.

With sweat pouring down my back, I run upstairs for a quick shower. Spending too much time on my wardrobe decision, I pop downstairs in gray pants and a black fitted sweater. Robbie is in the kitchen, peeking at my food.

Her long brown hair is arranged in two braids. She's wearing minimal make up, but whatever she has on makes her brown eyes pop and her glossy lips scream, "Kiss me." A white, low-cut sweater makes her olive skin even more appealing, and a short black skirt shows off her hours of running.

With a smile, she asks, "Is this all for me?"

Joking, I say, "And my dad."

With a kiss, she says, "Funny."

Lightly pulling on her braids, I kiss her one more time. She whispers, "Do we have time before dinner?"

Lifting her up on the table, we continue to kiss. She pulls off my sweater, and three loud rings almost ruin the moment.

I laugh. "The oven is preheated."

Pulling me toward her, she whispers, "So am I."

After a quick, but passionate rendezvous, I'm back to preparing.

Being a great catch, Robbie cleans the table. I'm squeezing lemon on the fish and taking the lava cakes out of the fridge.

Out of the corner of her eye, she sees a ramekin filled with chocolate. "You made my favorite!"

Shrugging my shoulders, I say, "Of course!"

Popping the cakes in the oven, Robbie takes all the other food to the table.

"Alex, this is amazing. Why don't we cook more together? We could run one hell of a restaurant."

After a few bites of taco, I feel full. "I'm going to miss this. I'm going to miss you. You know I went almost twenty years without this kind of love. I can wait five months for you."

Putting her soft, warm hand on mine, she says, "I love you, Alex. I have never felt this way about anyone. Maybe that's why I get so jealous of your college visits. I also know we are young. I want you to have crazy stories about the time you visited a school and grew this big business. I don't want to be halfway around the world wondering if this is the night that you can't say no. Is it the night he wishes he was single? Is this the night that some girl corners him and he caves? Irrational or not, I have those worries. I'm hoping and praying when I return, we get back together. We will email and talk. I need my updates on you."

All I want to do is cry right now. I feel a tear race down my cheek. "Why is my heart breaking and you're here, next to me?"

Pulling her chair closer to mine, she says, "That should be a song." With a sweet smile, she continues, "Alex, let's enjoy tonight. This food is amazing. I can smell the chocolate and your dad still isn't here."

Trying to be happy, "That sounds good to me." Passing her seat to remove the dessert, I can smell her perfume and conditioner. It's intoxicating. All I want to do is ravage her. Walking back, I kiss her neck. "You just smell amazing."

"Don't stop!" Turning her around, I carry her upstairs for round two.

We lay there cuddling afterwards, never wanting the moment to end. My phone ruins the moment; the ringing is continuous. With a confused look, I tell her, "It's Rick."

With encouragement, she says, "Pick up the phone! This could be it!"

"Kid, did you get that presentation done?"

With no hesitation, I say, "I have people working on it. The last draft was close."

With a stern voice, he says, "Send me what you have. They care mostly about revenue and projections."

Curious, I ask, "Who's they? Any estimate of what money we're talking about?"

With a long exhalation like he's annoyed, he says, "Probably a quarter to half of a million dollars. This guy is spreading money across the Chicago start-up scene. I wish he would just pick a few companies and invest more dollars, but he's a great guy. How's Mitch working out?"

My emotions are swinging like I'm on a rollercoaster. Trying to maintain my excitement, I tell him, "He's the best. He's a machine. He has this amazing combination of smarts and people skills."

"Great. Let's talk tomorrow morning."

The line goes dead, and I stare silently at Robbie. She grabs my arm. "Talk to me! What did he say?"

"How about we talk over dessert? Follow me."

Popping the lava cakes out of the ramekins, I carefully scoop vanilla ice cream and drizzle caramel. Then I lightly cover them with powdered sugar.

Laughing at me, she says, "You are ridiculous. Just bring me the chocolate!" Before digging in, she takes a picture.

"Rick has a guy that invests in Chicago start-ups. He's thinking about investing between two fifty and five hundred thousand."

Robbie's eyes sparkle with pride. "I am amazed by you. If you get the money, what will you use it for?"

Like my dad, my hands start the conversation, raising them up like a referee making the field goal sign. "I have no idea, but I will figure it out. I probably should get an office somewhere, hire a videographer, and get you cooking more. I should travel to Japan to checkout this manufacturer of high-end knives, hire two more sales guys, and a head of technology."

Shaking her head in disbelief, she says, "That is awesome. I can't wait to hear what happens."

"Me, too. Now, more importantly, how's your dessert?"

Robbie's plate is already clean. She holds it up, sticks out her tongue, smiles, and licks her plate.

Before she can answer, I joke, "You hated it?"

A chocolate mustache smiles at me. "It was awful. Can I have another one?"

Robbie blasts her favorite music station, some sort of house music, and dances while she helps me clean. I forgot how cute and silly she is. I need a little silly, as my mind is already focusing on the presentation for Rick.

Firing off a few emails eases my stress. Hopefully, Mitch, John, and our accountant Jerry will make the presentation look good. Jerry works with billionaires, so I'm grateful he's John's cousin. Without the family discount, we never could afford him.

Anxiety wakes me up earlier than usual. Quietly crawling out of bed, I stare at Robbie. She's out cold, softly snoring, with one naked leg out of the covers. Silently I walk downstairs and check my email. With no new messages, I head to the basement for a workout. Ideas flood my mind on how to spend investment money:

- *Add product lines*
- *Expand staff*
- *Rent office space*
- *Purchase software*
- *Create training for staff*
- *Hire a benefits company*
- *Hire a VP of Sales*
- *Visit Japan*

With no emails yet, I review my travel itinerary. Even though I'm going to Texas, I still have not reached out to Ellie. Mitch is coming with me, so that will be fun. We have The BBQ and Baker account, which is a growing restaurant. I'll be able to meet with them and with my influencers there. Jack has set up fun influencer meet-ups. Instead of paying these kids, we have fun events. Then I will go back to Madison, before heading to Indiana University.

"Hey Mitch. You're at it early today."

Sipping his tea, he hesitates. "I'm working from home and since you emailed me thirty minutes ago, I figured you would be around. I'm sending you the presentation. I think it looks good. Jerry's Excel skills are unmatched. He put together some great charts on growth, sales, and expenses."

Sitting in my sweatpants and hoodie, my eye starts to twitch. "Mitch, can you take me shopping? I need some clothes in case we get a meeting with investors."

Mitch pauses and laughs. "Wait, because I'm gay you think I can help you dress up? Like the guy in *Pretty Woman*?"

Laughing, I admit, "Mitch, I had no idea you were gay. Honestly. You just have the best wardrobe out of anyone I know."

Still laughing, he asks, "How did you not know I was gay? I wear sweaters with elbow patches, drink expensive tea, and live with a guy I refer to as Handsome Henry."

Coffee is shooting out my nose. I'm glad Robbie is sleeping, and Mitch is not on video. "You are ridiculous. Henry is very handsome, so I figured everyone called him that. And I also over-spend on coffee."

"Alex, you are the best. I will take you shopping. Review what I sent you and send it to Rick. He'll be honest. More importantly, what are you making for breakfast? Crepes are easy, but also look impressive."

Looking at my mom's cooking binder, I scroll to breakfast items. "Thanks. That is a great idea."

Continuing to help me out, my mom has a simple crepe recipe. Her magic food binder is a list of all her favorite recipes. She spent the last six months of her life printing up recipes. I've never looked at this because I memorized so many of them. This book is amazing. The title is *Cookies to Kale.* I feel the tears rolling down my cheek as I read her note. "I love you so much, Alex. This was the recipe I made the day you were born. Because you made me a sweet-eating monster, I made mine with chocolate hazelnut spread, and your dad had two with fruit compote."

Robbie loves sweets and fruit, so I'll make one of each for her. As I fill the pan with the second crepe, a naked beauty catches my eye. "Hey, I'm not done with you, mister. What's that smell?"

"Crepes!"

With a smile, she says, "I guess we could eat first. We have an hour before Megan picks me up for the ride home."

I grab the alpaca blanket and drape it around Robbie. I plop the binder/cookbook in front of her, while I finish heating up the fruit. Her eyes light up. "Alex, this is amazing. Is it okay if I take some pictures?"

"That would make my mom so happy."

Instead of sitting across from each other, we sit next to each other and turn page after page. She wrote notes on almost all the pages. Robbie's favorite page says, "This is a great meal if you need to poop."

Reading carefully, Robbie continues to read the notes, "There's too many for me to pick one, however this is going to sound weird coming from your mom, but these lava cakes are better than sex. Don't tell your dad."

With a serious face, Robbie gazes into my eyes. "It's true—those were amazing. How did you memorize the recipe?"

I smile because I'm thinking of my mom. "We made this all the time. It was her favorite. A close second to the Nutella cookies."

Laughing and crying, Robbie and I head upstairs for one last tryst.

A red Volvo sedan pulls up in the driveway and I can feel the sadness filling me up like a meal. Kissing me on the cheek, and hugging me tightly, she says, "I love you, Alex. See you in six months. I promise."

Hugging her tightly, I ask, "Are you sure you still want to go?"

Whispering in my ear, I can feel her tears. "No, I love you."

Watching her walk out feels so final, like we might never see each other again.

MO' MONEY

Work takes my mind off Robbie. It's been a nonstop day. Rick loves the presentation and Jim Miller agreed to meet with us. He's a young guy who worked for Uber in the beginning, cashed in his shares, started working for another start up that went public, and then decided he wanted to be a philanthropist investor/advisor. If this works, he'll be on our board of advisors. Well, he'll be the only member of that board.

A text from Jack interrupts my flow. "Can you call me?"

Jack answers right away. "Hey, thanks for calling me. I've learned you're always on a call, so I text first. Do you have a minute?"

Already, I know he wants to quit. He's done so much over the past few months. I ask, "You're quitting?"

A few coughs prevent him from starting. "I'm sick. I'm wearing myself out. I love this job—setting up parties, getting people to talk about your site, and finding friends at big schools. It's been amazing. I don't want to quit, but what about going down to working two hours a week? I'm going abroad in the fall, so I'll bring this to Australia. We should have an international site. Oh, and I have the perfect person for you."

Internally, I'm freaking out. He's added so much value and figured out I didn't need to pay the ambassadors. "I get it. You ignited my idea and the site took off so fast with your help. Thank you. Two hours will work. Who's your superstar?"

"My sister. I know it sounds like nepotism, but she's amazing. You also get a lawyer because she spent two years at a big firm, hated it, and now plans weddings."

Staring at the ceiling, I say, "I'll have Mitch interview her. I'll be too biased."

After a few more coughs, he says, "She has the biggest smile, is smart as hell, and knows everyone. When she quit her high paying job, she moved home, so she's close to the home office."

"If she has a little of your charm, we'll be fine. Send Mitch her information. I'll have him call her today. Does John need to quit, too?"

After a little throat clearing, he says, "Thanks, and John is fine. That guy is so organized. Aside from your daily chats, he only gives you a few hours a week."

Trying to get off topic, I tell Jack, "I think I insulted Mitch. I asked him to help me get clothes for this big meeting. I had no idea he was gay."

After laughing and more coughing, he says, "You're killing me. What guy calls their roommate Handsome Henry? I mean, he described Henry's dimple to us on a call."

I shake my head yes. "Oh yeah. I did think that was weird, but I thought he was jealous. You'll train your sister or whoever gets the job? I would love for you to do it in person."

"No problem. I need to hit the books."

"Feel better."

Taking a deep exhale, I try and forget about the sadness that feels like it's about to overwhelm me. Jack has also become my best friend. We text throughout the day, talk several times a week, and I'm going to miss that. And his energy is contagious, a call with him is like drinking an energy drink.

Concentrating is impossible; I've reviewed a document Rick sent me three times. A nervous leg bounce accompanies me as I focus on other work. I really like the international idea. Kids go abroad all the time and probably miss the comforts of home.

Three hours pass in the blink of an eye. I only look up from my computer because I hear the door open. "Mitch, you brought me lunch?"

The large Once Upon a Bagel bag is encouraging. "Matzo ball soup, bagels, and lox cures heartache and work stress. I'm not even Jewish, but I know that."

Laughing, I say, "Thanks! You are my hero. It's not a work north day though."

"I figured you needed it, and we are going to need to shop for breakfast with Jimmy!"

Surprised, I ask, "What?"

"Did you not check your email?"

Grabbing bowls and silverware, I explain, "I've been doing schoolwork. After I sent the email to Rick, I was too nervous to focus on work."

Staring at me like I'm nuts, he says, "Check your email boss!"

Scrolling down to Rick's note, I read, "Jim wants to talk. He lives in Highland Park. Can you guys do breakfast on Sunday?"

My next note is from Jim. "9am at the Little French Guy?"

My heart is beating so fast, it's concerning. Maybe I should've gone to college. Duke looks unbeatable this year. I could've been better prepared for this.

Mitch cuts into my self-doubt. "Earth to Alex! Come in Alex. Are you okay?"

Grasping my shoulder, I ask, "What if I'm not ready for this? What if we grow organically? What do I have that this guy really wants?"

Standing up from his chair, he says, "You are a badass! Stop talking like a little bitch. You have three companies. You're not even twenty years old yet. You're making money. You don't need Jim's cash. He needs you. He needs people like you to make him richer. Sure, he adds cash and experience, but you'll be fine either way. You're a boss! Literally. You have twenty-five people onboard and a ton of influencers and ambassadors."

Feeling better, I say, "Oh, yeah. Call Jack's sister. We lost our head of influencers. Well, mostly. He's giving us two hours a week.

He said his sister is the real deal. She was a lawyer at a big firm but burned out."

Mitch, scrolling through our budget asks, "The most we can pay her is forty thousand dollars. Is that going to cut it?"

Answering while digging into my soup, "Yes. He said she's making nothing planning weddings and we can offer her a percentage. The upside will be huge."

Looking back towards the door, I see a suitcase. "Where are you going?"

Holding one finger over his head he explains, "I brought you clothes that might work, but we can still shop. However, since we are having breakfast, I think a sweater and some jeans are fine. I think you'll fit in these. They were from my waif period."

Looking confused, I ask, "Am I that skinny?"

He shakes his head. "No, silly. It's not that I'm a whale, but you are probably twenty pounds less than me."

Opening the suitcase, I see my outfit. It's vintage Steve Jobs, a black turtleneck, and dark gray jeans. Mitch looks at me, and smiles. "I knew you would like a Jobs' outfit."

The clothes mostly fit. The jeans are a little snug, and Mitch laughs. "No, that's perfect. If you split them, it will be the best story ever. Maybe take a day off leg training."

Sitting down in my new outfit, I say, "Thanks man! It's from basketball. All I wanted was to dunk, so I spent hours jumping, sprinting, and squatting."

Looking at me a little too seriously, he questions, "And?"

"I can dunk. Not like MJ though because I've only done it in a handful of games."

"Nice! Okay, I'm calling Rachel now."

Trying not to eavesdrop, I focus on statistics. I'm glad I just took that class and analytics last semester. A month ago, we added a new line to the kitchen business, Proper Plates, and Whenplatesbreak. com and they are outselling knives, pots, pans, and flatware.

My mom was famous for breaking plates. From Target to Crate and Barrel, we had lots of different plates. Nothing matched. It was a family joke, and at poker when Joe suggested I added other products to increase revenue, it had to be plates. Since old customers are easier targets than new ones, we sent an email to anyone that bought anything else with a big announcement. "We Have the Plates!" Somehow that worked.

Advertising on the college site is also ticking up. Our sales plan is working, only slower than expected. If we get money from Jim, I would also love to hire a telemarketing company and just see if we can increase sales that way. I like that the site is growing organically, but it's just too slow.

Mitch pops back in the kitchen office. "She's hired."

"You already offered her the job? I don't get to interview people anymore?"

With a devious smile, he says, "Don't be so hostile. I was joking. You will get to interview her. I told her you would call her next."

Annoyed, I say, "I was insulted. I'm very stressed and now is not the time to fuck with me. Do I have to call her now?"

"It's up to you, Mr. Boss Man. Should I pick up your dry cleaning, clean the car, and get dinner?"

I answer Mitch with a smile and my middle finger. "Okay, point taken."

Now it's my turn to head into the living room that also serves as a private call room.

"Rachel, it's Alex."

I receive an exuberant "HELLO! I am so excited to meet you, Alex. Jack is obsessed with you. You have somehow changed his life. Seriously, that kid had no direction, and now he wants to major in business and work for you when he graduates. And he's dating your girlfriend's sister. I'm not even sure how that happens. Okay, I'm done ranting. What questions do you have for me?"

Since I've hired a lot of people recently, I fire off the usual interview questions.

"Rachel, do you really want to work for a start-up? It will be long hours and not the best pay. You'll also be traveling across the country visiting schools. If Jack gets his way, you'll travel the world."

After a deliberate pause, she says, "I'm in, Jack. I love to travel. Jack broke it down for me. He never traveled and was very successful. I'm also a lot more organized than him, so I can get this down quickly. What happens when you get bought out or go public? Do I get shares? Do you need legal counsel? I'm good at that side of the business. I just couldn't stand lawyers and working eighty hours a week, every week, to help a partner get richer. It wasn't for me."

Trying to answer her questions honestly, I say, "I have no idea. If you figure out how I can give everyone stock, then yes, you will get shares. If someone buys us out, we are all getting paid. Going public is a little premature, but I like your thinking."

Staring at the snow, I zone out as sleep deprivation is starting to get to me. "Sorry, you asked about law work. That is a yes. Right now, I mooch free legal help from a friend and have a junior lawyer do some work for us. It would be great if you could help there. Eventually we will need more legal help. What else do you have for me?"

The excitement still permeates through the phone. She asks, "What keeps you up at night?"

Without thinking, I tell her, "Everything. When will some kid get too drunk at a party we throw? When will this all come crashing down on me? Was skipping a four-year college a mistake? What do I really know? How can we get more sales on the college site? Why do knives and kitchenware sell so well? When is that going to slow down? Will increasing SKUs always lead to increased revenue? I'll stop there. Do you still want to work for me?"

With no hesitation, she says, "Hell yeah! You're real, Alex. I like that you rattled off that list. Do I start tomorrow?"

Confused, I ask, "Don't you have to give notice?"

Laughing, she says, "My mom will be fine without me. I just have a few weekends booked to be a day of planner."

This conversation has me feeling more centered. Rachel will be great. "That's hilarious. Jack failed to mention that you were working for your mom."

"Alex, I have loved working with my mom. Really, she's amazing. She has a great business, is super organized and connected, but I want my weekends back!"

"I promise not to take up too many weekends. Since today is Friday, stop by on Monday. Mitch has an onboarding program he's working on. You can give him some feedback. Have your brother train you. You can call him today. I know Friday afternoons he doesn't have any classes. And I promise the pay will get better."

"Thanks, Alex! Looking forward to Monday. Text your address."

And just like that, I have another employee. I yell into the kitchen, "She's hired! She's starting Monday. Can you have her review the legal documents for new employees?"

Sarcastically Mitch says, "Yes, Sir! Did she mention that I already gave her the job?"

It's so nice to have a coworker in the office.

"I love having you here, Mitch. Even if you bust my balls the entire time. You should leave soon. Traffic sucks on Fridays."

Opening the fridge, as if he lives here, he says, "You are low on pickles. Thanks for the advice. I wanted us to role play a little to prepare for Sunday."

Jotting down pickles on my grocery list, I respond, "I knew you were into role playing. I'm not getting tied up."

With a pat on the back, he says, "I knew you could be silly!"

Two hours pass by as Mitch peppers me with difficult questions. Flustered, confused, and anxious is not a healthy combination. I jot down more questions than I answer.

Drinking herbal tea to relax my mind, I ask, "Mitch, where did you find those questions?"

With an unusually serious look, he says, "Books on tape. No joke, driving out here and home a few times a week, plus driving to the loop, I like to listen to business books. A professor of mine had this list of the one hundred best business books, and I'm halfway done."

I'm impressed. "Send me the list! I also listen to books when I work out. TK sent me a solid list. Maybe this will be my free degree."

With his hand on my shoulder, he says, "Alex, you are one smart dude. Don't worry so much. You will be great. Worst case scenario is that we get practice talking to an investor."

Looking at Mitch, I have an epiphany. "This is all just practice. You are one hundred-percent right. We are making money. I'm paying bills, and learning. It's all practice. I feel much better."

Emails fill up from all the sites, and since I'm also customer service, I respond to all the issues.

"Mitch, add customer service representative to our wish list."

Deep in thought, he asks, "What if we develop a sales team? Since you have three related companies, we could build a cross-functional team. Sales, support, and product managers. I know I'm too junior to be a real head of sales, but maybe I can be the number two."

Taking the white board my mom used to write down meals for the week, we map out sales, marketing, and customer service teams first. Next, information and technology. Using my phone, I video call Dave from poker. Telling Mitch, "He's worked in start-ups and has his own company."

Like a true champ, Dave breaks down the structure of his last big firm. I take pages of notes. "Dave, thanks for giving us all this detail. I've been taking copious notes. We have a big meeting on Sunday."

Cheerful, he says, "I'm so happy for you. May I ask who you are meeting with? Maybe I can give you a few insights."

Unsure if it's cool to tell him, I respond, "Jim Miller. Keep it between us. Rick connected us."

Mitch, with the okay sign, reassures me I can share the information, a little on the late side.

Dave smiles. "He's a real nice guy. You don't need all the answers. He likes small companies like yours. He's super smart and if he wants to invest great, but if not, don't sweat it."

"Thanks, man." Dave waves goodbye and now I have a ton of work to do.

Mitch looks spent, like he just ran a mental marathon. "Go home, Mitch. The drive is going to suck if you wait any longer. I'm going to take these notes and clean them up."

With a hug, he says, "Don't kill yourself over this. It's just breakfast."

The door clicks, and I pour another cup of coffee into my Duke mug. Basketball flashes in my head for a second. My dad got me this mug after I got accepted there. I spent the rest of senior year drinking from it. I knew I wasn't ready to leave, but it felt good to know I got in.

Papers fill every square foot of our rectangular kitchen table. One by one, I type up the notes and organize them. My dad, along with most people have gone to bed. Robbie and I have a quick Facetime, and it's back to business.

The caffeine wears off at two a.m. Instead of heading upstairs, I sleep on the couch. Dreams float above me. It's like I'm watching a movie until I hear my dad coming back from a run.

The cable box blinks 8:30 a.m. It's the latest I've slept in years. Most of my friends could sleep until noon, but not me. Six a.m. has been my wake-up time for years.

Shocked to find me on the couch, my dad says, "I know you're not a kid anymore, but Alex, you need to sleep more. This is a huge meeting, and you don't want to yawn through it."

Slowly moving to the kitchen, I tell him, "I know. I got a little crazy."

He shakes his head no. "I remember your first big time competition. I think you were eight years old, and we had to drive to Naperville. You stole a flashlight, and we found you in the morning on the ground with this chess video game on your lap. You were out cold. It was so hard to wake you up. Later, you brought home a gold medal. So maybe you know what you're doing."

"I need coffee, stat. I promise that tonight I will hit the sheets early. I want to run through my notes and presentation a few times, and then I'm just going to relax."

Looking at the cookbook on the table, my dad turns serious. "Alex, would you be okay if I eventually married or moved in with Maddie? This might not happen, but would you be sad if we had a kid?"

"Dad, I would be so happy for you two. Really, I mean it. I would love a sibling. Maybe it would help make me a little more normal. The three of us should do dinner. I'm so proud of you. You're in a good spot."

Opening up the cookbook, my dad, turns to me. "Mostly, but I lost it the other day." Turning to the M&M cookie recipe, I read, "Dad's favorite." Then I see a tear in my dad's eye.

"Maddie and I were at a bakery in Glencoe that was selling those cookies. I started to cry. Every Father's Day, every birthday of mine, she always made them. I still remember that they had the perfect chew. Then you get an M&M. I had to walk out. It's almost three years and a fucking cookie makes me cry."

Hugging my dad real tight, like the way I would hug my mom, I tell him, "Dad, we're just doing the best we can. One day you'll eat those cookies and smile. And cornstarch was her secret."

A tiny laugh escapes his sadness. "That's what Maddie said." While we're hugging, my dad says, "Smell my hair."

Closing my eyes and smelling the sweet fruit flavor, it felt like I was with her. "I love that you still use her conditioner.'

Paging through the book, I see double chocolate zucchini bread. On that page is written, "This is the only way I could get you to eat zucchini. This was part of my plan. I made different baked goods with them, and then I slowly brought them onto dinner plates."

DEAL OR NO DEAL

Sunday morning comes fast. I feel prepared, which for some reason makes me nervous. Mitch comes over 30 minutes early, another reason to love him is for his promptness.

After nonstop talking for 20 minutes, the car ride to breakfast is completely silent.

Rick is standing outside the restaurant with Jim. Jim, who I learned is close to 50 years old, looks 30. He has a buzz cut, hazel eyes, and a great big smile. I feel like I'm about to break bread with Tom Brady. This guy is attractive, smart, and rich. I'm only a little jealous. Mostly because I'm watching him turn toward a silver Ferrari and lock the doors with his remote.

Reaching out his hand, he firmly shakes mine. "Alex, I'm so happy you could meet me this morning." He turns to Mitch. "Mitch, great to see you again. I think the last time I saw you was at Children's Hospital a few years ago."

Walking in, Mitch whispers in my ear, "I have no idea what he's talking about. I would've remembered this guy."

Jim shakes the man's hand at the host station. They share a laugh, and then we follow them to a table in the back of the restaurant.

The moment we sit down, a waitress holding coffee asks, "Coffee, gentlemen?"

Everyone but Mitch gets their cup filled. Jim cuts right in. "First off, great report. I loved what you sent me. We happen to share an acquaintance; your accountant has done some work with me in the past. It's impressive that he's on your team. I want to know your story Alex. How did this all happen?"

A sip of coffee, and a deep breath settles me down. This feels like the State Chess Tournament, except I'm dealing with much more social beings.

"Jim, I honestly have no idea how this happened. Right now, I should be in Raleigh finishing up my freshmen year. I stayed home because irrationally, I thought my dad needed me after my mom died. I started selling knives while going to junior college. With several one-on-one sales, I put my knives and a few other products online. I bought a few ads, made a few social media posts, and sales took off. Fast forward to visiting a friend at his college, I thought a Yelp type site geared to college towns would be great. The site is quickly growing in use. Lastly, someone saw how we were using social media for marketing and asked us to help them. Now here we are."

Rick interjects, "The kid is way too modest. Alex is smart and busts his ass. Kid's a leader. With a few bucks, he can grow these companies exponentially."

Rick then pauses. "More importantly, what if we did this breakfast thing family style? Egg scramble, bacon, pancakes, and fruit for the table? I know it might sound odd, but I love all breakfast food."

Jim asks, "Veggie hash too?"

Mitch and I shake our heads yes.

Turning to Mitch, Jim asks, "How did you end up working with Alex? How's it going?"

Mitch is looking stylish as usual in a fitted blue blazer with chunky black stripes, a white button down, jeans, and Ugg boots. "Before I took the job, I called Rick. He told me I would be an idiot to turn down the job, and he was right. This is an amazing company. We have all these synergies, great products, and services. We push to make clients happy. Alex pushes educating clients, he teaches them exactly what we do, so eventually they don't need us. That might sound bad, but it leads to referrals. And if I'm lucky, Alex will bake something amazing for me."

Jim turns back to me. "Was your mom, Sue? I think she made the desserts at my wedding, cake and all."

Once again, mom helps me out. "Yes, Sue Culp. She was an amazing baker and occasionally I make an old recipe."

Jim's eyes light up. "Can you make the Nutella stuffed cookies?"

I laugh. "Everyone loves those cookies. Of course."

Mitch, whose had them before also laughs. "His chocolate souffles are even better."

Jim smirks. "Make me those cookies, and I'll give you whatever you want."

"Deal."

A smorgasbord of food overloads the table and Rick lights up. Turning to Jim, I ask, "What's your story?"

Taking a little of everything, but mostly veggies and eggs, Jim smiles. "How much time do you have? I graduated from college and traveled for six months. That's when my loans started to kick in. I was in Australia at the time and a friend offered me a job at a software company. I worked there for three years in every role. I was ready to come home, so they told me that they would open a Chicago office. I had no idea what that meant, but I made it work. When the tech boom busted, they shut down the Chicago office, but kept me. I hung on for a while and a friend pushed me to work for Uber."

He takes a break to chew. "Things were bananas there. They grew so fast, I learned a lot, and moved on to SlapCloud, as CEO. My wife jokes that my ego and bank account blew up, but family time shrank. So, I quit. For the past three years I have been running a foundation and investing in companies like yours."

He takes a bite of the best pancake ever, which allows Mitch to cut in. "How do you decide where to give your charitable dollars?"

"Mitch, I sit down with my kids and wife, and we decide where to contribute our money. My next goal is to change philanthropy. All these rich donors ask nonprofits to fill out all these reports, show ROI, when they should focus on curing cancer and feeding the hungry. I want to develop a software that makes tracking easy, but that's another breakfast."

Rick jumps in, "However, when Jim invests, he wants updates. We want to see that ROI."

Stealing the last few berries, I clear my throat, "Money is great, and it will help spur growth, but what about mentoring me? Is that part of the deal?" I can't believe I just said that. Mitch also looks completely shocked.

Jim laughs. "Nice question, Alex. You actually read the presentations on my LinkedIn profile."

Laughing nervously, and bluffing, "I did my homework. Can you elaborate?" I feel sweaty everywhere. I didn't know people posted presentations there.

With dimples popped out, Jim rolls up his sleeve. "I'm not sure how much money to invest, but whatever the amount, I'll give you advice whenever you want and probably more. My goal is to get double my investment and then walk away."

With all eyes on him, Jim pauses. Taking another bite of the fluffiest pancake, he says, "This is like crack. Alex, where do you see the next step for your companies? I love how they all play off each other."

I'm still focused on him saying that he will invest. Mitch's eyes are bugging out like he just won the lotto. Thankfully, my poker skills are coming in handy, as I just keep it cool on the outside. Internally, I'm full on freaking out and hoping I don't puke.

I am trying to remember the question. "The next step for us is to beef up sales, support, and software. An office would also help. Everyone is working remotely and that works, but if we could all get in the same room, it would help. A COO would help, too."

The waitress comes to check on us, and we all look up. "Anything else, gentlemen?"

Rick answers, "Just the check."

As she pulls out the check, Rick hands her his card. "Thanks."

We all say "Thank you" to Rick.

With a serious gaze, Jim cocks his head to the side. "Tell me, Alex—did you ever want to give up?"

I'm so focused on building this company. I tell him, "No. I had some tough moments in the beginning though. When I was getting the site up for the campus stuff, I spent almost all of my savings. There was also one month that I took the little I had left, and slightly rolled the dice by buying more ads for the knife business. Luckily, it worked, because I made enough money for payroll."

Mitch looked at me in shock, like I was just hit by car. I think he wanted to tell me to stop talking, but I couldn't.

Jim was smiling. He'd worked for startups and understood that it's tough. "One day I thought it was over. I got a note in the mail and an email from a law office that I had to stop selling knives and a line of pots and pans. They were my top sellers by a lot. I spent the day on the phone with lawyers from two different companies." The stories pour out of me. It was when I first started selling copperware and switched to a better line of knives. I blocked that day out until now.

Wanting me to shut up, Mitch speaks up. "What's the next step?"

Jim stands up. "This week we meet and hammer out the details. I think it would help to have Jerry in the room, as he has a good sense of your financials. Rick should also be in the room, and then whoever else you want to bring, Alex."

Jim is waiting for me to say something, but I'm still freaking out internally. "Great! I can't wait. When do I get a car like yours?"

His beams his winning smile. "Any time you want to take it for spin let me know. I have great insurance. It wasn't snowing, so I thought it would be fun to take it out for a spin. When I sold some stock, I told my wife, let's both splurge and save the rest. She came back with new jeans, fancy shoes, and a dress from Lululemon. I went a little bigger."

Rick asks, "What happened when she saw the car?"

Jim continues to beam. "I thought her eyes were going to fall out of her head. Once we went for a ride, she told me the car was ours."

We exchange guys hugs, and I can't feel my face. I'm in shock. How did that just happen? He obviously had his mind made up ahead of time. The main person I want to tell this news to is on a flight to Europe right now. Good thing my dad's car is in the garage because he's the second person I want to tell.

The smell of cookies greets me as I walk into the house. Sugar cookies! He's making the M&M cookies! With a huge smile on his face, he says, "I thought we could celebrate with these bad boys!" My dad can follow a recipe, but he doesn't know how to adapt for dryness, humidity, or when you can substitute apple sauce or pumpkin for oil, but he's made many recipes when my mom had a big event.

"I got an investor! I have no idea about the amount yet, but we have a deal!" He picks me up and hugs me. It brings me back to grade school when he did this when the Bears scored a touchdown.

ROGER

With the money from Jim, and Rick helping me pro bono, I have lots of projects. Taking a moment to reflect on this journey, it's crazy to think that one post led to a poker game, and now those guys are my advisors.

Even though Mitch wanted me to hire a head of sales, I still haven't done it. Mitch is a natural, and Jim has really taken him under his wing. I'm slightly jealous, as Mitch gets more face time with Jim than I do.

My staff is now up by five more people. Most of them are in sales. Jack and John are the only part-timers. Instead of an office in the city, I am leasing, at a heavy discount, a space Rick had in Northbrook. He owned an importing company at some point in his career, and this was his storage space. The last tenant made it into a gym, but the owner retired a few years ago. Rick had been sitting on the space for a few years. It's perfect for me. There are two showers and a handful of old fitness equipment in one corner. My favorites include a high-end self-propelled treadmill, an old school stair climber, and boxing equipment. There is a double-end bag that connects to the floor and the ceiling. I've never used one before, but it's great for your reflexes.

An email from Robbie causes me to pause work. She sent me pictures from a trip to Paris and they are very guy heavy. She's been traveling a lot with this new group of friends, and they take trips all around Europe. I wonder if she is hooking up with Roger or Theo. They're the two guys in her new posse. Curiosity snakes into my head.

I decide to call Jack. "Jack, how are you buddy?"

With a yawn, he asks, "Alex! What's up, man? It's not even Friday. To what do I owe the pleasure?"

Debating whether to ask, I do it anyway. "Okay, I know that I said I didn't want to know about Robbie, but I have to know. Is she hooking up with Roger or Theo? What's her sister telling you?"

The deep exhale tells me he's conflicted. "The truth is that I don't know much. There are a lot of pictures of Roger and her online. I haven't seen anything sexual or even close, but ones where they are out drinking, on hikes, and sitting on trains. I noticed a few weeks ago and wanted to tell you. Remember, you are also on a break."

"Has Rose said anything? What does he look like?"

I hear a microwave or other device beeping. "I'm just heating up a snack. He's bald, seems short and thin. Um, I can't really think of much more. I looked him up and he goes to school in California. He looks like a party animal."

Taking his comments as clues, I'm putting everything together. "Thanks. Is he a party animal like you were?"

I hear him swallow. "Have fun and try not to think about it. I'll see you after your Texas trip. Are you still texting with Shelly?"

"She sends me an occasional text. Alright, fun it is. I'm going to text this girl I was close with goes to Texas and put Roger and Robbie out of my mind for a few weeks."

With a gulp, he says, "Can't wait to catch up in Madison."

I haven't looked at Robbie's Instagram account since she left. As much as I pretend to fight it, I have to see this Roger character. They are in a lot of pictures together. I miss her smile, touch and voice. She looks so happy. He has light blue eyes, thick eyebrows and a buzz cut. It does look like his hair is receding, but he's not bald.

I find myself texting Ellie without even thinking about it. She immediately responds, "OMG. How R U? This weekend I'm all yours! Can't wait. College has been great, but I miss home."

We text back and forth for another few minutes, but I can only focus on "I'm all yours." What does she mean by that? She was my first crush, and we had the best adventures. I had no idea about Skokie, Evanston, or really any suburb outside of my own, until we got our licenses and explored. Junior and senior year we hung out less and less because of all her boyfriends. I'm not even sure whether she is still dating Ryan.

Mitch asks me at least once a week if I called Ellie, so I text him the news. He writes back immediately, "Can't wait to meet someone you went to high school with."

Pushing Robbie out of my mind is tough, but I use my obsession to fill my mind. Reviewing all the daily stats is exciting, even if there's a dip. Sales are inching up for the website. No one thinks that will be my money maker, but I think it will be. We have an email distribution of 80,000. It hasn't even been a year yet. Website views, clicks, and the other indicators consistently grow. Kitchenware, although boring, continues to earn me the greatest revenue. Plates is growing steadily, we keep offering new lines, like bowls and platters.

With the long work hours and school, I have done zero work to prepare for my tips. Rachel, Jack's sister, has been a godsend. She planned the Texas influencer party and events. She also arranged for an event at The BBQ and Baker. Mitch is meeting with the owners while we are in town. This weekend will be a great way to show our reach. One hundred kids are coming to sample food and listen to live music. There's some sort of bracelet for the kids over 21 to wear so they can drink alcohol. Jack is designing a signature drink.

Rachel yells at me over the fans that hover 20 feet above us. "Hey, earth to Alex? You ready for Texas? I want you to review this itinerary."

Confused, I ask, "Why do we have to be at the restaurant at nine o'clock? It seems very early."

With a culpable smile, she replies, "It's something we wanted to do for you. Just, please roll with it."

Since I ruin enough fun with all this work, I tell her, "I'm game. I have three events. Friday night at the barbecue joint, a huge park for another meet up, and rock climbing. I hope we're insured for that."

"Relax, boss. We have waivers for everything, and the facility also has waivers. Mitch will meet you at the airport Thursday night."

Turning to Rachel, I ask, "What did I ever do without you? What happened to the poker event?"

At just over five feet, and maybe 100 pounds, you would have no idea what a powerhouse Rachel is. Brushing her dark hair back, so it holds behind her ears, she says, "Poker is too much red tape. Even if it's a charity event, there are so many rules."

Taking a second to dissect, I ask, "Are you power posing, Rachel?"

Laughing, she says, "Hell yeah!"

Rick, who often works here when his kids are in town, overhears our conversation and walks over. Rachel looks guilty, like she's six and did something naughty. With a serious expression, he says, "You guys have too much fun. Rachel deserves a bonus."

Walking back to the only office with a door, Rick disappears. I have no idea what he does in there, but he's laser focused. His normal routine is to say hello, grab some coffee, and then he hides in his office for hours without coming out. I want that kind of focus.

When noon comes, unless we have a meeting, we workout. Another reason I love Rachel is that she does whatever workout I'm doing. Mitch joins us when he's in the office. The other staff that regularly work out of the office are Barb our office manager, Tyler our artistic director, and Drew, who runs IT support. They disdain exercise. I think Drew is starting to think about exercising here, but he's anti-cardio and we only have a handful of dumbbells. He looks like a linebacker with broad shoulders, and he needs to turn sideways to get through doors.

Barb never gets up. She eats at her desk and sneaks to the bathroom when no one is looking. On Fridays, I order pizza for the office, and she pops up for the salad and one piece of pizza.

We are in search of the best pizza in the suburbs. So far, Pequod's is our favorite.

Since our webmaster lives in the city, he only comes to the office once a week. Usually, he carpools with Mitch. Even though he graduated from college two years ago, he's been building sites for years. He and Tyler chat all day long about design. Tyler, like Barb and Rick, is focused. Creativity oozes from his pores. You would also have no idea he's fifty years old. The guy wears shorts to work every day, has a full head of blond hair, and has a gym shoe collection that rivals pro-athletes. Two months in, and he has yet to repeat wearing a pair. If it wasn't for Jim's investment, I would've never been able to afford him. Like me, he loves to cook, so he also doubles as our product tester. I set him up with an affiliate site, where he earns commission on kitchenware, and through his foodie friends, he is killing it.

We are a team of misfits. Our board of advisors seems more normal, as it's basically my poker buddies and Jim.

Packing for my first college visit since Madison feels different. For starters, I have a hotel room, and work events to attend. Granted the work events are social, but it's still work. I won't be getting drunk and sleeping on a futon.

The hotel is close to campus and the barbecue joint, and since Mitch knows I like to walk places, he booked it. The price is also right.

Booking it to our hotel's free shuttle, all I want are food and sleep. Mitch, in his jeans, a suede fitted blazer and short boots, yawns. "I know you want to party tonight, but how about tomorrow with Ellie!"

Exhaling, nervousness sets in. I haven't seen Ellie since she left for college. Aside from a few emails, we haven't spoken. Once she started dating, I only got to see her a few times a month. She always tried to make time for John and me, but it was different. I think she still might be with Ryan. His name is Danny Ryan, but everyone calls him Ryan. He's at my school, Duke. The kid was nice, so I could never hate him. I was so jealous of him though. He swam, had long limbs, smelled like chlorine, and ran track. The reason I dunked for the first time in a game was because of him. Ellie was watching us play a pickup game at the park, and I dunked hard in his face. He fell back, and all I could hear was John yelling, "YOU GOT POSTERIZED!"

The adrenaline was pumping through me. I was ready for a fight if he popped up mad. Instead, he stood up smiling. "Damn, Alex! That was awesome." Guilt set in quickly, and I apologized.

Walking into our hotel, I ask Mitch, "If it's weird with Ellie and me, can you bail me out?"

Laughing, he says, "Don't be so nervous. Have fun, but of course, I can do that. I'll just say, 'Boss man, I need you.'"

Standing next to the registration table is a handsome cowboy. He has on boots, tight jeans, and a plaid shirt. With his curly blond hair and blue eyes, he looks like a Ralph Lauren model. Mitch looks startled. He says, "Bobby, man you look so different."

With a shy smile, "With football over, I lost my linemen belly."

They embrace. Bobby, who's almost a foot taller than Mitch, picks him up with the hug. Extending a hand to me, with a thick southern accent, he says, "Pleasure to meet you, Alex."

I was so stuck in my head, I totally forgot Mitch's crush was meeting us out. They met in college. Bobby was on the football team and never told anyone but Mitch that he was gay. Bobby's dad had a ranch in Texas, and since he was a kid, he was groomed to take it over. However, Bobby preferred to do coding.

Wrapping an arm around him, I say, "So nice to meet you, Bobby. Mitch told me all about you. I didn't know you were meeting Mitch tonight."

He gives me a warm smile. "I thought I would surprise Mitch. You can join us for a drink."

Holding my room key in the air like it's a golden ticket, I say, "That's very generous, but I am going to bed." A yawn follows my sentence, as proof of my sleepiness.

When you go to bed before ten pm, you wake up at five am, filled with nervous energy. The first thing I do is go for a run. Austin is cool. The main drag of bars and restaurants are close to the hotel, and campus is not much farther away. The only other people out now are runners. The streets are empty, and the campus is big and beautiful.

This campus is filled with potential for us. I take pictures of bars, shops, and restaurants to make sure they are listed on the site.

Grabbing a water bottle and bagel from the hotel, I run up for a shower. Statistics are on my mind.

A few light knocks on my door pulls my attention away from my computer. "Mitch?"

I open the door and he walks in with a big smile. "Hey buddy, are you ready to go?"

Per usual, Mitch has outdressed me. He's wearing a pink shirt with green stripes and linen pants. "Can we go shopping, for real? You always look so cool. So, did you have fun with the coding cowboy?"

Smirking, he says, "I'll just give you clothes. A friend of mine developed a personal shopping business. At the end of each season, whatever doesn't sell, he either gives to me or I get a ridiculous deal on."

Surprised, I ask, "Really? He just gives them to you?"

"Yes. I was his first model. He couldn't pay me, so he said if he ever made money, he would just give me clothes. I haven't really shopped in years."

I ask, "What about the cowboy?"

With his hands on his head, as if he is in disbelief, he says, "I don't even know what to tell you. This guy was my Ellie. We would sit a little too close and watch a movie. It's funny because women always loved him. He has movie star looks and football player muscles."

Walking at a good pace, I say, "I'm happy for you. Will you see him tonight? Can he come to our party?"

Breathing heavy, he says, "Oh yeah, I'm not sure if anything will come of this, but I'm rolling with it. Is Ellie coming?"

Trying not to get excited, I tell him, "I think she's coming to have dinner with me first and then we'll go to the party."

Walking up to The BBQ and Baker, we can smell smoke. I had no idea barbeque starts so early. The restaurant sticks out on a packed street. It's two stories, all white, and has huge windows. The door is unlocked, and we walk in like we know what we're doing.

Sitting down at a table, writing, must be Bo, the chef and co-owner. Standing up to greet us, he says, "You must be Alex and Mitch. Pleasure to meet you, boys." With a hand the size of a large baseball mitt, he shakes our hands. Bo's bald head looks freshly shaved, and his beard looks like he's either a rock star or an Orthodox Jew.

Mitch speaks first to Bo while looking at me. "Alex has no idea what you have in store for him, but he's going to love it. Is Jen upstairs?"

Bo brings his eyebrows up, like he has a big surprise for me. "Head up, Mitch. She's in school, so she only has a few hours before class. Find us in the kitchen and you can help out."

My eyes well up with excitement. "Am I cooking with you?" All I can think about is my mom because she would be so excited. When I graduated college, her plan was to open a bakery and sandwich shop. She would be so jealous and happy for me. The tears start to flow, and I don't know what to do. Mitch has already walked away, and Bo puts his giant hook of an arm around me.

With a warm southern drawl, he asks, "Are you okay, buddy? Mitch said you would love a day in the kitchen."

Using a napkin, I wipe my nose and eyes. Turning away from him for a moment, I say, "This is amazing. It's the best gift ever. Just give me a minute." I walk outside and completely lose it. I'm sweating through my polo, and the napkin I stole is filled with tears. I tell myself all I need is a few breaths.

Walking back in, Bo meets me with a glass of water, and I apologize. "I'm sorry." Continuing to breathe deep into my belly, I explain, "My mom was a baker." A few tears drip down my side. "She would've loved to do this. I don't usually cry at work or in front of strangers."

Bo points to a heavily tattooed arm revealing the words, "COOK 4 K." He wipes his eyes, too. "Keith was my older brother. My parents were dirt poor and were always working. Keith taught me how to cook. He died ten years ago, but I still lose it sometimes."

Handing me an apron, he continues, "You will still stink like smoke, but this helps keep you a little cleaner." He also hands me a BBQ & Baker baseball cap. "That's yours to keep. Come on back."

We walk through the kitchen and then outside, where huge ovens, pits, and grills crowd the back deck. Checking the temperatures quickly, Bo puts on gloves on and waves me close. "We make chickens, beef, turkey, and pork. The chickens are rotisserie, the rest we toss in a specific grill. I also like to use different wood. Cherry is my favorite. Grab that tray and hold it for me." He smiles bigger. "We'll see if your muscles are for show or work."

The aluminum tray looks like it's built to hold small children. Staring right into Bo's dark eyes, I say, "Load me up, Bo. What does Bo stand for?"

With burnt oven gloves, he unloads briskets on the tray. "There's a cart behind you. I was just messing with you. Roll it over." Dropping the meat on top of the cart, my muscles immediately relax. As I wheel it closer, Bo continues, "Robert is my legal name, but I've been Bo since the day I was born. Next up, we put the rubs on the meat, make some sauces, and then make pasta."

Following Bo back inside, I can see the burn marks on his arms. They line the inside of both of his forearms, like callouses. He's earned them all. "We let this rest twenty minutes, then chop it up. I like to keep it warm in its juices. Nothing is worse than dry brisket, right?"

The kitchen is spotless. An endless array of spices lineup every table, and there are huge fridges that store the meat. Behind another counter, weapons hang on a magnet. Those tools look like something out of a horror film. Turning to me, he says, "I'm grabbing some brisket first. I roast that meat all day and night on low heat. Low and slow, baby."

After moving the cooked meat on one counter, Bo pulls marinated beef from the fridge and places it on the counter with all the spices. "Alright boy, coat these bad boys with the spice mix in there." He points to three huge containers. "Don't be shy."

I shoot him a quizzical look and he reads my mind. "Alex, if you tell anyone this mixture, I'll use those tools over there on you."

Laughing, he continues, "Paprika, smoked and regular, onion powder, garlic powder, chili powder, celery seed, mustard seed, ancho chili powder, brown sugar, and of course, coarse salt and pepper. If people want a little more spice, I add that in before serving."

Dousing the beef in seasoning is followed up by placing it in the smoker. Then we clean off the table and season the other meats. The chicken is last because it cooks the quickest.

Pouring me some water, he says, "You're working up a sweat. I like it. Hey, how about at four p.m. you get a group here to test some of the meat? Do you have friends here?"

With a deep washing of my hands, I text Ellie. She responds instantly. "Count me in. I'll bring a few friends. Will we clean up before the party?"

"Yes, I'll need a serious cleaning. My coworkers talked the chef into letting me spend the day cooking."

She sends a smiley face and kiss emoji and says, "Sue is smiling so BIG right now."

This time, I think of my mom and keep it together. "I have friends coming! Thanks, Bo. Please tell me you'll be joining us."

Covered in dough, he says, "I'll say hello to them, but I have to check out the brewery before the event. I'm here for you for thirty minutes at eight o'clock. Then I'm out."

A woman with a pastry hat pops in. She's blonde, curvy, and smiles big. The name on her apron reads, Sue. "Hey, babe. Can I get this kid to help me next door? I hear he's a baker."

Kissing Bo on the cheek, Bo cuts in, "Alex, this is my wife, Sue. She runs the bakery. Sue, this kid is a work horse. Don't be stealing him too long. I want to show him how I make the macaroni and cheese and cornbread."

Smacking him on the butt, she says, "Don't you worry. I'll have him back in time to help with the blueberry sauce."

Pointing at Bo, I say, "I have to see that. I've never heard of that before." Sue and I exchange an awkward elbow touch. Her hands are full of flour.

Walking through a swinging door, I'm in another kitchen. This one is much smaller. It's just a little bigger than the one in my house.

Sue's dark blue eyes stare through me. "I hear you have a killer recipe for Nutella stuffed cookies."

This day is one giant surprise after another. "Sue, how did you find this out?"

With a warm southern accent, she says, "Darling, Mitch is a talker. I love the boy, but I would never trust him with a secret. I also have a cake for your girl."

I laugh. "Mitch really does have a big mouth. I'll share my recipe, but you have to share some Southern secrets with me."

Putting her long blond hair back into a ponytail, she says, "Deal. I have this whiskey-caramel bread pudding. Southern, sumptuous, and sassy—just like me!"

Baking with Sue feels like I'm in a dream. It's like I'm 8 again, standing on a step stool carefully folding wet ingredients into the dry mix. Patient, like my mom, Sue takes me through making bread. She places it near a window to rise, and then we cut up an old loaf for the bread pudding. She explains the reasons behind the recipe, and everything intrigues me. I feel like I'm asking her a million questions.

"Alright boy, I showed you mine. Now it's your turn." Handing me a pen and paper, I get busy.

With a hand on her shoulder, I tell her, "You need to really chill the dough and whip the butter well because it makes a huge difference. I've also tried a hundred different ways to stuff the cookies, but this is the easiest way."

With a serious look, she says, "Alex, be honest, can I use this recipe here?"

Euphoria hits me. "I would be honored. Let's make some cookies. Once we get them in fridge, I'll head back to the other side."

With her blue eyes pressing into me, "You should just work here. Seriously, Austin is awesome. We are growing and you have a lady friend here."

Laughing, I say, "Can we just make these cookies? I promise that I'll visit you."

Despite the limited menu, there is a huge lunch rush. Dinner is service, but lunch is self-serve, and there's a line out the door. I deliver trays of meat to the staff, and then head back to mix sauces, make pasta, and check on the grills.

I see Mitch standing in line and wink. He waves at me like a parent does when he drops his kid off at school. I can tell he's proud of himself for arranging this, and he should be. I haven't had this much fun in years.

When the rush ends, Bo and I sit down and eat. Warning me, he says, "Save your appetite. I know you're starving but trust me. You're eating at four o'clock and then again at eight o'clock. Your skinny ass will be sick as a dog if you chow now, too."

Bo made us sandwiches on a press. The bread is crispy, and the melted cheddar falls out of the sides as I take a bite. The sourdough holds up perfectly. "This is a great sandwich. Thank you, Bo! Today was amazing. What's your schedule like?"

Wiping the sweat off his forehead, he says, "This is a grind man. Sue is here at six. I get here at eight. In addition to the bakery, she makes dessert for our brewery. I work here from eight until four. I was working twelve-hour days for months, but I passed out one day. They rushed me to the hospital, and when I came to, I shot up and said that I needed to take out the meat. Sue turned to me and said that it's not worth it. I changed my hours, hired a great night manager, and life is much better."

Taking a sip of the peach tea we made, I agree. "I'm glad your life is better."

Reaching across the table, Bo puts a hand on me. "You were a huge help today. That lunch change was Mitch's idea. We used to have servers and it was an ordeal. Thanks, and boy are you born for this work."

Mitch deserves to be head of sales. Maybe he should have my job. How did he think of that?

Melting into my seat, the adrenaline is wearing off. Waking up early to run is catching up with me.

Sensing my fatigue, he says, "Alex, get out of here. I'll see you at four. You're young, but if you don't do this work every day, it will kick you in the ass. Take a shower or a bath, rest, and come back."

Before taking off, I run upstairs to see Mitch. Sitting at a table, solo, he lifts his head the second I pop up. "You smell like barbeque. I don't know whether to be grossed out or take a bite."

"I would hug you, but I'm covered in a mixture of sweat, seasoning, flour, and meat." Laughter pops out of me unexpectantly. "Thank you. This was awesome. I've never had a day like this."

Pumping his fist like he just hit the winning shot at the Masters, he exclaims, "I knew it! I'm so happy! Now it's time to lather up!"

ELLIE

Scrubbing, soaping, and repeating is a lot of work. Time passes quickly. I sleep for maybe 20 minutes, but it's the recharge I needed. Working in the kitchen is no joke; I have a new respect for chefs.

The restaurant looks totally different at night. The area where they do the lunch service is a bar. Bo is sitting there alone on a laptop. When I sit next to him, he puts his hand on my shoulder like we're old pals. "Alex, you were awesome today! Man are your cookies good. When we revamp the menu in a few months, maybe you can help us."

Without hesitation, I respond, "I would love to!"

Bo stands up and walks me over to a large booth. "Here's your table." Before I sit down, I see Ellie. With her short dark hair pulled back, it shows off her flawless skin. Like her three friends, Ellie is showing off part of her toned stomach, and her mini skirt shows off legs for days. I forgot how pretty she is.

Running to me like out of a movie, she gives me a tight hug and kisses me on the cheek. "Alex, when did you get all those muscles?"

Embarrassed, I laugh. "You should've seen me before I started my company. This is skinny. You look amazing."

Her three friends, Kate, Ria, and Sloan give Bo and I hugs. Ria, who's tall and looks like a Persian princess, says, "We love it here. Your Sunday Vegan brunches are amazing. How did you ever think of that?"

Bo, almost blushing, says, "Thank you ma'am. I give credit to Alex and his associate, Mitch. I told him my wife wants us to take off Sunday, but it's a great day. I told him the ovens could use a day off, so he came up with that entire social campaign on how you need to register to get a table once we post about it. I never thought Vegan and BBQ would be a success. People complain that they can't get in."

Bo continues to talk about how it books up in minutes after they post the menu. I only catch parts of his excitement because I'm texting Mitch about how much of a value he is to the company. He texts me back a kiss emoji.

A waitress brings us four pitchers and explains, "Peach Long Island tea, booze lemonade, BBQ Beer, and this last one is non-alcoholic blueberry pomegranate lemonade. It's my favorite. I'll be coming out the with food Alex prepared shortly." Samantha, the waitress, also hands us each a large water glass.

Bo gives me a hug. "Nice to meet you, ladies. Enjoy the food. Hopefully I'll see you all upstairs at eight o'clock."

Unintentionally, I ignore Ellie's friends. She cozies close to me, and I melt into her big brown eyes.

"First off, I'm very impressed you are friends with Bo. He is the darling of UT."

Taking a big drink of water, I try and calm my nerves. "Tell me everything. How's Ryan?"

She smiles nervously and takes several sips of the peach drink. "It's an interesting agreement. I know that sounds odd, but he does his thing and I do mine. During the summer we get back together."

Interrupting her, I say, "My old girlfriend asked me to break up with her while she's abroad. I thought it was crazy, but this seems to be the thing to do."

She puts her hand on my leg and I can tell that saying "old girlfriend" settled her. She continues, "It's a thing and it works well. I can also tell a guy I have a boyfriend if he's bothering me, and I'm not totally lying."

The food hits the table, and everyone digs in. I've been sampling it all day, so I only take a few bites. Everything tastes delicious.

Downing her first drink, liquor courage brings her somehow closer to me. I'm nervous I'm going to stand up and have a stiffy. She asks, "How come you've never tried anything on me? I had such a crush on you, Alex."

Surprise takes over. "Wait, what?" She shakes her head yes. "I asked you out, but you were too busy. Then once you got boobs, you always had a man."

Without moving her eyes from mine, she says, "But all I wanted was you."

Mitch and the coding cowboy walk in, which is perfect because I need time to absorb what Ellie just said.

The girls are staring hard at them. Ellie whispers in my ear, "They're gay, right?"

"How did you know?"

She laughs. "They're holding hands."

Immediately, I hug Mitch. "You are amazing at your job. We are going to pivot and offer consulting services to restaurants. Not just social, but revenue generating ideas like you did here with lunch. Robbie and I can help with menu suggestions."

Mitch smiles. He waves to all the girls and introduces Bobby. "Don't get up ladies. I just wanted to say, we'll be back at eight." Turning to me, he says, "Alex, I love how you are always thinking about business. Seriously, you have an impressive focus while surrounded by all this beauty."

As they walk away, I turn to Ellie. "Ellie, I had a crush on you. You always had a guy and our lunch dates freshman year didn't really escalate."

Grabbing my arm as if I did something wrong, she says, "Alex Culp, we were at the beach before the year started. A wave took down my top, and you turned away."

Laughing, I say, "Of course I did, I mean I'm a gentleman. I didn't realize that was an invitation. I was in awe though."

Dessert arrives just in time to break up our awkward moment. Ellie's eyes somehow get bigger. "The Nutella specials!" She gives me a surprise kiss on the lips. It was short and exciting due to so many years of longing for her.

Ria reaches out first. "Alex, Ellie has been talking about these since you texted her. Will they live up to the hype?"

Shaking my head, I say, "I don't get it. They're good, just not my favorite cookie."

With a giant bite, Ria stares me down. "Fuck, those are amazing."

All the girls agree. The only blonde, Kate, aggressively asks, "Tell me how you make these? I'm finding you on Facebook. Will you share the recipe?"

Grabbing me with a red manicured thin hand, she says, "These are so good."

The girls all laugh, and I shake my head and say that I'll share it.

The cookies disappear quickly and either her friends are bored, antsy, or it's the sugar, but they are ready to go. Sloan, who's been very quiet, says with a baby voice, "Thanks! We are heading to this other bar to meet Ria's boyfriend and his friends. Do you want to come with us?"

I stand up to say goodbye. "I have to stay here for a work event. You are welcome to come back. It starts at eight."

Ellie, without being asked, says, "I'm going to stay with Alex."

Within seconds of the girls leaving, Ellie leans in and kisses me. I haven't kissed any girl other than Robbie, and guilt is my first emotion. Although Robbie can be forceful, she's usually not like this. Ellie has me pushed up against the booth. Four years of lust is bubbling up to a crescendo.

She whispers in my ear, "Can we get out of here?"

Wasting no time, I drop 40 dollars on the table and we walk out.

Without much time to spare, we hop into a car and drive to my hotel. Stealing kisses in the car feels a little dirty, but I like it. Without much talking, we run up to my room.

The moment the door closes, Ellie pulls off my shirt and pushes me on the bed. She takes off her top, and I still remember how amazing her boobs looked only a few years ago. I didn't know what to do then.

Hopping on top of me, she says, "I've waited almost five years for this."

This experience feels like a dream from high school. If it wasn't for her nails digging into me, I would think this was a dream. Innocent Ellie is a freak. I cannot believe it, but I'm not complaining.

As we put our clothes back on, Ellie laughs. "I'm sorry I attacked you. I've never done that before."

Walking back to the bar holding hands feels comfortable. Absorbing the experience has left me a little speechless. She asks, "Are you okay?"

Pulling her to a bench outside the restaurant, I explain, "I'm in shock. For years, all I wanted was to rip off your clothes and kiss you. Rarely do dreams like that come true. I'm not going to lie, I didn't have you pegged as so aggressive but I liked it."

Her pale cheeks fill with red. "I had some liquor courage, but I also dreamed about you. That was actually better than I had imagined."

For the third time today, I'm strolling into The BBQ and Baker. The first floor is packed with diners. I guide Ellie upstairs and we run into Sue and Bo setting up. Ellie asks first, "Can we help?"

Bo looks cleaned up. He's wearing dark jeans, a promotional shirt, and a jean jacket over it. Sue is still in her work clothes. Feeling judged, she looks at me. "Hey, pretty boy. I had to work while Bo ran home and changed. Someone had to man the fort."

The four of us move tables and chairs around, and then place food trays under tiny heaters. Sue points us to the back kitchen. This one is small but has everything you need. Treats are piled beautifully on a folding table. "Don't be shy kids. Try one of the bread puddings. Alex and I slaved over those. The caramel melts in your mouth." With only a small bite, it's one of the best desserts I've ever had.

Ellie whispers in my ear, "This is almost as good as the sex. I can't believe I just said that."

I forgot how funny and carefree she is. I was always jealous of how at ease she was with everything. She was never embarrassed.

Once, she dropped a maxi-pad in the middle of class. Everyone was hushed, and she blurred out, "You'll learn about it in health class."

That's what I loved about her most. One Friday night, she picked me up and we went to see a Disney movie. I think it was the Incredibles. We were the only people there without kids. It was a fact she bragged about at school.

Mitch and Bobby interrupt my trip down memory lane. Mitch, for the hundredth time tells me the agenda. "Alex, you introduce and thank Bo. Bo says a few words. He introduces the performer. You thank all the kids for coming out, posting, and rating places. Keep it short. Don't be nervous!" Which only makes me more nervous. He continues, "Then the music goes on and people eat. Remind them to take a goodie bag for the road."

Confused, I ask, "How young are these kids?"

Laughing, he says, "Jackass, it's a swag bag. We are giving them a branded shirt, pen, mug, and a cookie."

Without thinking, I say, "It sounds expensive."

He shakes his head no. "It wasn't and we split the cost with Bo."

Sensing my nerves, Bo hands me a cocktail. "Take a few sips and relax. You're literally speaking for two minutes."

The room quickly fills. Half the room has a green bracelet, and the other half is red. I don't want to feel like a hypocrite, so I place my drink the table. These kids can google me and see that I'm 19 and under the legal drinking age.

The performer sets up his acoustic guitar and then pops next to me. "Thanks for having me play. I'm Steve. Nice to meet you."

Shaking Steve's hand, I say, "Nice to meet you. Thanks for performing. I have heard a few of your songs and love them."

Taking a few sips of his cocktail, he seems jittery. "The truth is that I've only played at Potbelly." He walks away, and now I'm worried. He looks younger than me.

Waiving me to the center of the room, I take the microphone. "Thank you all for coming out. We really appreciate it. I cannot say enough about all your comments and how fast you are growing our site. It's really our site. We created it to help college kids, businesses in college towns, and hometowns. Now I want to thank and introduce my new best friend and Austin's not so best kept secret, Bo."

The applause for Bo is loud. I step away. I didn't quite follow the script. Mitch winks at me in approval, like a coach or dad would. Ellie whispers, "That was great!"

Bo rattles off a few nice words and hands the microphone to Steve. With a smile, Steve says, "I'm taking your favorites and making them country." Sitting down on a stool, guitar in hand, he starts singing Billie Eilish, 'Everything I wanted,' and it's amazing.

Mitch and I stare at each other in amazement. Laughing, I ask, "Do you think we could sign him? This kid is going to be huge."

Mitch is still laughing. "I'm not sure we can form a label now."

Shaking my head, I explain, "Not a label. We make a section of the site dedicated to local artists. Whether it's music or drawing, we can promote them at events. We can work with their managers and get deals because they are fresh talent. Then they get found. People can recommend them like a great a wedding singer. Or Steve, future bad ass country singer. Take some videos and post them. If it doesn't get over one hundred views, I will drop the idea."

With his arm around me, he says, "Alex, I love it. I'll take a quick video and then take the night off. You have a beautiful girl and a successful event. Enjoy it. I will call Rachel tomorrow. I think she will be all over it."

My mind starts moving at a million miles per minute. I notice Mitch's backpack behind the bar. Ellie is talking to a few friends. With a tap, I tell them both, "I'll be right back."

Logging onto Mitch's laptop, I fire off a few paragraphs to Rachel. I really think this could differentiate us. Not only are we helping businesses, but we are also shining a light on performers. Not wanting Ellie to get mad, I send my email and get back to the party.

Mitch and Bobby are sitting at the bar with Ellie and Bo. I put my arm around Bo and Ellie. "Thank you, Bo! Everything about this day was amazing." Ellie squeezes my butt in agreement.

Bo puts his arm around me. "Thank you! You and Mitch saved my ass. We needed to get the word out on a budget. You did it.

Then this social craze with the vegan lunch. Everyone thought I was crazy for offering a vegan menu."

Steve takes a break from singing, swigs some water, and asks, "Does anyone like the Beatles?" The place erupts in cheers. The noise dies down, and in his southern charm says, "You may say I'm a dreamer ..." Again, boisterous screams sound off as he starts singing.

Mitch comes back to me. "Let's sign him. He can do all our events."

Laughing, I say, "Let's discuss this tomorrow. He's amazing and we can launch many careers."

Ellie is eavesdropping and pulls me aside. "I always knew you were going to be a big-time boss".

We sit away from the crowd. "Thanks, I have no idea where this came from. I always just went with the flow."

She shakes her head no. "You were cool if I said let's see a movie or grab pizza, but you always took charge at basketball and on school projects. Remember the recycling project? That was all you. You were always in control on the court, motioning people were to go, yelling out directions."

Flattered, I say, "Thanks. It's been a wild ride. I work a lot, but I'm really into it." Yawning, I feel the big day catching up with me.

Ellie smiles and kisses my cheek. "Can we sneak out of here?"

I take her hand. "Don't you want to stay with your friends?"

Leading me down the steps, she says, "I see those bitches all the time."

Running around the room, I say goodbye to everyone I can. I'm a little surprised how many people want to meet me. Ellie is being very patient, talking to a few of her friends while I pose for pictures.

After a few more pictures, I grab Ellie's hand. "Let's run now."

Walking back to my room arm in arm feels comfortable. Ellie tightens her grip. "This feels so natural. I cannot believe we never hooked up in high school."

Reaching the hotel, Ellie asks, "Quick swim?"

Confused, I respond, "Do you have a swimsuit?"

Before I finish talking, she's in her bra and boy shorts. Taking off my clothes, I join her. The water feels good. Thank God no one is around, because I'm feeling self-conscious, even with her kisses.

The stars come out, and although I'm ready to sleep, I feel invigorated. We hear a few voices and quickly jump out. Wrapping up in towels, we head upstairs. Being with Ellie is so easy. Not that things were hard with Robbie, but there's this built-in comfort level. I can't help but wonder what will happen next.

WORKING ON THE WEEKENDS

At 6:30 a.m., I sneak out of bed. My internal alarm clock is a little delayed. Throwing on shorts and a T-shirt, I head to the hotel gym. Mitch is sitting on a bench.

"Mitch, what are you doing here?"

Yawning, he says, "The cowboy wakes up at six to run every morning. I stayed in bed for another thirty minutes and figured, why not hit the gym."

Encouraging him with a pat on the shoulder, "What if we walk outside and talk? I want to know everything you know about restaurants."

Shaking his head like he's annoyed, he says, "Of course you do."

The fresh air feels good. It's quiet and not too hot. I turn back to Mitch, who already seems out of breath. "What's the deal?"

Clearing his throat as if he's royalty, he explains, "My uncle was in the business forever. He owned a few spots, from fine dining to fast food. With a group of his friends, they bought a bunch of Kentucky Fried Chickens and Popeyes. That gave me the idea for the lunch self-service station. Anyway, I helped here and there. I bounced between host and server most of my childhood. I did not like it because those hours suck and you're always on your feet."

"How did we never discuss this? Can we hire your uncle on as a consultant?"

Shaking his head, "The guy is eighty-five and lives in California. I'm not sure he's the man you want. Not because he's old, but he's just chilling and cashing those KFC checks. My cousin's a smart kid."

"Does he own fast food spots too?"

Laughing, "No, not Brian. He works in software sales but hates it. Maybe we could hire him."

Looking at my watch, I realize we should head back because I don't want Ellie to think I left her. "Let's head back. But tell me, why didn't he work with his dad?"

Stroking his always present scruff, "Brian loved the food business. He opened a restaurant after college with his dad. He lasted two years and burned out. I remember when we were in high school, his dad had this restaurant in Roger's Park. We had so many family gatherings there. Brian spent most of high school cooking, hosting, and cleaning."

Walking inside the hotel, Mitch follows me to the dining area and grabs some water. We are standing outside my room. "This is my last question. Why did he close the restaurant?"

Smiling, he explains, "He outgrew the space. It was a good reason. His dad wanted to find a bigger spot and Brian was done. I'll call him."

"Thanks! I'll see you at the park. Need any help setting up?"

Laughing at me, "No silly. We hired a company to do that for us. Show up, talk, and shake hands. I know you like to get your hands dirty."

Slowly closing the door, I try to be quiet. Ellie is somehow still sleeping. Hopping in the shower, I'm trying to figure out how music fits into the site. I think it's going to be easy to add. Maybe we can even have an events page that the influencers upload. I might have to pay them to do stuff like that. Better yet, they can email us, and I'll have the web guys handle it. Could we have an editable form? It's like my mind is overflowing with ideas. Spitting out all my ideas on paper wakes Ellie and I didn't even realize it until she taps me on the shoulder. She's naked.

With a dirty smile, she says, "Hello, Mr. Early Riser." Her sexual appetite is envious. She was lying on my bed, and all I could think about was work. Maybe I do need to get out more.

Laying on the bed, breathless, I wonder when she's going to leave. This is all I wanted for four years, and now I care more about checking our daily statistics than sex. I really need a therapist.

Pulling me towards her, she asks, "Earth to Alex. Did I just break you?"

I shake my head no. "You did try, but I'm just thinking about work. The projects never end. We have this investor now, and I feel like I can't let him down."

Tossing on her clothes, she says, "I'm so proud of you Alex. Don't overdo it. You have that tendency to focus so intensely on one thing that you miss out."

Confused, I ask her for an example.

Stealing a few sips of my water, she says, "Chess championship, junior year basketball, selling candy, building the treehouse, car repairs, and I could go on."

Putting on clothes, I say, "That candy was for charity. You're welcome! We won the competition, and it was low sugar candy, which you said would never sell."

Tying her shoes, she jumps up. "That was it, Alex. That was when you could've made your move. I was single during the entire project. We spent all this time at your house and in my basement. You didn't try anything. All you could think about was the best locations, driving to Wisconsin because the cost of candy was cheaper, lower taxes, and about a bigger profit margin."

Thinking back, she's right, all I wanted to do was win. "Winning that competition was an obsession. My mom just died, and I needed a win. You know what I mean. I just needed something to take my mind off being sad. Yes, you were awesome. No one, including John, knew how to treat me. You just listened and hugged me. We listened to sad music together and I loved you for it. Depression is a real bitch. And I wish I tried something."

Sensing my aggression, she says, "I know and I'm sorry. I didn't want to upset you, but I just want to make sure you enjoy your success. It's okay to celebrate the little successes. Who planted that competitive bug in you?"

"My dad. I don't think he meant to, but he beat me at everything. I didn't have a sibling to play with, so it was him. I remember that I loved when I beat him at chess. My freshman year of high school I beat him at basketball. Funny thing is that he was so happy and proud of me. That made me feel like a real asshole."

Laughing, she says, "Well, you are a real asshole. I have a crap ton of homework to do. What if we do dinner with the cowboy and Mitch? Is that too much Ellie time?"

Kissing her, I say, "No, that would be great." She gives me a vice grip hug, and then heads out to campus. I feel a little guilty that I didn't take her to brunch, but work awaits. Maybe I do have a problem.

Taking my laptop to the pool area, I sit down and work. An inadvertent nap hits me, so it's a good thing I was in the shade.

Between reading emails and checking the stats, I hear Ellie's comments. Am I unbalanced? She's not wrong. Before basketball season started, I studied all the teams we played. Thanks to the internet, there were games out there on everyone. John and Ellie told me I was ridiculous and that this wasn't the pros. I was obsessed. It worked, and I had the best season. We won almost every game until we got bounced in the playoffs. Division three schools were recruiting me. Maybe I should've played senior year.

Rachel's text pulls me back to work mode. "Have fun. Take pics!"

Today's event is our fun fest. Rachel found a company that sets up outdoor ping-pong tables, bags, lawn darts, and volleyball for corporate outings. She thought this would be great. Food trucks are going to come by for a late lunch. The event is booze free, so that makes me less nervous that someone will get hurt.

Walking towards the park, I can see what looks like a few hundred kids. Being our first event like this, I'm okay if it's on the smaller side. If we get good pictures, these events will grow.

Mitch, with his large camera, is all over the field. I notice that we have a small stage. I see Steve the singer, and I am surprised, I didn't know he was coming to this. Running up to him, I say, "Hey, I didn't know you were coming. You are amazing!"

Shaking my hand, he says, "Thanks, man. I had a blast night. I picked up some business from the party. Two fraternities asked if I would sing at their house parties."

Patting him on the back, I tell him, "That's awesome. I told Mitch we were going to make you famous. I'm not sure you need the help."

His smile is ear to ear. "Thank you, Alex. I just needed an opportunity. This is step one. Anyway, Mitch asked if I could play a bit during lunch."

Snapping a picture of Steve and I, Mitch adds, "I'm following your orders. We are making this guy a star, one UT event at a time."

Kids keep coming in and there must be five hundred in attendance by now. Staring off into the crowd, I'm amazed. Mitch pops up next to me. "Hey Alex, can we talk about Steve for a moment?"

Smiling, I ask, "What did you do?"

Guilty, he admits, "You were right, the music on the site is a great idea and Steve is awesome. I sent a friend at a music label a snippet. He loves it and wants the kid to come to New York. Are we, his managers?"

I'm excited but not sure how to react. "You were not a fan of my idea, but now you're his manager. I don't know anything about business, but I know even less about the music business. I say we help him out, but not sure we can become a talent agency. However, we should get him a lawyer. I don't want him going at this alone. I'll call Mike."

A dejected look forms on his face. I add, "You did nothing wrong. You are awesome. He can be your first guest on the podcast."

A surprised smile forms. "I thought you said there are a million podcasts that no one listens to. Why should we do one?"

Putting my arm on his bright blue polo, I explain, "If you want to do a podcast, start a talent agency. I'm all for it. As long as your priority is what we're building."

Shaking his head yes, he says, "Thanks. Even though part of me feels like you only want me to do the podcast so you can say, 'I told you so.'"

COOKIES KALE & COFFEE

Laughing, I admit, "Oh, I'll totally do that. And I love how you did a total one-eighty with the music."

Walking away, I dial up Mike. Since I've started my business, he's been more helpful than I imagined. He answers on the first ring. "Kid, if you are ringing me on a Saturday, you're in trouble."

Walking away from all the noise, I say, "Mitch and I found this kid who can sing. He sings pop songs in country style, and it sounds amazing. He's so good that a label in New York wants to meet him. I don't want to send him alone."

I can hear his deep breaths. "I'll text you Tamar's number. She represents a bunch of Chicago actors and one singer in LA. If he doesn't get a deal, I'm charging your company for her time."

"Mike, you are amazing. Thank you. Bill me." Half joking, I continue, "Now if he gets a deal, will we get a cut?"

With no emotion in his voice, he says, "Of course you get a finder's fee."

Hanging up the phone, I run back to the stage. Mitch introduces me and I momentarily freeze because five hundred people are staring at me. Mitch pats me on the back a little harder than he should, but it works.

Regaining my composure, "Thank you for coming. Thank you for visiting the site. Thank you for the hashtags and the posts. This event is really a way to say thank you, keep you active, and build this college community together. Have fun today!"

The sweat flows everywhere as I walk off the stage. Mitch laughs. "You'll get used to it."

Walking around the park is fun. These kids are really getting into it. Watching them compete makes me want to get in the game, but between taking pictures with Mitch and talking to Tamar I don't have the time.

The company running the event is doing a great job. They are also taking pictures and tracking winners. Everyone gets a shirt, but Tyler designed a winning shirt for one team. College kids love free shirts.

Food trucks and a bunch of restaurants are handing out samples. I grab a bottle of water. I'm starving, but I'm not sure we'll have enough food. Luckily, most students head out once the event ends. A handful stick around and listen to Steve. He starts off with Madonna. I thought "Like a Virgin" would sound odd as a country song, but it's awesome.

"Tamar, I know you got the video of Steve, but listen to this..."

After 10 seconds, I put the phone back to my ear. "What do you think?"

"Alex, he's awesome. Now let me enjoy my Saturday. We've already got everything planned. You don't have to sell me."

HITS AND HITS

Waking up Sunday morning, I pop out of bed and log onto my computer. Before working out, I check out the stats. I double check everything. Our single greatest day ever for College Comforts was yesterday.

That event exploded the site. All my emails are from our advertisers who are either thanking us or asking for more space. Our plates and other kitchenware for students set a record for daily sales. I knew this site would be a good thing, but just didn't know how we were going to make money. Affiliate relationship sales are also a record. I might be able to pay Jim back earlier than expected!

All I want to do is tell Robbie and the guilt is killing me. I had a phenomenal weekend with Ellie. She was a fun date at dinner, great at the Friday night event, but I still love Robbie.

We usually only email, but I decide to call her. She picks up right away and her warm voice is concerned. "Everything okay, babe?"

Trying to control my emotion, I explain, "We had two events so far in Texas and they were amazing. We had the best single day on the college site yesterday. Visits and sales are off the charts!"

I can feel her smile through the phone. "That's so great! I'm so happy for you. I miss you."

"Robbie, I miss you, too. Have the best time."

I can hear others talking the in background. Robbie, sounding rushed, says, "Hey, don't forget about me when you go public. We are heading back from France. It was gorgeous. I'll see you in a few months."

The line goes dead. Emotional confusion sets in as professional success, lust, and love cloud my mind. Lifting hotel weights helps ease my mind. I text my therapist/dad's girlfriend, Maddie.

Her advice is simple. "Celebrate success. Have fun. You can be in love with Robbie, and still have fun with Ellie. Robbie asked for a break. Love is tough. Don't beat yourself up. CELEBRATE!"

Walking back into my room, Ellie shoots up. "Alex, do you ever sleep? When did you become a vampire?"

Sitting on the chair across from the bed, I ask, "How do you do it with Ryan? Do you feel guilty?"

Her huge smile relaxes me. "Alex, I had the best time with you. I've wanted this for years and it exceeded my expectations. I still love Ryan and this summer will be filled with him. But I'm not even twenty. I want to have fun and experience college. It was hard at first, but now I consider myself lucky. These deals don't happen often. Enjoy the moment."

Already feeling better, I say, "Thanks Ellie. I'm new at this. Breakfast? My treat. Yesterday was the best day of sales and visits to the website!"

Winking at me, she says, "I like having a sugar daddy. This has been the cheapest weekend for me. Thanks. Also, the coding cowboy is my new best friend!"

I'm confused. "Really?"

"Alex, he's the best. He's getting me an internship and said we're going to do lunch once a week."

From the shower, I yell, "Glad to hear it! Do you think you can come with me to Madison? John would love to see you. He's a little player now."

I can hear her brushing her teeth. "John? Good for him! He's so cute and I was always surprised he didn't date more in high school. He was just too shy."

Walking to breakfast I feel like a CEO. My phone is blowing up. First Tyler calls. "The site is back up. I just increased the bandwidth. Josh actually did it, have to give him credit."

Hanging up with Tyler, I click over to Rachel. "Alex, what a day! Keep it up. The pictures got a ton of hits. I'm having Josh work on the talent section of the site."

Ellie cuts in as I hang up. "Wow, you're big time. Are you sure you have time for this?"

Taking her hand, I reassure her. "Yes, I'm sorry. This is not normal. I have one more." I take Mitch's call and he's loud!

Almost yelling, "FUCK! We brought down the site. I'm getting calls and emails from our advertisers. We are going to do a weekly newsletter and most of the space is sold. See you at the gym."

Adrenaline is pumping fierce inside of me and I'm concerned I might bust. Ellie points to a pulsating vein in my neck. "Are you okay, Alex?"

"I have no idea what cocaine feels like, or any drug for that matter, but this high is incredible. I'm trying not to let it get to me. I know I should be happy, but all I can think about are my next steps." It's like when I won a chess match but couldn't stop playing all the other moves in my head.

Two bagel breakfast sandwiches are dropped on our table, like our waitress is mad. With no emotion and gritting her teeth, she explains, "I'm sorry about that. It's my first day."

Laughing as she walks away, Ellie adds, "Enjoy the win. I think that was always hard for you. I remember when you hit the game-winning shot against GBN. You had one epic fist pump and then, when I congratulated you, you said, 'Time for GBS.'"

I shake my head in agreement. "That was my only buzzer beater. The only time I took the last shot, I somehow made it. Also, it was the only ball I ever saved."

Nostalgia fills my mind. I'm watching my greatest moments of high school. I see my last judo match, the game I scored 20 points, Ellie hugging me from behind at prom, John and I playing video games, my parents sitting in the stands, the time I got in trouble for telling a kid to fuck off when he made fun of me for playing chess, and all of the group projects.

Brunch ends and I don't want Ellie to go. She hugs me so tight that it's hard to breathe. This entire weekend has been wonderful. From baking to business success, to hooking up with Ellie, it has all turned out great. I know my mom is looking down on me with pride. She told me repeatedly, "That girl is crazy about you. Who cares about her boyfriend? She loves you."

With a kiss, she says, "Thank you, Alex. No bullshit, this was one of the best weekends of my life. I want you to keep being big time, but like Ferris Bueller said ..."

I know the line from the movie well, so I cut her off. "Thank you, Ellie. It's been amazing spending time with you. You taught me a few things. I'm going to enjoy the ride more, I promise."

One more hug, and I watch her cute little round butt walk away. I still can't believe we had sex.

The climbing gym is huge. This event is smaller than the one in the park. It's for our most dedicated influencers and their friends. Before walking in, I grab a giant coffee. This weekend has been fun, but a little too long.

Since I already checked the stats, and I'm 30 minutes early, I boulder. I wish there was a gym like this near me. All you need are shoes and chalk. They have huge fluffy mats to land on if you fall.

About 20 kids sit with Mitch and the manager, who has tattoos like he plays in the NBA, huge piercings in his ears, and no body fat.

I climb down and join them. I can hear whispers. "That's the owner. He looks so young."

After introductions, we get right to climbing. There's one tall and lanky girl that dominates every wall. It's like watching Spiderman train. She's fearless at times. She even jumps when she can't reach a hook.

Mitch taps me on the shoulder. "Hey, this week was awesome. The momentum will be building. We have Illinois, Indiana, and Madison, and then we need to hit other schools. I'll work with Rachel on a list."

"I need to focus on the business. Can someone else travel with you? It's a two-man job. I wish Jack was older, as he would be awesome at this. What about Rachel?"

He slumps his head. "Rachel will be fine. I think it's good for people to see you. This is your baby. Once things really take off, you're not going to be able to get away."

"Okay, I hear you. Let's climb. I think our food is getting here soon, and then it's off to the airport, right?"

Thirty minutes more of climbing is no joke. My hands, arms, and legs are all fatigued. Getting here early might not have been the best idea.

Mitch is snapping pictures while I ask the kids why they are so involved with the site. A slightly awkward kid from Jersey, Tommy, tells us the meet ups we plan helped him meet his friend group. A girl from California, with a golden tan, wanted to meet people without joining a sorority. The amazing climber emphatically says, "I'm a Journalism and Social Media major. I started posting things on your site to get practice." The last person who speaks is Jeremy from Chicago. His buddy Jack, who is from Northbrook, told him he had to spread the word.

"Jack told me that he worked for this company. I told my parents, and they sent me cookies from a place back home and bought me gift cards from local spots. It's been great."

THE LEGEND

The adrenaline of Texas has only begun to wear off, and now we are headed to The University of Wisconsin–Madison. I am looking forward to spending time with John and Jack. This won't be like last time. We are hosting an ultimate frisbee competition and having a smaller event at an Italian restaurant for a pasta making course. Two events in one weekend will allow for a little more down time.

Ellie and I have only exchanged a few messages, and that's for the best. After seeing all of Robbie's pictures with Roger, I'm okay with what happened, and I don't feel guilty flirting with Shelly. She told me that I'm her plus one for pasta making and I'm on her frisbee team. We have a stacked team. It's me, Jack, John, Shelly, Mitch, Shari, and Judd, who owns the bar where Shari works. I already told the team via email that I'm not going out Friday night because I need to be fresh for Saturday.

The website continues to grow. Event marketing, even the smaller ones, are helping us grow. Jim has been very happy with the results. In other exciting news, Steve, the singer, is negotiating a contract with Mitch's buddy. Tamar has been emailing me all week with updates.

Between my dad and my poker buddies, it's like they are fighting to prove who's prouder of me. I feel guilty that most of the poker game is spent discussing my company. Then during break-fast and dinner my dad congratulates me on my success. I'm still barely able to pay myself. I'll celebrate once I can move off my dad's insurance.

Mitch and I decide to drive out to Madison at 3:00, so we miss most of the Friday traffic. The week has been so busy that the moment we hit the highway, I pass out. The light rain bouncing off the car keeps me asleep the entire ride. I wake up feeling completely refreshed.

Mitch watches me wipe the sleep out of my eyes. "I'm sorry, Mitch. I thought I would sleep maybe twenty minutes. I cannot believe we're almost here."

Concentrating on the road, he says, "No worries. I didn't feel guilty listening to country music."

"Bob got you into country in one weekend?"

With a guilty laugh, he explains, "No. I always liked country but forgot about it. He reminded me how awesome it is."

Looking at him, I ask, "Is he your boyfriend now? Since we have an office, I don't get as much one on one time with you."

He grips the wheel a little too tightly. "I have no idea what's going on with us. He wants a relationship, but I'm not sure that's what I want. Long distance relationships are tough. What's up with you and all of your girls?"

Shaking my head in disbelief, "A year ago, I would've never imagined hooking up with Ellie, dating Robbie, and someone like Shelly being into me. This is nuts. Ellie told me that was the greatest weekend of her life, but she's with Ryan. Robbie is happy with my work success, but across the pond galivanting around with some dude. Shelly is so flirty. I have no idea what's going to happen with her."

Looking me in the eye at a stoplight, he says, "I guess the expression is true—'pimping is not easy.'"

"Not for this chess geek. Hey, if it rains Sunday, where are we doing this rock paper scissors tournament?"

He lowers the music as if it's about to get serious in here. "Plan B. Judd's bar does not open until later on Sunday. He offered it to us, but it will be tight. He said that he can fit us in if he moves around tables. The forecast is sunny, and the rain is dissipating."

Scrolling through my emails, I explain, "I feel guilty leaving. I should be working all weekend. We have a lot of interest in ads to put on the site. Josh, Simon, and Tyler have been working on it all week. Also, we need to send out an email about the ads you sold. I hope we don't get a lot of unsubscribes on the first go."

Mitch attempts to relax me. "Dude, we have thirty thousand email addresses and we're still growing. Some people will unsubscribe. Our open rate will be fine."

A smack on the door alarms both of us. Rolling down my window, I say, "Jack, you asshole. You scared the crap out of us. Do you have a tracker on us?"

With a goofy grin, he says, "Of course. Come on, we have reservations."

Jack and John lead us to a restaurant a few blocks away. We are meeting Shari and some others after dinner.

John, as if he's a historian, is detailing my last visit. "Mitch, it was so epic. He literally carried this girl home. That's after he tossed two huge Ohio State fans on their ass. We have a pool guessing what Alex will accomplish this weekend."

I try to play off the attention. "This weekend we will bring more visitors to the site, and we'll win the frisbee competition."

In case Mitch didn't know, Jack brags, "Alex does not lose. Well, he does not like to lose. Last time we played darts, and he was pissed that it took twelve rounds to beat these drunk girls. He also does a fist pump when he wins basketball games, and it's amazing."

Being the only one old enough to legally drink, Mitch gets a cocktail. Like the excellent salesman he is, he listens closely before adding his own stories. "Trust me guys, I have seen this guy in action. At the bouldering event, he showed up thirty minutes early to warm-up. His buddy TK came over a few weeks ago. Alex knew TK would want to shoot around, so in preparation, Alex took two to three hundred shots a day in preparation."

I defend myself. "Hey, I took the first two games of horse."

COOKIES KALE & COFFEE

The smell of basil and garlic fills the air. I can tell this is going to be a great meal. The owner, who is wearing jeans and a checkered shirt, stops by the table. "Hello, I'm Evan. You must be Mitch and Alex. We are very excited for the pasta class. We've done a few classes already and everyone really likes it. Sunday afternoon is quiet."

I chime in first. "Thank you for hosting the event. We are excited! How are the leads coming from the site?"

Pulling up a chair, Evan sits down and gets comfortable. "We get a lot of parents buying gift cards. That was the goal because this place isn't cheap. When we do coupons on the site, we offer a limited number, and they always sell out. Mitch suggested creating another company that only does pizza and market it through the site. We tested that out a few times, it was great, but I want to focus on dining. My next venture is a pizza and pasta pickup and delivery spot. I'll totally use the site for that."

I can tell what Mitch is thinking. This is a college town and affordable dining is what people want. He needs to let it go. Instead, he says, "Evan, it's great to meet you in person. Whatever help you need, let me know. We just added a restaurant consultant and we're adding a nutritional expert."

With his eyebrows hunched, he says, "Tell me about the nutritional expert."

Since he's my neighbor, I cut in. "This guy is super smart. He spent thirty years working in a lab as a chemist. His son has epilepsy, so he's been making ketogenic food for decades. It helped his son and transformed his body. He decided to quit the lab and started making healthy meals. His focus was the workout scene, but the bulk of his business is helping those who are severely obese."

Amazed, he asks, "How did you connect with him? I would love to learn more."

Proudly, I respond, "He's my neighbor! My mom was a baker and they used to cater events together. Dean taught my mom how to bake with monk fruit, almond flour, and other fringe ingredients."

A waitress whispers in Evan's ear, "I've got to go guys. We'll be in touch. Enjoy the meal and order whatever you want. It's on me, fellas. See you soon."

John points at me. "Free meals! The Alex folklore builds."

Sitting at dinner with my best friend and my new friends feels great. Until Robbie came along, my life was depressing. Aside from John, I had no one.

Sitting back, watching my new crew eat, is unbelievably comforting. I never had a crew before, and this feels right. With way too much pasta in our stomachs we head out.

The moment I walk into Judd's bar, I see Shelly. Playing hard to get, she waves at me, and I feel obligated to come up to her. Her ripped abs sneak out at the bottom of a short shirt, and her black leggings conform to every perfect curve on her legs.

"Alex, you're looking skinny. Don't try and out lean me."

Kissing her on the cheek and then stepping back, I say, "It's great to see you, too. I need to find Judd and Shari. Then I'll be back."

With a smile she says, "Shari's working the back of the room. We'll stop by in a bit."

With a simple smile, I leave her and head to the back. Shari spots me while pouring a pitcher of beer at the back bar. Immediately, she places it down and runs towards us. I get a running hug. I feel several jealous eyes on me—most notably, Shelly's.

"Alex! I'm so happy you stopped in. There's a table in the corner that I saved just in case. I have big news. I have to check on a few tables and then I'll fill you in."

Waving to the guys to join me, I sit down. While everyone chats, I worry. Is Shari going to quit? I already offered her a full-time position once she graduates.

Placing a pitcher of some sort of lemonade drink on the table and a pitcher of water, Shari joins us. "Boys, I'm moving to Chicago! I have a roommate lined up and an apartment! I can't wait to have in-person meetings!"

Relief spills out all over my face. Mitch is also excited. "That's the best news I've heard all day! What area are you moving to in Chicago?"

Full of excitement, she says, "A few blocks north of Wrigley Field. I have a parking spot and an in-unit washer and dryer and dishwasher! It's close to the train and I'm not too far from the highway or Lake Shore Drive!"

After everyone fills up their glass, I toast Shari. "To big moves, big sales, and big-time fun!"

After only a few sips of lemonade, I stick to water. Is it bad that I really want to win tomorrow? Second place would be best. I want a team of influencers to win. I know Jack is an athlete, but I'm not sure about the rest of the team. John has quick feet, so that will help, but the rest are wildcards.

John brings me back to the conversation. "I'm really getting into data and looking for trends. You had a huge spike with hits while you guys were in Texas. That's only starting to slow down now. I'm guessing, if you hit big schools every other month, in a year, we might average over five hundred thousand hits a week." He pauses and we all stare in disbelief. "Give me three more months and I'll have more accurate estimates." Taking a sip of his drink, he holds up one finger. "Wait, I'm also researching the best days for hotels, restaurants, and clothing stores to advertise. I think we can provide blueprints and it will increase sales. We are not just taking your money, we are telling you how to best invest it."

Mitch opens his mouth before I can. "John, you are my hero."

Business talk is interrupted by an old friend, Natalie. Approaching our table out of nowhere, I see her dark skin and abundant cleavage on display. "My knight in shining armor visits and doesn't say hello?"

I stand up and look for Shelly. I signal with my head for her to come save me while I give Natalie a hug. "Natalie, the ninja. How are you? Has anyone else carried you home recently?"

She laughs politely. "No, I've cut down on the day drinking. I learned; I can't keep up."

Shelly makes it to the table. "Hi Nat. Alex, are you ready to go?"

I turn towards the table. "Don't drink too much because it's a big game tomorrow. Natalie, have a great night."

Shelly offers me her well-manicured hand, and we quickly walk outside. Turning to me, she is almost my height in her heels, "I'm going to get a lot of shit for that. You realize that girl lives a door down from me."

Feeling confident, "Well you won't have to see her tonight."

With her head cocked to the side, she asks, "Oh, is that right? You think you have a sure thing over here?"

Before I can answer, she kisses me. Wrapping her arms around me, a twinge of guilt sets in. I remind myself that Robbie wanted a break ... and Roger.

With are fingers linked, I ask, "Where are we going?"

"You'll see." The campus is buzzing with kids, bars, and restaurants. It's a different vibe than Texas. There's not live music around every corner, but a lot more diversity. Ten minutes of walking takes us to the AC Hotel.

We head to the bar, which luckily does not ask for ID. Shelly's friend is a waitress and takes us to a table. The crowd is dressed nicer than me, but Shelly fits right in. With an openness I'm not used to, she asks me, "What's going on with your girl? How are you doing with all this business stuff?"

I feel remarkably at ease with her, which is weird because I was really intimidated last time we met. "Robbie and I are on a break. It was her idea, not mine. I miss her. She's still the person I want to call about wins and losses. I know she's having fun and traveling around with a new guy. I'm just trying to not think about it."

Her hazel eyes sparkle. She is only paying attention to me and not glancing at her phone. It's nice and unusual. "What about work? Do you ever have Alex time?"

Thinking, I say, "In the mornings I usually work out alone. I listen to a book on tape and just escape. However, I end up jotting down a ton of notes. My dad was all for me dropping out of school, which of course led me to taking night classes. I have no idea if that was his intent. By the fall, I'll be done with my associates degree, so I can spend the next year focused on business."

Putting lip balm on her full lips, she asks, "So you work all day, take classes at night, and travel for work on the weekends?"

COOKIES KALE & COFFEE

Laughing, I explain, "Yes, that's my life. With all my credits from high school and starting college classes during the summer, I can graduate soon. Why not hammer this out? If next year goes well, I'll investigate online programs. If business tanks, I could probably get into an even better school."

My phone buzzes. "It's Mitch, and we are staying at this hotel! He has my luggage."

I text him back, "How can we afford this place?"

A smiling emoji hits me back. "They are an advertiser!"

Shelly talks to her friend as I run to see Mitch, check in and get my luggage. Mitch greets me with a hug and reminds me, "If you want to compete, don't stay out too late."

Patting him on the shoulder, "Thanks. Are you any good at frisbee?"

Cocking his head to the side, he says, "Maybe? I've been waiting for you to ask that for days. Rachel and I had a bet that you would want to practice in the office."

"I've been practicing with my dad for a few weeks. Tell anyone, and I'll deny it. I'm good with both hands. That should help."

Shaking his head in disbelief, Mitch walks away.

Walking towards our table, I see an older guy in a nice suit flirt with Shelly. She's really striking, and I get it. She waves to me, so this time it's my turn to save her. I smile at him, and he mutters something like "Lucky guy," and we walk away.

With her arm over my shoulder, she asks, "Want to check out your room?"

I wonder what's going to happen next. "Sure. Tell me about you. You asked me a million questions. How did you pick Madison? What are you studying? What are your intentions for the evening?"

Laughing, she says, "I had a friend from high school that came here. After one visit, I was hooked. The people are chill, the school is great, and it's close to home. I have no idea what my major will be. I like business or psychology. I would love to do a combination of both. I was also supposed to walk on to the basketball team."

Surprised, I ask, "Wait, what?"

She laughs. "I was a three-sport athlete in high school. I played soccer, basketball, and tennis. The summer before college, I just worked out with weights and let my body heal. I had no pain, I actually grew boobs, and boys actually started talking to me. But I just didn't have it in me anymore. I scrimmage with the team sometimes. I'm a weekend warrior now."

"Impressive! Anything else to share?"

The hotel room is small, but it has a great view of the city. When the door clicks, she says, "Just my intentions. Well, they're not so innocent."

For the first time in months, my watch alarm goes off before I'm out of bed. Growing up, I was required to be downstairs by 7:05 a.m. Not that I was sleeping, I was usually watching chess or basketball clips, but I didn't want to get in trouble, so I set my watch. It worked like a charm.

My eyes search the bed. There is no sign of Shelly. Did she leave when I feel asleep? That can't be safe. Scanning the rest of the room, I notice the bathroom door is closed. "Are you okay, Shelly?"

Yelling, she answers, "Yes. I didn't want to wake you. You looked so peaceful."

Turning on my computer, I say, "Thanks, this is late for me. You really wore me out."

Laughing, she says, "That's what I do. So now that you know I'm an athlete, do you feel like we could win this thing today?"

Searching the statistics I tell her, "Hell yeah. We are going to smoke these guys. I'm not sure about Shelly or Mitch."

Walking past me with only her underwear on is a sight to see. "You are, like perfect."

With a big smile, she says, "Thanks, this is me chunky."

Confused, I tell her, "You have abs. Don't be crazy."

She shakes her head. "I'm fine with it, really. I'm not crazy salad girl. I just know what my body is capable of. I had abs like you. I'm lucky it was a combination of genetics, diet, and way too much exercise."

Tossing on exercise shorts and a shirt, Shelly sits next me. "Want to hoop it up for real?"

With a cocky grin, I say, "Jack said you were good in high school. Don't worry, I'll go easy on you."

After we speed walk to her dorm as a warmup, she changes, grabs a ball, and drives us to an outdoor court. At this hour, there's no one out here but us.

It's perfect weather today. The sun is shining and there's a slight breeze. Taking turns warming up, I'm in awe. Shelly does not miss a shot. I might lose this game. Hopefully, my height and quickness will make this competitive.

We trade hoops. She's like Jordan, hitting fade away jumpers and left-handed layups. We don't call out the score, but after 40 minutes, we both know I'm up by two. Sweat drips down her face and she steps behind the three-point line. "How about if I make this, we call it a tie."

"Works for me." Before I finish my sentence, the ball swishes through the net.

With a familiar cocky grin, she says, "Not bad, Alex."

GAME TIME

The park is filled with college kids. Not as many as Texas, but there's at least 200 people here. There's no place for me to talk, which is nice, the events coordinator has us sign in and points us in the right direction.

We are all in athleisure wear, except Mitch. He has on a teal polo, and I can't tell if his gray pants are for the office or exercise. They are branded with some fancy sportswear logo, so I'm assuming it's for working out. Before our match starts, we warm up. Everyone can catch the frisbee well, and Judd can throw it the entire field. For an out-of-shape bar owner with a gut, he has a cannon for an arm. Shari is quick and Jack hasn't dropped a pass yet.

The first game is easy. I'm pretty sure they are drinking beer when we take breaks. I have no idea the score, but we are winning by a lot.

Two hours pass in what seems like the blink of an eye. We've played several games and are now in the finals. While on a break I catch up on emails. I have no idea how my inbox gets flooded, on a Saturday. Most are self-generated reports. Our product lines continue to grow, and we are somehow in 100 schools. The data never stops coming in. Good thing John is into analytics.

Jack yells, "Put it down!" I drop my phone as our challengers reach the field, they look like pros. Tall, lean, and athletic. Even the girls on their team are almost my height. They all have white shirts on with nicknames on the back, and sweat bands on their head that say, "ROZELLE" a nod to Jim McMahon and the 1985 Chicago Bears. I have a slight crush on this team.

All the other competitors are watching us, like this is the Superbowl. It's hilarious. We hired a few food trucks to come, I thought that would be the highlight.

We win the coin toss and have them throw us the frisbee to start. I figured that if we have any chance of winning, we have to score first. And we do, on a beautifully diving catch by Jack.

They respond with a score of their own. This game is a lot more running than I expected. Judd is falling behind, but with his strong arm, we capitalize on a few scores.

With a minute left in the game, it's tied. I have no idea how we've kept up with them. They are close to scoring again. Shelly somehow tips a pass, Judd catches it, and with his quick release he tosses the nugget all the way down the field, and all I can think, don't drop it. Using both hands, I catch it and the crowd goes wild.

I hear one, possibly drunk kid yell, "That's the fucking CEO!"

The entire team runs to the goal, and we are celebrating like we won the world cup. Jack and John both take off their shirts. Mitch is staring at me with a hint of disgust, "I thought we agreed—second place."

Shelly, shaking her head, "Fuck that." I like her more now than I did before the game. We shake hands. I grab Judd some water, he looks pale. "Thanks, Alex. I need to exercise more."

Jack chimes in, "Are you kidding me. You're like Aaron Rogers. Where did you get that cannon?"

Laughing like he stole it, "Four years of high school ball, lots of darts owning a bar, and karate."

The food trucks take off before we leave the field. Judd offers us free lunch and drinks. His restaurant is quiet until dinner time.

Everyone relives the game as we wait for the food to come. I'm just listening. Everyone is so happy. This was a memorable event.

As my lawyer/event planner always says, a good event, is a safe event. I'm thrilled by the attendance and that no one got hurt. Maybe we keep these events more like bags, less likely to blow out a knee tossing a bean bag.

Jack starts breaking down everyone's game. "Alex is like Randy Moss—he runs by everyone, jumps up and gets the ball. Shelly is Khalil Mack, knocking down passes, sacking the QB. And then you have John. He's like a spider monkey, somehow getting open, streaking down the sidelines. I can't forget QB one: Judd. Seriously, looked like you were taking smoke breaks, and then all of a sudden with no effort you flip it fifty yards."

Shelly turns to Jack, "What about you? You had a solid tourney. A few picks, a bunch of points. You're like Larry Fitzgerald. Consistent. You'll go across the middle." Everyone laughs.

I pull Mitch aside as the others compare stats, "I know you didn't want us to win, but look at that camaraderie. Everyone is so happy."

Mitch, like an older brother puts his hand on my shoulder, "Alex, this was a lot of fun. I've never won something like this in my life. This will be my winning story. But we still would've bonded if some random kids won. Think about marketing, those kids were awesome. We got great pictures of them, and they would have this awesome story to tell their friends about."

I see his point, "I get it. Listen I have the team manager's phone number. We'll have a pic of them on our site. Let's get an interview of all their players. We can still market them. Enjoy the win."

Sitting at the table, I'm starting to like Shelly a lot. Robbie is still my number one, and I had a great time with Ellie but there's something about Shelly. I can't explain it, maybe it's the jock thing. She's like one of the boys, but really hot. Maybe it's the curiosity aspect. I know everything about Ellie, and that was comforting but not intriguing.

When lunch ends, we all separate, except for Mitch and me. We walk back to the hotel in silence. From the basketball and then four hours of running around, it's tiring. Mitch also looks spent, "Mitch, you played great. Seriously. You had three pass breaks, ran in two scores, and threw three scores to me alone."

Surprised at my memory, "You were keeping stats?"

Thinking for a minute, "Only a few. I don't even know why. Or how many scores I had."

Standing right in front of me, "Alex, you dominated. Are you kidding me? Jack was pretty good, too. You were in a zone. Don't let this get to your head, but MVP. I mean, you were down field the second Judd had that pick. It's like you knew."

Trying not to let my ego grow to large, "Thanks. My dad repeatedly used to tell me, have fun. You don't have to win. But that's all I want to do. I've never been a rub it in your face guy, I just hate losing. And honestly, all I do is work and workout. The benefits of not having a social life."

Reaching the hotel, Mitch and I separate. Laying down on the bed, I pass out.

Waking up, it's dark outside. I slept through dinner. My phone is filled with messages from Mitch, Shelly, Jack, and John. Returning the texts quickly, I hop online. Another huge spike in hits to the site.

Returning emails, and assigning work takes me to nine. Everyone should be at the hotel bar by now. With a quick shower, I toss on a polo and jeans.

The team is sitting around a high table. The sun gave Shelly a beautiful tan. She's wearing a little makeup and her eyes look huge and inviting. I stand next to her, and I can smell her sweet perfume. She smacks my butt, like, we're still on the sideline. "Well rested?"

Everyone is sipping on champagne like we won the Superbowl. "Best nap I've had since the ride to Madison. It was a long day. Please tell me, I'm not the only one who crashed."

Everyone raises their hands. Shari, raising her hand, "I have to run to work. I just wanted to thank you guys. That was super fun. The last time I won something athletic was High School Cross Country. And man, if I didn't have the endurance base, I would be at home right now, like Judd."

Jack, smiling, "Ha. I knew he wasn't going to make it out for this drink. I shot him a text. He said his wife put him in a bath."

John sneaks between Mitch and me. He puts his arm over my shoulder, "Alex, I'm happy, you're happy. You deserve it. You had two rough years, shitty. You can deal with anything now. And this success is earned." Taking a sip of his drink, "But you should know, I'm still faster than you."

Laughing, it feels like water is about to shoot out my nose. It's a good thing I'm not drinking. "John, thanks. I appreciate it. I appreciate you. Seriously. You were always so caring. Above and beyond. Never called me out for crying. I owe you. And I'll race you right now."

Grabbing my hand, Shelly leans into me, "John, are you taking Alex home tonight?"

With a confident grin, John practically yells, "Yes I am. Back off, my man!"

Starvation hits me, "Guys, what if I order some room service, and we watch a movie in my room or something, is that lame?"

Mitch shakes his head yes, "I'm so fucking tired. We ran a marathon today."

Shelly who's dressed to impress, leans into me, "I'm so happy you said that. I'm going to pass out in your bed. Is that okay?"

With a yawn, I reply, "That's cool. I want a rematch on the court, though."

With a serious look, Shelly asks, "Hey, can you teach my sorority self-defense?"

"You're brilliant. What a great thing we should offer on the site." I kiss her on the check, "What an idea. We are going to do that across all our campuses. You live in Buffalo Grove, right?"

Shaking her head yes, I continue. "Next time you come, I'll show a bunch of stuff. In the meantime, I'll find a teacher for you here."

PR MACHINE

Shelly didn't just give me one idea; she gave me a million. Why don't we have Campus for Good? With a lot of help from Rachel, we start building an area dedicated to volunteering, tutoring, donating, and filling needs in different communities. Aside from influencers, we have community ambassadors. They are all volunteers who help build up their community.

Initially I was concerned no one would want to do this for free. Jim loved the idea and offered a grant from his foundation to offer a stipend and budget for the volunteer projects. His only request—nowhere do we mention his foundation or him. I was amazed on all fronts: one, that he has a foundation, and two, the anonymous nature of his giving.

Mitch has taken on more responsibility as I work on building our philanthropic arm. Stories pour in every day; from those we help and the volunteers about how thankful they are to have an opportunity to give back. All campus visits now include a community volunteering event.

Tyler hovering above my desk, "Hey, we need to talk about Campus for Good. It's growing faster than our other site."

Confused, I ask, "And that's a bad thing? Let's sell advertising on that site, too, and donate some of the sales to the local community."

With his hands out to the side, like I'm robbing him, "That's awesome. But does it look bad if this site is more popular than the other one?"

He already knows what I'm going to say, so he continues, "Dumb question. I'll get a quote on how much this will cost."

Rachel eavesdropping, asks me, "I'll research setting up a 501 (c)(3)." Reading my blank stare, she explains, "That's just what a nonprofit is. Maybe we take donations. Or we could have a foundation instead. I'll see what requires less red tape." She pauses, and then ads, "I'll also look into starting a donor advised fund."

Turning towards Rachel, "Thank you! I have no idea what that is but fill me in later."

Looking out into the office, I see everyone working hard. The only problem is, I need them to work harder. I'll have to ask my poker bodies how to get more out of everyone. If revenue jumps, I'll give out bonuses.

Pulling a chair up to the web guys, Tyler and Simon look a little surprised. They're usually asking me for money, more servers, or some software. I always say yes. My usual request from them is improved speed and more white space. "Gentlemen. How does it feel to be at full staff? Josh, we can't wait for you to be full time."

Simon, cutting through the bull, "What's up?"

"I need marketing and PR help. I have a few interviews coming up, and we should put them on the site. Either of you guys write?"

Tyler raises his hand but says nothing. "Ok. Work with Mitch. I'm fine with search, and buying ads, but I need help getting things posted, spreading the word."

Tyler shaking his head yes, finally adds, "I can write. I already do the editing for the site."

Simon is looking at me like I asked him to kill a dolphin or something. "Simon, why do you look so pissed?"

"Alex, we have twenty different sites now. We have been outsourcing some work, but we are drowning. We need a team of people. Get me a few coders, designers, and a helpdesk person. I can't fix paper jams and keep this shit rolling."

Rubbing my hands together, in the hopes it gives me an idea, "This quarter is going to be our biggest in revenue. You build a plan, who we need, what it will cost, and some alternatives. We could have an intern at each school work on this. We pay them, they help with design. Of course, using our template. Great experience for them, cheaper labor for us, and a pipeline of talent."

With a little relief on his face, "Thanks Alex. The past few months we've grown like crazy, but our staff has not increased. I need help."

Josh cuts in, "I'll be starting full time in two weeks. I have a friend, who's ten times better at this than me. Can we get someone a work visa?"

With my hands in the air, "Maybe? Talk to Rachel."

Growing fast is a good problem to have, that's what I tell myself. Since I've been back from Madison, I've had no time to wonder about Robbie, think about Shelly, or text Ellie.

TK was supposed to start working soon, but a few teams in Europe want to sign him. I can take that money and apply it to technology, but I need more sales guys to bring in the revenue to pay for IT. It's a vicious cycle. What's really weighing on my conscience: I have to see if Mitch would restructure his contract. He's making almost double what I am. And yes, he deserves a lot of it but when he started, I had no idea what compensation should be and that he would sell so much.

The stress is starting to weigh on me, I can feel it like a heavy coat that I can't take off. I can't even enjoy the press because I feel like the rest of the team is pissed. When I'm quoted in the paper, I always give the team credit but I'm afraid they resent me for being so out in front.

Ignoring my anxiety, I answer my phone. "Jim! How are you doing, buddy?"

Pushing the negativity out the window, I smile, hoping he senses optimism. "Alex, can you do a longer lunch today?"

Now I'm nervous again, "For you? Sure."

I can sense his happiness, "Okay. Grab your gym bag. I know you brought it in case I flaked. I'm outside."

Once a month we have lunch, I'm not sure he realizes that our lunches are the highlight of my month. His confidence and advice always seem to put me at ease. We are also growing, which he enjoys. I feel like each lunch is a free class in entrepreneurship.

The first thing I see as I walk outside, his muscular arm hanging outside his Ferrari. He's wearing a brown sleeveless shirt and black shorts. "Where are we going, Mister Muscles?"

With an embarrassed smile, "You'll see. How are things?"

Without meaning to, I feel myself word vomiting, "The IT guys cornered me, they need more help. Three more bodies. Mitch's salary is like double mine. The insurance for our community events is more expensive than the social events. That site is also getting more hits than the other ones. We are getting a lot of press, well I am, and I think that's pissing everyone off. And ads just topped kitchenware sales. So that's a win."

With his perfect smile, "Welcome to start up culture. Everyone sees the shorts, and flip flops, and has no idea that you're working twenty-four seven. You have the dollars. Hire more staff. And I have an idea about Mitch."

Taking a sip of iced coffee, Jim continues, "Tom Brady—that guy restructured his deal several times, so they could have more talent on the team. Approach it like that. And don't say cut, re-structure. Offer him stock in place of some of salary. Rick can help you with that."

Sitting in a sports car of this caliber is cool, flying down streets, not so cool. You feel every bump, every turn, and the acceleration is so quick it's like being on a rollercoaster. Of course, Jim, one arm on the wheel, aviator glasses on, just smiles and keeps racing.

Approaching a park, Jim slows down and parks. He pops the small trunk, and it's so tiny the basketball is about all that fits. "I thought we could play some ball, then grab lunch."

I can feel the tension in my shoulders ease up. This is my kind of break. The ball is brand new. It almost sticks to my hand as I dribble. On this perfect Spring day, we're the only two people out here. With a smile, Jim asks, "I heard you're pretty good. How about we play to eleven, by ones?"

Taking a few practice shots, I can see Jim has great form. He has a nice arc on the ball, but his dribbling is not the best. Internally I'm thinking, do I always size up the competition?

"Jim, I'm out of practice, but that works for me. Loser has to buy lunch."

Shaking his head no: "I'll buy either way. But I get the ball first."

His first shot rattles off the back board, right into my hands. With one juke, I'm passed Jim for a layup.

"Not bad kid. Remember, I've got over twenty years on you." Trying to snake around me, I steal the ball. I can tell this irritated his competitiveness. He tries to steal the ball back, but he's too late.

Looking at Jim with a smile, "Like Jordan, I've got mid-range."

"You weren't even alive when he played." Giving him some space, Jim hits his next shot.

"I think he was on the Wizards the year I was born." Taking a step behind the three-point line, I drain my shot.

Jim laughs, "I didn't realize you would embarrass me."

Shrugging my shoulders, "I'm not even keeping score anymore."

Faking right, Jim goes left and takes a step back shot. I grab the rebound and he yells, "Fuck."

Dribbling the ball through my legs and behind my back, "You do not like to lose either. It's killing you."

With a quick step, I slash to the middle and drop another basket with my left hand. Jim fires an angry arm in the air. "I don't like to lose, but I knew you would beat me. I just thought it would be good to get you out of the office. Are you left-handed?"

Shaking my head, no, "My dad told me, if I had a few left-handed shots, I would be hard to defend."

I leave him an open shot and he sinks it. With an exhale, he stares deeply into my soul. Well, that's how it feels. "I like how you're building community, increasing volunteerism at schools. I heard at Indiana you had a team make five hundred lunches. And you're building equity. You need to take a day off. Enjoy the success. Plan some fun stuff for your staff. Sounds like they're stressed out."

Sinking a shot deep behind the line, "Thanks, Jim. I needed this. I'll have more fun. Not that I'm a boring guy; I get really focused."

Attempting to make a shot from where I did, Jim misses but keeps talking. "Most people are not like that. They need some distraction, plan one happy hour or bags tournament, or something every month. Don't turn into one of those companies that everyone starts drinking at four but a little fun might ease your stress."

Getting his rebound, "I can do that. I've been reading all these management and leadership books. And it's like obvious advice, tell the truth, challenge staff, ask them how they are doing. I need some insider tips."

Guiding me back to the car, "You'll figure it out. Don't burn out. Even in my prime work-acholic state, I took a day off for softball. In six years, I never missed a game. That's how I met my wife. She was subbing for a friend. After the game, we all had drinks. The rest is history. You drive stick?"

He hands me the keys, "Yes, but are you sure about this?"

With a grin, "I have insurance."

Snapping the seatbelt in, I forget everything. Jim puts his hand on my shoulder, "Slow and steady. You'll be fine."

This car is probably over six figures. Then I remember I drove Joe's car. "One of my poker buddies trusted me with his fancy car. I'll be fine. See I have a hobby and friends."

Laughing, like I told the funniest joke, he adds, "Really. Most of those guys are a half century older than you. And they talk business the entire game. Rick told me."

Whizzing through the neighborhood feels good. We normally eat at this brunch place in Winnetka, so I head there. With the slightest pressure on the gas, I'm at 90. I slow down, and a cop pulls up right next to me. He rolls down the window, and all I can think is that I'm going to get a ticket.

Jim is calm. The cop looks at the car, then me, "You have one cool dad. Drive safe. Beautiful car."

I finally exhale, "Dad, thanks for letting me take the car out."

Rolling his eyes, "Do I really look old enough to have a kid your age? And how are you driving this car so well?"

"You could have a kid my age. And my real dad taught me well."

We sit down at a table with a *Chicago* magazine on it. Jim scrolls through it while I read the menu. He always orders the same thing, veggie omelet with a pancake on the side. With a Stern voice, "Alex!" I turn my head, and there's a picture of me in a baker's hat from Austin. The title: "Young CEO gets his hand dirty."

With a proud smile, "How do you not tell your investor about this?"

Shrugging my shoulders, "I totally forgot about that. The interview was a month ago. I never heard back from the writer, so I assumed there was no story. The funny thing is, that day, was less work more fun."

Jim looks deep in thought, then turns to me. "What if you brought a ping-pong table in the office?"

With my hands in the air like I won something, "Yes. I have a table at home. I'm sure my dad wouldn't mind. Great idea."

WELCOME BACK

The simple addition of a ping-pong table and a few more staff members has boosted moral. No one is really that good, or competitive, aside from Tyler and me. We have lots of battles. I usually win, but he has beat me a few times.

Work has not slowed down, but time has. Today Robbie is coming back! Knowing that she was coming back, to stay with me before school starts, made the last two weeks feel like months. I've said nothing about Roger, but it's all I want to know about. Mitch has suggested I don't ask, and I only say I went out and had some fun. No details, no names.

I feel guilty about my two trysts. I enjoyed them, but it wasn't the same. There's no doubt I would rather have Robbie than anyone else. I guess she feels the same or she wouldn't have asked to stay with me.

Sitting at O'Hare, with half a dozen Nutella specials, I'm nervous. Standing outside my car, scanning for Robbie, my eyes tear up when I see her. Remarkably, she's more gorgeous then when she left. With golden skin and dark hair, her smile is brighter than before. Running, like she just returned from war, we hug. It's tight, strong, and euphoric.

Before I can utter a word, "I missed you so much, Alex! You look so skinny! I got chubby and you got leaner, it's not fair. God did I miss you. I was so nervous to call you—what if you found someone else."

Pulling out the tray of cookies, "I missed you. All these crazy business highs and lows—I wanted to share them with you. I was worried you'd replaced me."

Shaking her head, "I could never. All I did was travel, eat, eat some more, and drink wine. It was great. I learned a ton about Europe and their cuisine. I joined this olive oil club. It's the best, and I have some amazing balsamic vinegars."

Looking at the cookies, her dark eyes seem to expand. "Ah. Those look amazing." Biting into one before I can put her luggage in the trunk, she adds, "Nothing like this over there."

Taking out her camera, she snaps a picture of the plate, and sends it to a friend with the words "STILL LOVED!" Within a second, I notice it's Roger. My heart sinks in my chest, caving into my spine.

Noticing my concern she begins to explain, "Alex, Roger is ...," pauses to take another bite, and then continues, "... just a friend."

Hopping in the car, "Jack might have mentioned him to me."

Laughing, "You are so jealous. I'm not the only one." Taking the last bite of her cookie and still laughing, "He's gay. But that's cute. I can see it on your face."

I swallow. The only reason I reached out to Ellie was because of Roger. The only reason I hung out with Shelly: Roger.

"Alex, we were also on a break. And that had to be the dumbest idea I've had. I was unconcerned with men, except you. I kept thinking because I was so adamant about taking a break, and you are so damn cute, I would come home, and you would be enjoying the single life. All these women's hanging on you. I'm sorry."

Taking Mitch's advice, "I worked a lot, I had some fun. And I missed you. Work never stops. I'm trying to make the office a fun place that's also profitable. The cutlery business is still doing well, but web ads for the college site are outpacing it. Finally. Mitch is like this force of nature driving sales. And the IT needs are constant."

Pulling into my garage, Robbie puts a hand over mine. "Are you happy? There's always college."

Grabbing her luggage, "I'm sadistic. I love it. It's this roller-coaster of success and failures, every single day. Two more years, and it's time for something new. I have no idea what or why, but I want this to grow big, and then sell it or have someone else run it."

Smiling with her eyes and mouth, "Perfect. I'll graduate then, and I can take care of us for a while."

With a kiss that sends goose bumps through my body, we head inside. Streamers and a "WELCOME BACK" sign greet Robbie. My dad and Maddie have made dinner, and hugs are exchanged. My dad picks her up when they hug.

Robbie, surprised, "Thanks everyone. I really missed this. Jerry, you were so nice to me. I knew your son for a minute, and you opened up your house to me. I don't think you realize how much it meant to me. I cooked in here. I learned some great recipes overseas and brought you guys amazing oils and stuff."

I always give my mom credit for the amazing things she taught me, but I've learned so much from my dad. The little things, like how to drive stick, his style of child rearing is my style of management. He gave me all this freedom and then warned me it could all disappear. I'll never forget, one night I was playing chess with some older kids in the neighborhood. He texted me, "Where the fuck are you?" My friends thought it was funny. I told him where I was and what we were doing. His response, "Wear protection." Like me, he was broken for a few years but other than that, I can't complain.

After Robbie talks about her trip, my dad inquires, "What's up with your business?"

With a huge smile, "I owe you guys a thank you! Dean has been awesome. All my clients love his food. We are going to meet this week to talk about some new menu items."

Raising my hand, as I've barely gotten a word in edgewise, "I forgot to tell you dad: I hired Dean."

With a head shift, "For what?"

I can feel the enthusiasm pouring out of me, "We are offering restaurant's menu planning, help making their food healthier, local sourcing, and how to grow their own spices and in some cases vegetables. At first it was just for the health stuff, ends up Dean is really connected. Through his previous life, he knows farmers across the country. We are not only improving menus, but we're also saving them money, and getting them fresh produce and meat. And I hired Mitch's cousin to work with him. This guy's dad owns a ton of fast-food restaurants. He grew up in the business. A ton of knowledge and a great salesman."

Robbie, beaming with excitement, "Alex, that's amazing! You have created all these lines of revenue that feed off each other. Jerry, did you ever think your son would start a business before he was twenty?"

With his hands in the air, "No idea what Alex would do. He's always been a thinker. That's what helped him out in chess and sports. He's planning the next five moves in seconds. Watching him grow has been amazing."

Maddie cuts in, "I remember when Sue catered desserts for a party I was throwing. Alex was probably nine. I walked inside and he's covered in frosting. Wearing no shirt, an apron, and shorts. He's methodically decorating a cake. Squeezing this piping bag and writing in cursive. The funny thing is, next to him, on the table I can see he practiced ten times. And I knew then, he was going to be successful."

All this attention is making me nervous, "Thanks. I appreciate this love fest. It's making me nervous."

Robbie wonders aloud, "Why?"

With a warm smile, my dad answers, "Alex does not like compliments, or to lose."

GOOD NEWS BAD NEWS

Waking with Robbie next to me has been wonderful. Everything she does is cute; that's how I know I'm in love. Even when she snores, it's this light, cute sound, like you would expect out of a baby snore. It only happens when she drinks too much, which is not often.

Trying not to wake her, I grab my clothes and head to the basement gym. She needs a full hour of sleep more than me. I'm not sure if that's jet lag or just her.

Mixing Greek yogurt and flour, I make bagels for us. The house smells amazing, I almost feel guilty when she exclaims, "THESE ARE AMAZING!"

"They are protein packed, too! You should make them for your clients. Dean taught me the recipe." Robbie's phone buzzes. No one ever calls her before 9. Concern forms on both of our faces.

"Rose, what's the matter? What test?" Tears roll down Robbie's face. Starring down at the table, as if she's looking through it, she can barely get the words out, "Will ... she be ... okay?"

I hand her tissues and extend my hand. She's squeezing so tight, I want to pull away, but I don't. I know this call.

"Rose, I'm coming home today. NO. Today." She hangs up the phone and wraps her arms around me. I can feel the tears on my shoulder. The sobbing, the shaking, and the nose sniffling—I remember it too well.

Saying nothing, I just hold her. She takes three big breaths and peels herself off me. "She's going to be okay. Breast cancer. They just got confirmation, and the good news is that it hasn't spread to her lymph nodes; it's still early. The doctors are going to remove the tumor, double lumpectomy, maybe chemo, radiation, and reconstruction surgery." Starting to breathe normally, she starts looking for flights on her phone.

All I can think about are the many doctor visits where I heard good news, bad news. I wish they didn't sugar coat things. All the good news would give us hope. I won't share this memory with Robbie.

"Can you take me to the airport at ten?"

Placing my hand on top of hers, "Of course. What else can I do?"

Her beautiful eyes are red, and filling with more water, "How do I do this?"

"I'm going to tell you everything I know. My mom was stage four. They said they were going to save her, but I knew better. Your mom is going to get through this. You need to tell her you love her, and smile. And try to only cry with your sister. I'll send you an email with things that helped my mom with nausea, fatigue, and loss of appetite. Weed helps. My mom was against it at first, but then she got into it." I laugh, "She was so high once, it was hilarious. All she wanted were Cheetos and tacos. She begged me to take her to Taco Bell. It was like ten a.m., and I was researching twenty-four-hour Taco Bells."

I'm not sure what's happening. I'm trying to be strong for Robbie, and somehow I'm finally able to talk about this without breaking down.

Robbie calls her mom next. She asks to squeeze my fingers while she's on the phone. Forcing a smile, Robbie makes small talk. "Hi mom. How are you holding up?" Pausing, I can hear her mom playing tough. The typical "I'm fine" response is all Robbie can get.

Robbie squeezes my hand tighter, she scrunches her eyes shut, as if she can reverse the flow of tears. "Mom, I'm your helper. This is what family is for."

Hanging up the phone, she breaks down again. I get it, the next few months will suck. Calmness falls over Robbie, "She's going to be okay. I'll take care of her. My aunt and her husband are professors, and they are in Ireland for six months, I saw them when I was aboard. I'm going to take care of my mom until she gets back."

Holding her hand, "Let me know what you need from me. Your aunt might want to come home and help earlier."

Smiling, "I love her, but unless my mom was on her death bed, she wouldn't leave a project early. Besides, no one will take care of her like me, and I don't want Rose to miss out on her first semester of college. I'm going to be a junior. Since Covid, schools are much more open to e-learning."

As Robbie runs upstairs to pack, I text my dad. Since Maddie only lives a few doors away, they pop in minutes later. Hugging my dad tightly, I lose it. My dad whispers, "You have to stay strong for her okay. Once you drop her off, cry, scream. I'll be here."

Pulling it together, "I know. I've been keeping it together." Maddie gives me a smile and walks upstairs. No one is better at these conversations then her.

Unintentionally eavesdropping, I overhear Maddie giving Robbie her number. I imagine at this point, Maddie has one hand on Robbie, offering a friendly smile. I can't hear Robbie crying anymore. Making myself useful I put together some snacks for her trip.

When they finally walk downstairs, my dad hugs Robbie, and her eyes well up again. Trying to make her less sad, my dad comments, "Get it all out. That way, when you see your mom, you'll have no tears to give."

Maddie sees the tray of bagels and asks, "Any chance these are extras?"

I answer, "Help yourself!"

Maddie laughs, "I cannot believe I use to make food for you guys, not knowing you were an amazing cook. Did you ever eat my casseroles?"

My dad shakes his head yes. "We ate most of them. Well, I did. They might have had too many carbs for Alex. And he's pickier than me."

Robbie turns to Maddie, "Why did you make the food, and talk to Alex so much?"

With a serious look, "Sue and I always chatted. She was one of the few neighbors that was nice to me. When she learned I was a psychologist, she asked that I look out for Alex. It was funny, she said I could date Jerry too. That he was a wonderful husband. Then she added, he's broken but I know he's getting help."

With surprised eyes on Maddie, "I had no intention of dating Jerry. Really. I always thought he was handsome and sweet. I might have had a little crush, but I thought dating him would be weird. But after each dinner I dropped off, I found myself more and more interested in Jerry. The guys I normally meet, wanted one thing and were awful conversationalist."

Smiling, my dad says, "I was a mess. I drank too much. Depression swallowed me whole. And then one day looking at Alex, so impressed by his composure, that day, I said it was time to change. And some prodding from Maddie."

Holding nothing back, I comment, "You were a hot mess. I was had no idea what to do."

With disappointment on his face, "I'm so sorry. I was supposed to take care of you, but you took on caretaker. I felt so guilty knowing you were here instead of school."

Looking at my watch I realize it's time to go. "Dad, this experience has been amazing. I would never have my own company, never met Robbie, it worked out in my favor."

With hugs exchanged, we head to the airport. Silence fills the car. I don't know what to say, and Robbie's just flipping through photos of her mom on her phone. I remember when I found out about my mom. I went mute. It took a few weeks before I could speak at school.

Grabbing her suitcase for her feels like an ending. With her hands wrapped around me tightly, I do not want to let go. Tears start to form again in her large brown eyes. "I love you."

She walks away without looking back, and I feel my heart ache. The pit of my stomach fills with sadness.

JUST THE TIP

Sitting at the kitchen table, studying, my dad glares at me, like I stole something. "What are you doing? It's Sunday. Have some fun!"

Laughing, "Homework calls!"

Now I get the puzzled look, "I thought you were taking a break from school?"

Pointing at him, "I had a lot of AP credits and started taking classes the day after high school ended. When you said quit school, it oddly motivated me to get my associate degree. I'm now working on my bachelor's degree."

Still confused, "How do you not tell your dad you graduated? We should celebrate. I thought you were full throttle businessman?"

Closing my laptop, "I know nothing. Success was a matter of luck, persistence, and good advice. I'm taking finance and tax accounting right now. I had no idea I could basically loan money to the Fed overnight."

With a warm smile, "Good for you, Alex! These are things we should discuss. Just because you're CEO doesn't me you don't share these things with me. And you still need to have fun. How's Robbie?"

I can feel the sadness fill around me. We don't talk that much. She's seeing a therapist but she's not in a good place. I totally understand.

"She's okay. Her mom was paired with a survivor her same age, through this not-for-profit called Imerman Angels. Sounds like she's doing better than Robbie. Money is also tight. I helped her set up a web page for her cooking. She's getting a few customers."

A frown forms on his unshaven face, I haven't seen this look in over a year. "It's hard. Just offer her an ear. Nothing you can do."

My phone buzzes. It's Mitch. I hear heavy breathing. "First off, it's okay. Everything is okay. Don't freak out."

My mind races. He was in Indiana this weekend, fixing up a house with students. "What happened at the site?"

In the background I hear announcements, like he's at a hospital. My blood pressure and heart rate begin to rise. Mitch, a little frantic, "This kid, he thought he was funny. Took a piece of wood through the saw, then it kept going and clipped off his fingertip."

Calm rage, if there is such a thing, takes over me, "What? Is he okay? Tell me everything?"

I can almost feel Mitch exhale, "He's fine. Sewed back up. The contractor tossed it on ice, a nursing student applied a tourniquet. Hand surgeon fixed him. He'll have nerve loss but that might come back. Full use will also come back. Another kid got a video. This kid feels awful, too."

My dad is staring at me, begging for info. "Dad, a kid got his fingertip clipped. He's fine. It's all good. You can exhale."

Mitch yells, "HI, JERRY!"

Snapping back into action, "Did you call Rachel? What's our liability? Did he sign the waiver?"

"I called Rachel. She's already spoken to Mike. We are good. Kid's fault, one hundred percent. We also have insurance. We are golden. Not sure about the PR fallout."

Mike's number pops up on my phone, "Got to go, Mike's calling."

The moment I click over: "Relax, kid. We're fine. The kid is a fucking idiot. However, I strongly recommend no more building homes."

"Mike we were on pace to build fifty homes this year. We are improving neighborhoods. Making a difference. We can't stop because one idiot saws off a finger."

With his usually cynical tone, "Kid, it's great that you want to build houses, pick up trash, recycle, but limit your exposure. It's not worth a lawsuit. And increased insurance premiums. This shit is real. People are stupid."

Since I just learned about insurance, I sort of get it. "Okay. Maybe we just sweep and paint."

"Hey kid, Steve is making us money. Thanks for the intro. Kids got talent. Painting is fine."

Mike always hangs up first. He's not into small talk.

As my phone starts ringing again, my dad laughs, "That's why I don't run a business."

Before I can say hi to Jim, he spouts off, "I'm not calling about finger gate. I'm glad the kid is fine, but did you see how many people were at your event?"

In the back of mind, I'm trying to figure out why he's calling me. "A lot of people. We have events twice a month at most campuses now. One is social like the frisbee competition and the other is volunteerism."

Cutting me off, "I know. College campuses are often used as test markets. Large companies want to try out a new fizzy drink, Trident has whacky flavors to test, and the list goes on. Why not have them sponsor your events?"

Laughing, "Jim, we have sponsors for all events! Saves us a ton of money and we make a little."

Jim, not amused, "Why not do one a week? And what if I could find you more sponsors."

Thinking, "I could staff up. More sponsors would be great. The pictures and videos are great content. We do a talent contest that always gets people. Oh, I have a sighed artist that could appear."

Once again interrupting my flow, "I don't need the play-by-play Alex. Think big! Someone is going to copy your plan, steal some business, and I want you to be big enough to buy them out. We'll discuss at lunch."

Hanging up the phone, and closing my laptop, I turn to my dad, "Let's have fun."

Hugging me, "Starved Rock. Get away from the office. Hike?"

Rucking is my dad's newest fitness kick. The mornings he doesn't run, he loads a bag filled with rocks or books and hikes. Like he's in the army. Hours after leaving, he returns home drenched in sweat and starving.

"Sure, dad." Scanning the pantry, I grab jerky, nuts, and granola. The fridge is my next stop—I grab grapes, apples, and water.

Watching me, "You're too good to me, Alex. After the hike, we hit that place for ice cream. We'll earn our scoops."

Before we hit the highway, I feel myself fading. My eyes feel too heavy to keep open, and I give in. I think I need to get driven around more often.

SHARING THE WEALTH

Thanks to another investment from Jim, our office has grown, but we are still busting at the seams for space. One of the few benefits to COVID: People are more than okay working from home and rarely coming to the office.

When I ask who wants to work from home, 10 hands shoot up. That should buy me another six months before we need new office space. Jim is trying to convince me to buy a building. His thinking is, if we get bought out, I can rent out the building and keep making money.

While viewing our stats, Jim calls. "Hey, let's go car shopping."

Insulted, "What's a matter with my Honda? It's only twelve years old with a little over a hundred thousand miles."

I hear Jim tapping on his desk over the phone, "Kid, why not splurge a little. Enjoy your success. I'm not saying you need a Bentley."

Money has never meant anything to me. "I'm prouder of the fact we're inspiring young people to volunteer. That we've raised close to a million dollars through fundraising. Sure, most of that money is from our sponsors but still, we made it happen. What do I need a car for?"

The tapping stops, "Okay. I can get you a great deal if you ever want a new ride. No pressure. It's also fun to test drive." Without a goodbye, he hangs up.

I've been putting off this next item for days, paying Robbie. She was in so many videos, that sold a lot of kitchenware, she deserves to be paid. I know she's going to fight me.

"Hey Robbie, how are you today? How's your mom?"

With a pause, "She's responding well to treatment. The doctor has been impressed. Once he said Keto diet might help her, I've gone full throttle. Your neighbor has been a huge help. From how to get fat adapted to recipes, he's been a great resource." Despite trying to comfort her, Robbie's sweet voice makes me feel calm. We only talk once a week, and it's almost always me calling.

Our conversations are usually about her mom, and Robbie usually leaves out how she's doing. Typical caretaker. I press, "What about you? Make some new friends? How's eLearning?"

With a short breath, "It's fine. I'm actually able to bang out work pretty quick. My mom is still working part time for the insurance and when she's not working, it's sleep. Not to sound like a stiff but I don't have time for friends."

Here goes nothing, "You remember those videos you shot for me?"

Laughing, "How can I forget, I see the ads all the time and it was the most fun I've had cooking."

Hopeful, "Those videos have helped quadruple sales. I had no money then but now I need to pay you for it."

Here comes the push, "Don't be ridiculous. That was fun, and I've used those for my benefit as well."

Slightly lying, "Well my CPA, you know, the other Jerry, told me I need more expenses on that business. I have a lot of revenue, but my only expenses are ads. This sounds odd, but you'll be doing me a favor."

Laughing, "You are so full of shit. How much money do you want to pay me?"

With most negotiations, you start low, and hope to meet in the middle, I'm doing the opposite. "Models can make a fortune when they shoot so many videos. I want to pay you nine thousand two hundred and fifty dollars. According to Jerry's calculations, that's fair."

Loudly, "WHAT? Come on. I did them as a friend. I can't take that much money. It feels wrong."

"How about seven grand and we call it a day." I know she needs money but would never ask. Her dad has helped with her with college but since her mom used to make the same as him, there was no spousal support. And her mom is not working full time.

"You're ridiculous. What's the number you thought I would take?"

With no hesitation, "Five grand; but I really need to pay you seven for tax purposes."

Laughter starts to build, and it's the sweetest sound I've heard in months, "I can't believe how ridiculous you are. Thank you. I would pay you back in sex but not sure that would help either of us."

Fantasizing, "I could be in Minneapolis in three hours. Pick me up from the airport?"

Before she responds, I send her the money and email her an invoice, so it seems more legit. "You work fast. Thank you. I will always love you, but I'm afraid if I see you right now, my heart couldn't handle it. And I'm a mess. Maybe one day."

My heart feels like it's splitting in half. I feel tears losing the battle to stay in my eye, "I've been there. I'll always love you too. Next week?"

A long pause is followed by tears on her end, "Yeah. Next week."

Starring at the celling, I try and will the tears back in. Mitch has been pushing me for weeks to ask out our intern. I feel wrong, I'm the boss. His theory, she's only working at the office twice a week and the internship ends in a few months.

It's been months since Robbie left, and she's told me she's not in a place to date. Trying to push my first love out of my heart, I message Mandy to stop by.

Mandy looks nothing like Robbie. I keep telling Mitch she's not my type, his answer is always, "Bullshit." Mandy has wavy blond hair, ocean blue eyes, light skin, and these red cheekbones that make her quite stunning.

Her pearl white smile and sarcasm greet me, "Great. The boss wants me in his office." Joking, "Should I close the door?"

Answering her, "Yes," surprises her. She closes the door and sits down across from me. I try to look her in the eye, she has a blouse on, and it's needs to be buttoned, just one more button to keep eyes in the right direction.

"Whatever I say, you can say no. This is not like, you'll get fired, you'll get a bad review, I'll tell your professor you suck. None of those things will happen. With that said, would you like to grab coffee after work?" Even though Mandy is smiling, and Mitch swears she's into me, I'm nervous. I've never really asked a girl out, aside from Ellie.

Shaking her head, no, "Dating the boss. I'm not sure Tyler would approve. He's very jealous. Coffee, no, Dairy Bar, yes. I'm an ice cream girl."

My heart has yet to slow down, but I'm trying to play cool, "Cool. I don't even drink coffee. Well, that's a lie, I drink too much coffee."

Standing up, leaning on my desk, I try desperately to maintain eye contact. Mandy, with her hands out, "How about tonight? I'm staying at my parents, and they live close to here."

"Sure. One condition, you stop calling me boss, especially on our date." Slightly shaking her head yes, she walks out.

Before I can get back to work, Rachel and Mitch come in and close the door. Rachel hands Mitch ten dollars. "Did you guys have a bet if I would ask out Mandy?"

They are both laughing like toddlers do after a fart joke, Rachel speaks first, "Mitch called two months I took the over."

Embarrassed, "You guys are the worst. I probably should've waited until the internship was over. Just ice cream. I got off the phone with Robbie, and it's time for me to move on."

Rachel cuts in first, "I thought for sure you would call Shelly. Jack told me you two had a serious connection."

Laughing, "We text. She's dating some frat boy. She's a great catch, funny and a great athlete but I can't keep up with her."

Rachel points at me, "Mandy was a stud volleyball player. She took a year off to model and when she went back, didn't have the fire anymore."

Mitch, rolls up his sleeves, "I knew she had to be a model. Those cheek bones, and she's my height."

Putting my hands on the desk, "Do we have any work to discuss?"

Mitch offers advice as they both stand up, "Just have fun. She's just a girl looking for a nice guy. Plan dinner if the drinks go well."

Waiting until five, takes forever. I made dinner reservations just in case it goes well and told my dad I might be home late. He's staying at Maddie's and that's when I realize this could get confusing. Maybe I should call Mandy, Amanda.

Usually, the day speeds by but I can't take my eyes off the clock. I'm usually here until 6 or 7, but when 4:59 hits, I message Mandy. "What time do you want to head out?"

Making me sweat it out five minutes, "I was thinking of going for a run first, no pressure but you can join me. Earn that dessert. PS—I know you have workout clothes with you."

"Done. Five fifteen. head out from here?"

A thumbs up hits me back. Now I need to figure out what to do for 15 minutes. I usually wait until everyone is gone to read John's emails. They require my complete attention. Along with stats, he's taking data analytics classes. Reading through his email I lose track of time.

Standing in front of me are legs for days, a lean midsection and ripped arms popping out of her tank top. "Sorry I got caught up in this email. You look like a pro athlete."

Smiling, cocky, "I do triathlons. I heard you're an athlete. We'll see."

"So, it's going to be like that. Alright. Loser buys ice cream?"

She's now laughing, "Sure."

Mandy leads us to a local high school track. It's empty at this hour. With that same cocky smile, "Since you're an athlete, eight hundreds. Two minutes rest."

I have not had a workout like this in years, but I can't let her show me up. The first two times around the track I win. The next four, she smokes me. It's not even close. My legs, lungs and even arms are dead.

My stomach is knotted up like I have the runs. Instead, I puke. Laughing, she asks, "You okay?"

I gargle water, take a few sips. "Much better. Two more, right?"

"Alex, we can be done. If you don't do these sprints regularly, it's hard."

Shaking my head, "It might look like slow motion but I'm not quitting."

The next two sprints are more like jogs, but I make it. She takes a tablet out of her bag and drops it in my water bottle. "Electrolytes. You'll feel better soon."

The nausea has passed since I puked, and by the time I finish my drink, I feel much better. The cooler temperature also helps. My embarrassment fades as we hit the office. Turning to her, "Well, that was humbling. You've got some wheels."

Her cheeks are a little redder than usual, "I'm sorry. That was a dick thing to do. I mean that workout humbles everyone. You up to eating?"

Covering my face with my hands, "That was brutal. I need a shower, but can we first do dinner at Glenview House, and then dessert?"

Putting her hand on my sweat-soaked shoulder, "You really do need a shower. I'm going to run home, shower and I'll meet you there."

Further impressed, "Really?"

Laughing she adds, "I'm just kidding. We'll shower together and then head there."

Sensing I misheard that, she back tracks, "Sorry, I mean we can both shower here, and then go. You have to buy me dinner before we shower together."

Fatigue sets in the moment we sit down to dinner. Mandy fires off the first question, "Is it true that you dated the model in the kitchenware videos?"

Gulping my water, "Yes. She's not a model. She was my girl-friend and a cook, so it made perfect sense to use her."

Ripping off a huge hunk of bread from the basket, "She's gor-geous. What happened?"

Controlling my sadness, "Her mom got sick. She left to take care of her, and we drifted. I tried for months to keep it going but I understand. Rachel said you were a model. What was that like?"

The waitress scurries away after bringing us more bread. Mandy answers, "Hashtag me too is no joke. I'm too short for runway work here, but not in Asia. The guy sold it to me and my parents as a great experience. I was spotted on the beach playing volleyball. This scout said he could help me get college paid for. He left out the free cocaine and ecstasy and the sex for money. I'm not joking. I was fifteen. My mom came with me on the first trip overseas. It was innocent. The next trip was three days and that's when shit got crazy."

A natural storyteller, I'm drawn completely in. "What happened?"

Taking a swig of her iced tea, "We get invited to this party of this super rich guy. We are in Japan, and all these movie stars are there too. Things seem normal, but coke and other pills are everywhere. Our manager was encouraging us to have fun. I'm training for my first tri so I use that as an excuse. This other dumb model is like, sure. She takes a pill and her hands are like all over everyone. Some older dude, with his hands all over her, whispers in her ear, they take off. There was one other model there, and she did some blow and then fucked a guy in the bathroom. It was too much for me. I left. I signed a contract for six months. And my amazing mom came with me each time after that."

In complete shock, "That's like a movie. Wow. Good for you, for walking away."

We both destroy our meals. Mandy's stories are so engaging. With some chewing, she adds, "I was on a shoot once, and this guy, no idea what he was doing there, asks my mom how much I charge for sex."

The only response I have: "No way."

With raised eyebrows, "Ice cream?"

Taking a stroll to the Dairy Bar, my phone buzzes. "Call me ASAP." And it's from Rachel.

Turning to Mandy, "I have to call Rachel. Not sure what emergency happens at this hour."

Understanding, "Go ahead."

Before I get a word in, "Your new hire, Brian, took a picture outside a strip club, and posted it to our campus account. I deleted it. He's running an event at Illinois tomorrow. What do you want me to do? I have a kid on campus helping but we need an adult. Mitch is in Austin."

"Fire him. I'll leave in the morning. Send me the itinerary and contacts."

Before it's our turn to order, I'm off the phone. Mandy is gazing up with intense curiosity. "Can you figure out what happened?"

Rubbing her blond locks, "If I had to take a guess, you fired Brian for doing something stupid."

Impressed and a little surprised, "How did you know it was him?"

Giving a duh look, "He's an idiot. He came on way too strong his first day. When I ignored him, he stopped talking to me. He gives frat boys a bad name."

With two giant swirl cones, we sit down on a bench. I can already feel my leg muscles tighten. Trying to change the subject, "How are my leg muscles already sore? Why did you push me so hard?"

Laughing, "Push you? Are you kidding me? You came out tough the first three, maybe four runs. I thought you were a runner. And then you puked. Why did you push it so hard? For real. I'm in training mode. I was a Division One athlete. What are you training for?"

Thinking back to the run, she did say several times, I should scale it back. "Ego, competitiveness. I always want to win. I was stupid. Not sure what's a matter with me. My parents never pushed me into anything except judo. They were the best when I won or lost."

With one hand on my shoulder, "My mom ran track at college, my dad played football at a small school. They are both uber competitive. They pushed my brother so hard he cracked, quit all sports. Since he was older, they did the opposite with me. It created a monster. When you beat me those first two races, I turned on the jets to beat you. Once you puked it was easy though." Laughing, she apologizes, "Sorry. I didn't mean for that to happen."

Walking her back to her car, I have no idea if this was a bad or good date. I had fun. I think she did. Asking for honesty, "Was this a good date?"

Pulling me into her, Mandie whispers in my ear, "This was fun. Thanks." With a sweet kiss on my lips, she pulls away. "Is it weird I want to say, 'Thanks, boss'?"

"It's wrong, but I get it. I got to pack. See you in a few days."

SCALING UP

Six months later, while taking a work break, I look at pictures on my phone. This past year has been nonstop. Mandy and I had some fun dates, but since she took Brian's spot on the team, we stopped dating. It felt wrong. What I lost romantically, I gained in fitness. Mandy is now my trainer. She works out about six of us, either at lunch or after work. The amazing thing: I work out less now, but I'm in better shape.

Jim has been pushing me to open an office in Silicon Valley or Austin, he wants to capture the talent out there. We have a few employees out there, but he wants 20 staff in the west coast. Real estate in California is more expensive, but we do a lot of work there.

Contemplating this move, Jim calls, "I found you a building in Evanston, should you buy."

Confused, "I was just thinking about California. I thought you wanted me to open an office out west. What's up?"

Pausing for what seems like forever, "Alex, I still believe you have to grow out west, but this is huge. It's a building with twelve rental units, and a restaurant. The rents might cover your mortgage. West will be there in a year or two. This office has plenty of space. The owner died and kids don't want to keep it. Now is the time."

"Send me the rents. It's a simple formula to figure out the price and if it's worth it."

Jim laughs, "How do you know everything?"

Trying not to sound cocky, "Truth, school. I just took an investments class, and we talked about real estate. Fresh in my head. My dad has a friend that does inspections, think we could do a walk through? And how do you know these people?"

While emailing me details on the building, "I know the kids from growing up. Good people. I'll text you when you can check it out."

The second Jim hangs up, I call Chuck and look at my balance sheet. We've been saving up for another office for a few months. "Chuck, how are you? It's Alex."

A deep voice answers, "Good kid. How's your pop? He still dating your neighbor?"

I find it funny; he doesn't ask about me, only my dad, whatever, I need his help. "Chuck, can you check out this building I might buy. It's a rush job, kids want to unload it, their dad recently died."

"What's the address?"

Before I can spit out the entire address, "That's a great building. About twenty-five years old. It's probably been through a bunch of maintenance five years ago. If so, that will save you a lot of money. If you don't buy it, it'll go fast."

Thinking for a moment, "Chuck, is it crazy to buy a building this big?"

Laughing, "No. That location, you'll get renters for sure. Think about what you want your office to look like."

While Chuck and I talk, Jim texts me, "Anytime today, tomorrow or Thursday."

"Short notice, can you check out the building with me the next few days?"

With no hesitation, "Today noon, then you buy me lunch?"

"That would be great!"

Inhaling, Chuck adds, "Tell Jerry I say hi."

Sitting in my chair, staring out at all the people, I see Rick. He's working with a chiropractor who wants to rent in our office—perfect timing.

Catching myself running to Rick's office, I slow down. My heart is beating like I'm sprinting. The adrenaline leads me to knock hard on his door.

A grumpy "Come in" greets me. I pop in and Rick smiles. "What's up, kid?"

Too nervous to sit down, "Jim wants me to buy a building in Evanston. Numbers look good. Twelve units and a restaurant can help offset my rent. Is this too big a move?"

Putting down his notebook, Rick cocks his head to the side, "Go for it. You are busting at the seams here and you have a bunch of people working from home. It would be nice to have an office large enough for big meetings."

Feeling more relaxed, I ask, "What will you do with this space?"

Turning in his chair to the window, "See those guys? They are working on chopping this office up. At first, I thought I could take my office and fix it up for this chiropractor. Maybe I can turn this back into a gym."

A light bulb bursts in my head. "Is it stupid to take a star employee and help her with her dream?"

Smiling like a proud parent, "That's great. Some companies have dream or goal programs where they help employees achieve projects outside the office. It's wonderful. Keep me posted. Good luck!"

Picking up the phone like I've already left, Rick dials his wife, "Hey, babe. Lunch?"

Walking out filled with energy, I stand in the middle of the room, "HEY EVERYONE, CIRCLE UP HERE!" Expecting no one to listen, I'm happily proved wrong. "We have a new program called Dreams. Some call it a big hairy audacious goal, but I'm calling it Dreams. I'll help you achieve whatever it is you want, and I'll form a team to help you. I'll email everyone soon."

Half the room looks at me suspiciously, like I'm on drugs, the offer half claps. I have one employee in mind, that hopefully, will respond. I was trying to plant a seed.

Strolling back to my office I formulate my email, asking for helpers and goals.

Rachel pops in my office, "You okay, Alex?"

"Close the door." With the door close, "I'm looking at a bigger office in Evanston. Don't tell anyone yet. Am I crazy?"

With a wink, "Crazy smart. Best move I ever made was to work for you. And I love the dreams idea, but are you okay losing staff?"

"Yes. We are going to make people happy, and they will tell their friends that this is the best company to work for. Our goal is to build communities, I need to focus on this community. I'm so obsessed with sales and growth; I forget about the staff. What's your dream?"

"I want to be a CEO."

"Rachel, you are more than halfway there. When I quit, this is yours, if you want it."

Again, looking at me like I'm crazy, "Are you quitting?"

Without waiting a second, "Not yet. I need to make some dreams happen."

DREAMS

Four years later: Waiting for Jim at Furious Spoon, I'm fidgety. The smell of ramen soup is intoxicating. I order some dumplings. I know he likes them.

Autumn Jim is stylish, he has on trendy jeans, a tan V-neck shirt, and a vest over it. After a quick hug, he sits down and smiles. "Hungry? Why did you want to meet? You already outgrown Evanston?"

"I'm starving and the smell was getting to me."

With an inquisitive look, "What's up with your Dreams initiative? Mandy's fitness business seems booming."

Nervously smiling, "Yes. She was my first success story. With the help of our video and web team we set her up for online training quite well. And Rick did a great rebuild for her. With the chiropractor and massage rooms, her rent is low, and she gets referrals from the doctor."

Slowly chewing on a dumpling, "That's great. What's your take?"

"Ten percent from the web sales. She also donates ten percent to charities that help women and girls. With her products selling so well, in a few years she will donate fifty grand. That does include her clients donating as well. She was really surprised at how her clients and friends have taken to her charity."

With a quick glance at his phone, "What about that house flipper? She still work for you?"

Shaking my head yes, "Gwen is still in the office. She's part time now. Marv, the maintenance guy at my building helps her. It's funny, his goal was to pay for his grandkids to go to college. Between helping her and working for me he's socking away a lot of money."

The steam rises off our soup, I feel my nerves settling. Jim's head shakes with pride, "Alex, you've really created something amazing. What's up with Mitch's fashion blog?"

Mixing philanthropy and business development, Mitch has created a great website. "Mitch's site is growing by leaps and bounds. It started out as a fashion blog to promote LGBTQ+ designers. And now he has famous artists talking about their journey. He has a mentorship program and raises money to educate schools on being more inclusive."

With his hands above his head, "That is awesome! I love how you've built an organization around achieving dreams. You figured out if you invest in your employees, they work even harder. What are you going to do about the offer?"

The offer. That's all I've been thinking about since last week, when Jim told me a group of investors wanted to buy my campus business. "I've done a lot of thinking. I've averaged 14-hour days for five years. We struggled, we've grown, and my favorite part has been the philanthropy. The foundation is mine, so I'm going to keep it. I love helping people achieve dreams, now I need to learn how to do that for more people."

Playing poker all these years, I can usually judge fascial expressions well, I think Jim's a little shocked. "They want to buy because they think this can be huge. You sell now, might mean you lose out on millions more. And they want to keep you on."

Laughing, "I never cared about the money. This sale will make me richer than I ever imagined. And this is going to sound odd, but I miss baking, and relaxing. And the only reason I see friends, is because I hire them to work for me."

Slurping some noodles, "Okay. What are you going to do with the building and the café?"

"Gwen is going to manage the building for me. The café has an office in the back, I was thinking I could open a coffee and bakery shop, run my charity back there."

Jim lets out a few laughs, "You do make great cookies. Who's going to run it?"

"I have no idea. I interviewed a few restaurant managers but haven't found the right fit."

By some miracle, I pull out my wallet before Jim and he actually lets me pay. With a smile, "You're about to be wealthy, I'll let you buy. For the record, we are still doing lunch once a month. I might have someone you can coach. Good luck with the bakery."

BUTTERFLIES

Jack's favorite bar is empty, except for him, the bartender, and me. This is his bon voyage party. When he started working full time, he told me his dream was to travel the world. For a few months, our Friday Dreams meetings were about travel. He saved up all his paychecks, and now he's headed around the world—with Rose.

With a hug, "I can't believe you are still dating Rose. You were the biggest player."

With his trademark dimples, he smiles and says, "When you know, you know. She was so sweet. And so cool. I mean, what girl really likes football and beer? Oh yeah, and she loves to bike, and hike. It's like this dream combination."

Taking a sip of his beer, his smile disappears, "You know Robbie is coming tonight? You cool with that? I can't believe you two haven't spoken since she left for Paris."

Sadness fills me up. "You know, I tried so hard. And when her mom was better, she, like, forgot about me. Does she have a boyfriend?"

Laughing, Jack continues, "I'm not playing that game. Last time, the guy from Italy. I can't believe he was gay. I'm so sorry about that. But you never would've experienced Shelly."

The bar slowly starts to fill up. Friends from college and high school swarm Jack. I sit alone, sipping my drink.

A pat on the back interrupts my loneliness. It's Rachel. Before she can say anything, "Rachel, you ready for your dream?"

Looking at me confused, "I never told you my dream."

Giddiness bursts out from inside me. "Three or so years ago, you said, 'I want to be CEO.'"

Her hands drop to her side, and she's not smiling, "Wait—what are you telling me, Alex?"

"I told the buyer I would only sell if they retained you as CEO for four years. That's the industry average."

Still confused, "What about Mitch? He has worked so hard and brought in so much revenue."

Reassuring, "They only want the campus company. He'll run the restaurant consultancy business."

In shock, "What about you?"

"I'm going to be able to give a lot more money away. The foundation is mine. I'm still going to sell kitchenware, and you'll have to come to my café!"

With the world's biggest smile, "Taking over the restaurant space—nice. I don't know what to say, which is unusual. This has been the most tiring yet amazing ride." A hug follows her sentence. It has been a long time since someone squeezed me that hard. I think of my mom, and how not only did she hug this tight, but she would be so happy at this moment.

A kiss on the cheek follows. Without any hesitation, Rachel climbs on the bar, "Hey, everyone, I'M A CEO!"

Clapping and whistling erupt from the now busy bar. While wiping up tears of happiness, it hits me like a bolt of lightning.

She's more gorgeous than she was when I last saw her in person. And her smile is cuter than the last time I saw her almost four years ago. Robbie catches me out of the corner of her eye while walking in. She walks right toward me, and we hug for what seems like an hour. Tears pour down her check, she whispers, "I'm so sorry. I never thought my mom was going to live." She then stares me up and down, "You look amazing! You got your muscles back."

Her wide smile melts me. Without letting me talk, "After mom was cancer free, and I graduated, I moved to Paris to cook. I was sure she would get sick again, and I would be back at home. I needed a break. I didn't want this to ruin Rose's life, so I took on a lot. I was broken."

Wiping away her tears, I ask, "What brought you back?"

Smiling, "You. And I don't really like France. Don't tell anyone. Oh, and we have to do that Pilates session with Susan."

Joking, "What if I was married or had a girlfriend?"

Whispering in my ear, "I would kill the bitch."

Laughing, "You want to run my bakery?"

COOKIES KALE AND COFFEE

The stress of selling a business has kept me nervous for weeks. The deal took a few months to get done. According to Jim, that is record time. Debating who gets what, the lawyer fees, the finances—thank God I have good lawyer and CPA. I still retain a bunch of stock, and now Jim, Mike, Rick, and I are the board of advisors.

Mitch has retained his sales staff and a few admins. John, of course, stayed with Mitch. He's working on a degree from the University of Chicago. His dream is to use data to solve the world's problems, from fighting disease to ending poverty.

Building out the restaurant keeps my days busy. Having lived through the pandemic, I realize you need multiple forms of revenue; carryout and dining isn't enough. I'm cutting down on seating and increasing the kitchen size for catering and a boxed lunch program. Using my connections, I've set up four clients for lunch service, and we will ship our baked goods around the country. Since my chef is an expert at healthy meals, we also supply meals for keto, high protein, or calorie-restricted dieters.

Even though seating is limited, I have room for a few groups of card players. The poker guys won't be there, but Joe's wife has two groups that want a location for their games.

My dad is even more excited than me because I'll be using my mom's recipes. Although he moved in with Maddie, he tells me often, "I will always remember and love your mom." I know she's looking down on your café with a huge smile.

I'm a little mad at the old man. He kicked me out a few months ago. He's renting the house to a family. The wife is on a four-year project with a pharma company, and I don't think he was ready to sell. With a hand on my shoulder, he told me, "Alex, love you buddy, but you need a life. Move to Evanston or the city."

Currently I'm living a few blocks from the office. I had no idea when I bought the place that I would sell my company, but I'm glad I splurged on a two-bedroom. The best news: I have this roommate, and other than threatening to kill my pretend wife, she's an angel.